THE LAST PLACE YOU LOOK

Norma Curtis was born in North Wales, but now lives in London with her family. Her first novel, *Living It Up, Living It Down*, was awarded the Romantic Novelists Association New Writing Award 1994 and selected for WHS Fresh Talent in 1995. It was followed by her second novel, *Quality Time*, which was successfully published in 1996.

The Last Place You Look

NORMA CURTIS

HarperCollins*Publishers*

HarperCollins*Publishers*
77–85 Fulham Palace Road,
Hammersmith, London W6 8JB

Published by HarperCollins*Publishers* 1998
1 3 5 7 9 8 6 4 2

A catalogue record for this book
is available from the British Library

ISBN 0 00 225625 8

Typeset in Galliard and Photina by
Palimpsest Book Production Limited,
Polmont, Stirlingshire

Printed and bound in Great Britain by
Clays Ltd, St Ives plc

Dedicated to
Neville Jenkins, 1928–1975, and Rowena
my dear parents

and to Paul

ACKNOWLEDGEMENTS

To Dave and Elaine, Dr Selina Gellert, Rachel Hore
thank you

PART ONE

This side enough is toasted, so turn me tyrant . . .

St Lawrence

Chapter One

'Lose a father, gain a bench,' Faye said, resting against the weathered seat and glancing at the inscription. There were so many commemorative benches in the area that the council had put a stop to them, but of the ones that had made it, she knew them all by name.

Her two children watched her in impatient silence, saving their breath for hurrying. In the chilled smoky winter air it puffed out of them like empty cartoon speech balloons and trailed away.

She got up again and rubbed her aching shoulder. 'Let's go,' she said. Her son slung his bag over his shoulder wordlessly, his eyes distant. Somewhere along the leafy walk between home and school Samuel had left her.

Isabel, being four, reached for her cold hand, and tripped occasionally as they walked, but it was nine-year-old Samuel that Faye looked at, expecting one day to see the actual transition from son to pupil taking place. Perhaps it was in the hope of preventing it, she thought, smiling slightly, her cheeks stiff in the wind.

Not that it mattered. Not that it should have mattered. This sense of separation was some old fear revisited, but she wasn't comforted by that. Clean sheet, she thought, reaching the road, gripping Isabel's hand more tightly and standing shoulder to shoulder with her son.

He hurried across slightly ahead of her. His mind had moved on to his friends and the day ahead and by the time they reached the black, wrought-iron gates of the school the parting, for him, had already been made.

He didn't kiss her or even say goodbye and she watched him walk away, tugging at the navy blazer that was bunched up by his bag strap as he merged with a bobbing crowd of boys.

She watched their heads for a moment, tracking his progress by the sun shining weakly on his coppery hair.

'Mummeee?' Isabel was hanging onto her hand restlessly, tugging her fingers to bring her back.

Faye felt her knuckles pop and she looked down at her small daughter, resisting the impulse to pull her hand away. 'Yes, let's go. We're nearly there.' She could see the yawning black-glossed doorway of the nursery that adjoined the school, fifty yards away at the most.

Isabel whimpered feebly. Unlike Samuel, school took her by surprise every day. 'I don't want to go,' she said desperately, twisting behind Faye's legs, ducking under the blue coat, pressing her face into the denim of Faye's jeans.

Faye felt a small, concentrated circle of heat from Isabel's mouth at the back of her thigh. She straightened slowly and looked up the road. Cars were pulling in on either side. For a few minutes at the beginning and end of the school day, the Highway Code didn't exist. Next to her a green Rover stopped dead in the road and a boy of about nine, Sam's age, stumbled out, face red with embarrassment or the stress of being late. He slammed the door and dodged around her, nudging her with his bag. The grudging line of cars moved slowly on. She could feel the heat radiating off them; a combination of exhaust fumes, dust and the worries of the occupants.

Late for work, she thought, staring at them. She reached and caught hold of Isabel's hand, suddenly impatient. 'Miss Maitland will be wondering where you are.'

Isabel pouted. 'You're hurting me.'

Faye relaxed her grip and Isabel's hand slid out, free – she had seen Sasha, her friend. Faye slipped hers into her warm pocket. She too could see Sasha and she watched as Isabel ran to meet her.

'Bye, Mum,' Isabel called from the gate.

Faye raised her hand and gave a wave.

It was just turned nine and already the traffic was thinning. Faye paused and glanced up the road. She saw Vicky, her friend and one time fellow-smoker, talking to two other mothers at the top of the street. Faye felt inside her handbag for her cigarettes and sunglasses.

The sunglasses were for hiding behind. She put them on, shook a cigarette out of the packet and cupped her hands around the lighter. The first cigarette of the day . . . it was always the best.

She shook her tinted auburn, curly hair away from her eyes and felt the winter sun unexpectedly warm on her cheek. Tilting her head, she could see part of her face reflected metallically back at her in the dark lens of the sunglasses: the curve of her brow-bone, fair down shining silver, encroached on by the wiry, neatly-laid hairs of her eyebrow. A silver river of a crease led to the black pool of her eye. She watched her magnified, reptilian eyelid blink swiftly. Dazzled.

She exhaled slowly and started to walk back, her blue coat billowing out behind her. Shaking off the feeling of having left something behind, she came alongside Vicky and the other women.

They were still deep in conversation. Vicky glanced up and smiled. Her gaze flickered towards the cigarette and away again. And back. 'Faye, we're going to the gym at eleven. Care to join us?'

Faye glanced at her watch regretfully. 'Oh, I'm busy this morning. But thanks.' Walking on with a sense of relief at the ease of the lie she took another puff. At the top of the road she turned right, looking briefly at Alf's bench. She gave a quick glance towards Samuel's window as she passed – habit again, it was too high for her to see into – and strolled along the lane that took her home.

By the time she got back, Nick, her husband, had gone to work.

It was never the silence that she noticed, she thought, listening to it nevertheless as she hooked her bag and coat over the banister. No, the silence could be drowned out. It wasn't the silence, it was the space. After the turmoil of breakfast the house seemed to have been burgled; robbed of people, it was left bare.

She walked up the stairs into the white living room and picked up Samuel's red pyjamas from the floor. They seemed to have retained the shape of him – more sloughed than dropped. Folding them up, she lifted her face to the light and felt a sense of peace wrap round her.

The ceiling above her was studded with constellations of coloured spotlights which gave the room atmosphere when wanted, but she used them less and less. More important to her now was that there should be no shadow. Nick said she was suffering from seasonal affective disorder and she liked the thought of that, that it was so simple.

She put Samuel's pyjamas on the arm of the chair. Her newspaper was on the desk and as she reached for it she saw that the red light of the answerphone was flashing.

She pressed the message button.

An echoic, non-descript background noise played back, out of which her own voice suddenly spoke clearly: 'No, I don't know where your shoes are. Sam, I can see your fountain pen from here, it's in your blazer pocket, look!'

There was no disguising her irritability, she thought, grinning, at the same time feeling the shame of being caught unawares. She took a navy scrunchie from her wrist and tied her tangled hair back while she carried on listening.

'Is there any mail for me?' That was Nick.

'Telephone bill, it's on the table.'

'Sasha hates Polly Pocket.' Isabel.

'Have you got everything, Sam? Your homework? It's not gym today, is it?'

'No, but it's swimming tomorrow. If we forget, the school secretary's not allowed to ring you up to bring it any more.'

And further background noise.

Faye sat on the arm of the chair, prepared to be patient. She knew what had happened, someone had hit the memo button. She'd had to play back fifteen minutes of passing traffic once, waiting for the two beeps at the end so that she could erase it. 'Right, we're off.' That was her. 'Kiss Daddy.' So that she could have her turn, she thought, grinning again. More background noise.

'See you later.' That was Nick, his voice low and warm, post-kiss. Movement, and then the door slamming, and silence, except for the sound of traffic.

She got up off the arm of the chair and stood by the machine, waiting for the two beeps. The silence was broken by the sound of the phone ringing, and for a moment Faye reached out to get it, but no, it was still the recording.

'Hello?' Nick's voice. 'Susie.' It was a statement, identifying the caller, his voice subdued. 'No, no, it's all right.' Subdued, but reassuring. Listening. Then, 'Look, let's talk about it. No, no, that's not what I mean, I just think –' there were a couple of clunks, as though the telephone cord was hitting the table. 'Well –' more silence. No movement now. 'No, don't.' His voice was so subdued as to be almost inaudible. 'We'll talk about it. Today, yes, today. Yes, I can, I'll ring you from work. Please, just wait until we can talk about it. Yes. Yes. Okay. Bye.' Bang, shuffle, and another bang, not so loud.

There was a silence, followed by Nick's voice saying something over and over. It grew clearer as he walked about: 'Shit shit shit shit shit.'

Faye stared at the machine. The two beeps came and after a moment the tape rewound, ready to give her the memo again. The red light blinked. It looked surprised.

The crushing sensation of having suddenly been damaged in some way kept her immobile. She waited, and her brain, shocked into inaction for those first moments, slowly jolted into some sort of life again.

And then it panicked.

Susie? *Susie*? She'd been going to ring her. Theirs was an office friendship that had survived long after she'd left. She'd go to the gym with her again, once her shoulder was fixed. Susie. What would Susie be doing ringing Nick? Stupid question, nothing new about that, the story of the husband and the friend, the old ones are the best, aren't they? Who said that? See, that was the thing about clichés, they were so often true, so true . . .

. . . and suddenly she felt her head quieten again.

Unease, ragged, like smoke in wind, came and went.

She needed a cigarette. Her handbag had gone. She ran down the stairs and it wasn't lying dumped at the bottom. Panic. Coat pocket? Please – and yes, they were there with her sunglasses. She took one out and sat at the bottom of the stairs and lit it with a shaking hand.

Relief.

The first inhalation made her cough, and her mind free-wheeled along that thought for a moment, the cough and the ache in her shoulder and her recent visit to the doctor and the doctor's first question: do you smoke? As though it was the sole cause of all the ills in the world. So, she'd said I do smoke, and they'd given her a chest x-ray. Disapprovingly. And on her next visit they would suggest that she give it up.

She turned her hand and stared at the ash at the tip of the cigarette; the memory was an interesting detour while it lasted, but it led her right back to the main point: Susie ringing Nick. Susie ringing Nick about something he didn't want to do, actually that was what it had sounded like, she recalled, feeling the nicotine kick in, watching the smoke lift lazily and twist as it neared the ceiling.

And now what? Well, she could make the beds while she was down there in the upside-down house, as Sam's friends called it. But she really needed to think, so instead she went slowly back upstairs and into the kitchen, flicking the kettle on and getting the instant coffee out of the cupboard; it was Ishmael's advice, of course, using action to get rid of melancholy. She looked for a cup and found a Flintstones mug and poured in a random amount of granules straight from the jar, before stubbing her cigarette out in the sink where it died with a hiss.

She poured the water into the cup and stirred. The coffee tasted foul.

She took it back into the living room where the answerphone still winked knowledgeably. The sun had passed the trees outside the window and the beams of light that came into the room were polluted with haze and dust. Something about the sunbeam made her turn to look sharply at Nick's silver crucifix on the wall. It was hanging in the shade, dusty and slightly tarnished, part of the room. One of those things that, if someone moved it, no-one would miss for weeks.

But there it was, oddly reassuring considering she wasn't a Catholic herself. Just before Christmas Nick had stepped up his visits to mass. He was a good man, she had to remember that. She turned her back on the crucifix and walked towards the window, her footsteps sounding oddly loud on the carpet.

She fell back into thought and the ring of the phone was so shocking, such an unexpected interruption that it stopped her in her tracks. It wasn't until the answerphone clicked into action that she hurried to pick up the receiver, pulling it so sharply that the phone fell off the desk, tingling as it dangled as though there was a bell loose in the microchips. She grabbed it mid-swing.

'Faye?' Nick's warm, deep voice sounded close and amused. 'What's going on there?'

For a moment she was so surprised that she couldn't speak. When she'd listened to the answerphone Nick had become a stranger to her. Now here he was, hers again. 'I dropped the phone,' she said.

'Oh. You sound as if you've been running.'

'I was trying to get to the phone before the machine switched on.'

'Right. Listen, if you go to the shops could you get me some black shoelaces? I snapped one this morning.'

Faye rubbed her eye with the back of her cold hand. Against the darkness of her eyelid she could see him crouching to fasten his shoes after the phone call, angry, agitated, pulling that thin black shoelace a little too hard and feeling it snap off in his hand. Shit shit shit shit shit . . .

. . . but it wasn't real. The picture faded and she was half-smiling to herself. The familiarity of his voice made it seem very possible, now, that she had made a mistake; she was quite willing to settle for an explanation knowing the suspicion would go in time, drift off and be forgotten. So she said, mostly out of curiosity, 'Nick, did Susie ring earlier?'

She waited, and in the silence of his hesitation the stranger Nick and the familiar one slowly merged.

8

After a long pause he said, 'Yes.'

'Someone hit the memo button,' she said. 'What's happening? What's going on?'

Another pause and then he said briefly, 'She's got problems with her love-life.'

'Really? Why's she telling you?'

'She wanted a man's perspective.'

Faye looked around for her cigarettes, tucked the phone under her chin, found them in her back pocket, contemplated the last one. 'You said you'd ring her from work . . .' Digging deeper, she waited to hear the impatience in his voice, or failing that, to be told she was being absurd.

'I just wanted to get rid of her,' he said, and gave a short laugh.

'I'll give her a ring, see if I can help,' Faye said casually, laying a trap of sorts.

'Fine,' he said. 'You should do that. And don't forget the shoelaces, will you?'

'No, I won't. Bye.' She replaced the phone, took the last cigarette out of the packet and threw the packet in the kitchen bin. Still uneasy, she went back to look at the answerphone. She could have misheard it.

Nick was a Catholic and the Good One of his family; his elder brother was the Clever One and his younger sister was the Crazy One. Edith, Nick's mother, spoke of them just like that, as though they were strangers she was trying to get a handle on. Faye liked being married to the Good One. Fairy-story-like, it seemed to imply a charmed life, and that's what they lived, didn't they? A charmed life with good children and light everywhere and no shadows. Nick worked as a loss-adjustor. She, after a couple of false moves into theatre design and Mahler Industries, was newly self-employed, designing lighting for other people's houses. She was happy, now.

There was nothing wrong.

She could listen to the tape again, but she wouldn't.

She could ring Susie and find out about the man trouble, have a chat and arrange lunch if she wanted to, but she didn't.

Instead she pressed erase, keeping her finger on the button and listening to the whir. When the tape had rewound and come to a stop she felt relieved but slightly resentful, too, of the machine which had got her worked up. She pressed the off button and the red light went black.

9

She carried on looking at it because it seemed familiar. It reminded her of something.

It came to her after a moment.

It looked like her eye had looked, earlier that morning in the reflection of her sunglasses.

Chapter Two

Unravelling.

It doesn't feel like a memory, this unravelling. Soon be done, Faye thinks, concentrating on her knotted thread of life. She knows she is concentrating too hard to be asleep but she has drifted from the present into some time past, past but not resolved.

She wipes her eyes. The wind is blowing hard, twitching the hedges and bulging the black smoke away through the trees. Stiff-legged and blistering, the lady's chair burns in a haze of orange and green flame. Cracks, like a stick hitting railings, pierce the air above the roaring. A sharp explosion sends black scraps of burnt curtains into the air where they fly like crows.

Faye watches them sail on the wind. A backdraught is blowing towards her the smell of incense as the varnish on the chair smoulders and bubbles, and her face is tightening with the heat.

Those curtains shut out the light for seven years, protecting the vivid pink of the rose-patterned upholstery whilst its owner and her daughters passed like shadows in the muted colours of the stale dark. She wishes her mother were here to see them flying charred and tattered from the skeletal orange cavern of the lady's chair.

She wishes she could see with her own eyes how pointless it has been, all that living in the dark, when the curtains haven't saved the furniture after all.

Chapter Three

Nick sat back in his black vinyl swivel chair and covered his face with his hands. It wasn't the sort of day to be working. He had been so nearly caught by Faye he hardly dared believe he had talked his way out of it. He groaned at the memory.

Well, that was it for him, he thought. He picked up the phone and dialled Susie on her direct line at Mahler Industries.

She answered immediately, her voice light and flirtatious. 'Hel-lo?'

'Susie.'

'Nick, is that you?' He could hear the smile in her voice. 'So, are you going to come round tonight?'

'Susie, it's got to stop.'

'What has?' The smile in her voice faded to grey.

'Us.'

There was a long silence, and then she laughed. It was a slightly mocking sound. 'Before we've even started?'

He didn't reply. It had started for him. For a long time she'd tugged at his thoughts. At first the distraction was niggling, irritating and as constant as an itch waiting to be scratched. Oh, he'd kept his thoughts on Faye and pushed those of Susie aside, but he'd been aware of them all the same.

She used to call round for Faye and they would go to the gym together and he imagined, when they'd gone, the things they might say, maybe about him. He'd also imagined them flirting with the instructors. Or, and this was worse, he imagined them taking it seriously, working on the weights until it hurt, until they were self-centred and sweating and hot with effort, not thinking of him at all.

Around November Susie had started calling round earlier, one week full of excuses for it, then the next without, until it was the new way of things, her being early and flirting with him, using her sideways glances while Faye was still looking around for her Reeboks or kissing Isabel goodnight.

It had meant little to him then, except that he no longer felt left out. Why it had it changed? He wanted to tell her she was a gnat-bite, a dog-bite, a love-bite, a sharp shock in his good and striving life.

'Well that's that then,' she said. 'Got to go.'

Clunk. He kept the receiver to his ear for a moment, and then replaced it slowly. He groaned. What had he done?

'Suffering?' Ralph asked, coming into his office unannounced and dropping a file onto his desk.

Nick mustered up a weak grin. He stroked his hand over his cropped dark hair, noticing that Ralph's, once again, was curling over his collar. Ralph liked acting the boss without looking the part. He looked bohemian. He believed it made him seem younger. Truth was, he looked fifty with long hair or without.

'Hangover,' Nick said briefly, rubbing his temples. He was relieved he had the kind of face that always looked as if he were suffering – or failing that, the kind of face that looked cruel. It was a paradox caused by his hooded eyes.

Ralph was looking at him without curiosity, his mind on his job. 'Have a glance at this, will you,' he said.

Nick looked at the file. Albert Hall, the label said. Man or monument? he wondered, and then thought: suffering. Ralph had meant nothing by it, it was just a greeting, but it was funny that he'd used that word. See, Faye used to tell him he had the eyes of a Madonna, to tease him.

And Susie said he had the eyes of Tim Roth.

But he *was* suffering. 'Ralph, I'm just going to pop out for some Resolve,' he said suddenly. It was a private joke with himself that was wearing thin.

Ralph placed his large, hair-flecked hand flat on the file. Now he looked concerned. 'How long are you going to be? I want you to take a look at this before lunch. Can't you scrounge an aspirin from Beverly?'

Nick looked through the open door and saw Beverly's blonde head bent over her desk. Beverly was a swift and efficient secretary but he didn't think she would have a cure for a fictitious hangover. He stood up and began pulling on his jacket. He had to get out of there. He felt stifled, by Faye and by Ralph and now by Susie, who had sucked all the interest out of the day. Out of his life. 'I won't be long,' he said to Ralph. 'It can wait ten minutes, can't it?'

Ralph stepped in his way between the desk and the doorway and for a moment, face-to-face with him, Nick thought something would happen.

But then Ralph stood aside, backing down, Nick saw with relief.

'I want it back before lunch,' Ralph cautioned.

Nick didn't turn, but he was aware of Ralph's speculating eyes upon him as he left the office.

Whatever Ralph thought, whether he believed the Resolve story or not, the truth would have come as a definite surprise.

Nick was going to church.

The Church of Our Lady of Lourdes was sandwiched between an estate agent's and a row of houses. It was also behind Marks and Spencer, and Nick often saw women in there with their heads bowed and their stuffed-full white-and-green carrier bags placed next to them on the seat.

It was a red-brick building, dark inside, and although it wasn't in his parish the doors were always open and he was thankful for that. He slipped into the subdued coolness and saw the church was empty and as he genuflected his heel slipped out of his shoe. He went down the aisle to the front, slid along a newly polished pew and knelt.

His head told him that he didn't have to ask for anything; God knew. But he had to put it into words for himself; he wanted there to be no misunderstandings. 'What can I do?'

He was startled that he'd said it aloud. He turned to look behind him but the church was still empty, polished pews stretching back unoccupied as far as the doors. He intertwined his fingers and rested his hands on the back of the pew in front. He rested his forehead on his hands. Behind the cool skin the frontal bone felt heavy and dull. *Help me.*

Where to start?

He shut his eyes and saw images of Susie, waiting for Faye and giving him those sideways looks, as though they were sharing something, a secret, a joke. Flirting. She hardly ever looked at him direct and yet after seeing her he could play back everything she'd said, whole sentences, like a script.

Then Faye had felt as though she'd pulled a muscle in her shoulder and had stopped going to the gym, so that should have been the end of it.

But it wasn't for Susie.

She'd rung him.

He'd met women like her occasionally but the crucial difference was that he'd never been attracted to them. Never before. Susie was different. She was neat. Her shirts were always tucked in. She was always made up and had manicured nails. Her hair was dark and glossy and straight. She mostly wore black, or sometimes brown.

And she wanted an affair, only that, nothing more, just a small part of him, ha ha, and just a small part of his life. She didn't want Faye to know because this was just between them, and she didn't want to lose Faye any more than he did and when she said that, she did look at him, with dark, sincere and shining eyes.

And it seemed so possible, the way she said it. It had opened something up in him, but it hadn't been the truth, had it? She'd rung him at home and Faye had heard them.

A long time ago he'd prayed he would become immune to her.

Then he'd prayed she would leave him be.

And now?

He lifted his head up from the darkness of his clenched hands and opened his eyes. The light hurt them. Help me, he thought again, staring at the rose window, because I don't want to lose her; forgetting that was supposed to be his prayer.

He expected an answer. In all these years he hadn't asked for much. He'd adopted Samuel, his sister's child, and saved his wife from her childhood darkness and been the good son and asked for nothing in return. Never before. But he was cashing it in.

He was asking now. He didn't want it to stop. He wanted Susie in his life and he wanted to give her what she asked of him: time, love, himself. *I love her*, he thought desperately. A world without her would be cold, dark, empty and endless and he could feel it settling in him now. *Help me, I love her. Amen.*

Nick got to his feet dizzily and held onto the seat to maintain his balance.

Now he was standing, he wondered if he was going mad. The rose window seemed glaringly bright.

How can it be answered? he asked. He had a wife. He had a wife whom he loved and who loved him, or had done, once.

The church was still empty as he walked between the squatting pews and paused to dip his fingers in the holy water. The air cooled the wet cross on his brow.

15

Outside he pulled up the collar of his navy jacket. Though sunny, it was very cold. He'd lost track of time and he glanced at his watch.

He hurried back to work. Ralph was watching for him covertly from behind his paper-covered desk, looking at his hands as he came in through the door. Nick patted his pocket, as though the packet of Resolve was tucked neatly away. Ralph got up out of his seat and followed Nick to his. As Nick sat down he leant over the desk and put his hand on the file, patting it. 'Lunchtime,' he said ominously.

Nick nodded.

Ralph continued to lean, looking into his face.

Nick finally met his eyes.

'Did you get your Resolve?' Ralph asked softly.

Nick looked at him but there was no sign of irony on Ralph's face, only concern.

Nick shook his head and reached for the file.

Chapter Four

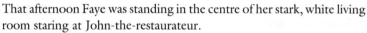

That afternoon Faye was standing in the centre of her stark, white living room staring at John-the-restaurateur.

John-the-restaurateur was staring at the ceiling, perplexed by the array of spotlights studded across it. 'And what,' he said, 'can you follow people round the room with them? Like spot dancing?'

Faye closed her fingers over the remote control. 'Yes, and they'd have to do a turn,' she said. There was no reaction from John. 'No,' she amended, 'they're just for colour.'

'Yeah – so what colours you got?'

'What colour do you want?' She pressed the remote and flicked. A wash of citrus green coloured the room. She felt saliva shoot into her mouth as a response. Flick. Purple. Flick. Blue. Flick. Red. She grinned suddenly. It was her greatest toy.

'I like that one,' John commented.

'This red? It's a good red, it's got a touch of orange in it, keeping it warm.'

'Warm, yeah, you wouldn't want the vice squad to see this room all lit up like that.'

Faye laughed and switched the lighting off, so that they were standing in the cold white space again. She felt the relief. The white tingled like peppermint, or paddling in a cold sea that burns the ankles. She walked towards her bleached oak desk and her foot slipped out of her shoe and she thought of Nick and his broken lace. She stepped back to retrieve it, glancing at her visitor.

John was still blinking at the ceiling. 'Makes a difference,' he said. 'Could be a different room. How many colours would I use, saying I had it put in?'

'That's up to you. Different colours for different sections, depending on the time of day. No-one wants red at lunchtime, for instance. And you'd have to mix them with white so that people could eat their food. Coloured light by itself is too dark to see by.'

17

'Yeah, although I suppose it'd appeal to some.'

'You have to go by what appeals to you,' she said. 'It's your place.'

He flushed slightly. 'So you think it'll improve the place, lighting like this?'

'Me? I haven't got a say in it at all.' It was the opposite of sales talk but her indifference often worked to her advantage. It wasn't her style to push people into things they didn't want. She saw John's gaze rest on her, taking in the navy jacket, navy trousers, turquoise cotton shirt, and drift up, baffled, to check out her expression. He wanted to be talked into it.

Eye to eye, now, she said, 'It's your decision. I can come and look at the place if you like, see what it lends itself to.'

John pressed his lips together and shook his head. The shake was to show his uncertainty. 'What if the lighting turns out to be a dud?' There was a pause. 'That's not to say you're a dud.'

Faye grinned. She liked discomfort in others. 'Well the fact is, you might be better off getting a new chef.'

'I've got one of those. Mick Daniels.' His voice was warm with the pride of insider knowledge.

She was smiling when the phone rang. She handed John the remote before picking up. He switched the lighting to red again. Faye tucked the phone under her chin and folded her arms. 'Nick.'

'Just checking on how you are.'

'I'm fine.'

'You've got someone there, haven't you? I know you can't talk. See you later.'

She replaced the phone. He always rang her in the day, and she was still smiling about it when a blue-black shadow filled the seats of the chairs next to her and pooled in the corners. She was bathed in it and an oppressive sense of hopelessness settled fixedly in the room. The ceiling seemed to have lowered to just above their heads. She shuddered. She knew she couldn't live with a colour like that for long.

'Shee,' John said, wondering, backing over to her desk. 'Heart-attack navy. I saw a rose that colour, you seen them? Ugly, I call it.'

Faye nodded in the blue of despair, twilight going into darkness. The colour of shadows.

Yeah, she knew all about darkness.

John switched off the blue.

The daylight in comparison was dazzlingly clean and cold, and she shivered. John gave her an uneasy glance.

'Feels like it's still hanging around, doesn't it? It makes you want to give the walls another coat of white.' He stared up at the spotlights. 'Get this on the market and you'd put the Dulux dog out of work.' He tapped the brochure. 'Yeah, well, I've got it all here and I'll let you know when to come round.' He cocked his head to one side. 'Ever thought of going into film lighting?'

'Theatre's where I started out.' And hated it, she thought; the absence of windows, being in a large black box, blind and stifled. She was about to tell him more when something caught in her chest and she started to cough. Embarrassed, tears flooding her eyes, she patted her chest until she recovered. 'Sorry,' she said, her voice still croaky.

He was looking concerned. 'You want to give up,' he said gently.

She laughed. 'Over my dead body.'

He shrugged. 'Your choice,' he said.

Chapter Five

Edith Reading adjusted the gold shepherd's crook brooch so that it sat better on her black wool coat, and stepped back from her hall mirror to judge the effect.

Her hair still had a hint of red warming the grey, and, with it newly set, she felt she could be – (anyone?) – someone.

Someone.

She kept hold of the thought.

She wasn't vain, no, not by any means; her worst enemy couldn't call her vain, she was sure of that. Apart from the brooch, her only other pieces of jewellery were her wedding ring and the small crucifix around her neck. No, she wasn't vain. If she wanted to look nice, in keeping with the occasion, it wasn't out of vanity but respect for the deceased.

Not that she knew him.

His name was Bernard St John Dalby and he was a writer, she believed, so although she didn't know him, she knew of him.

The memorial service was to take place in St Margaret's Chapel, Westminster Abbey, a popular venue. She would have a snack in the Army & Navy afterwards.

She checked that she had her purse and keys in her handbag, then opened the front door to see a young woman standing by her garden wall. Edith's mind skipped a little, but the young woman didn't acknowledge her and a moment later carried on along the pavement.

Edith turned and locked the door behind her. It was a fine day for a service. Morning ones were the best, she always thought, the same as funerals; ones before lunch. They gave her an appetite that wasn't at all satisfied by a cup of tea.

She didn't see the girl as she walked to the bus stop. She caught a number 24 bus, which was right on time, to the Abbey.

*   *   *

People didn't wear black for memorial services any more, she'd noticed. They used to, once. She always did. She liked tradition.

She mingled outside the chapel and slowly filed in with the others, looking for a familiar face without success. The trouble with writers was, one couldn't recognise them. Even author's photographs could be misleading, showing them in their thirties looking moody in black-and-white before they'd lost their hair.

She genuflected and took her seat. She looked at the order of service. She didn't care for modern ones but this was satisfyingly familiar: JS Bach, Toccata and Fugue in D minor BMV 538; St Anne Fugue in E flat; Hymn, 'The King of Love my Shepherd is'; Reading, Romans 8: 35–38 – she hoped it was read by someone with a vibrant voice; Sung, JS Bach/Gounod, 'Ave Maria' – a little too popular, perhaps.

She glanced around, scanning faces. Now, Salman she would recognise, although she didn't think much of him. He was costing the country such a lot, when having a shave would have made him unrecognisable to even his mother. She was surprised the British government hadn't assassinated him before now. Kingsley Amis she would have known, dead now though, of course. Nice funeral. Perhaps she would recognise his son, from the service. She should stick to actors, she thought.

The Army & Navy restaurant was full, but she waited for a table, smelling the yeasty aroma of the bread rolls which accompanied the tomato and basil soup. It reminded her of her husband and the yeasty smell that hung around him after a Friday night at the White Lion. (It was called the Dandy Lion now, supposedly some sort of joke.) A table became free and she sat down and ordered.

She sipped at the hot soup slowly. It scalded her lips, a surprisingly satisfactory feeling. She began to feel that her body was actually connected to her again.

The feeling of not having done the right thing came back to her. It was the second time that week. The first was over the grandson of a woman she used to meet at the hairdresser who had died of a virus. His name was Shane Gilpin, and he was twenty-three when he went. Those were the facts that she knew. She disapproved of gossip, but she'd been told he hadn't died of a virus at all, but of a drugs overdose. With a virus, of course, the police didn't normally put a plastic ribbon across the front door, so it looked as though Barra the hairdresser had been right. She'd known Barra since she was Barbra, because Barbra's father

Den had told Edith that they were calling her after Barbra Streisand. At the time, Edith had turned her nose up at this, but not half so much as she had when Barbra had said she was dropping the 'b'. Despite that, she was a good hairdresser, average on the styling but very up-to-date on information.

She had called into the funeral home to pay her respects. She wasn't alone. Shane's family was well-known, and she was one of many locals filing in through the door. When she'd reached him (crossing herself) Edith had been surprised to see Shane was in his coffin wearing a brand new suit and spotless trainers, as if, she remembered thinking at the time, he was going to climb out of there and go to some job interview.

(That would be the day.)

Less of a surprise was the rolled-up cigarette behind his ear and a can of Tennents in each pocket.

She had been absorbing the scene when Wendy McIlroy, Shane's mother, had come in, her eyes red, glanced at the line of people and asked them all who the hell they were. It had been an uncomfortable moment, Edith thought, taking her handkerchief out of her sleeve to rub her brooch to a shine.

Presently she could drink no more tea. It was time to go back. She felt a great deal better, more like herself.

On the way home she went to the butcher, Mr McMahon. 'Two thin lean lamb chops, please, Mr McMarne,' she said, pronouncing his name very deliberately. So many people erroneously called him Mr McMa-hone that she liked it to be known she was aware of the correct pronunciation.

The butcher hacked off two chops for her and presented them on a piece of greaseproof paper for her to see.

They looked fleshy. Flesh-like. 'They're not quite as thin,' she said doubtfully, 'as I normally have them.'

'You want them thinner than this?' the butcher asked in a way she wasn't sure she liked at all.

Small pieces of pale flesh were stuck to his white overall. (Flesh? Meat. She always ate meat. A meal wasn't a meal without meat.)

The butcher tossed them up, still on the paper, and caught them on the turn, to show her the chops from another angle.

'I'll take them,' she said, because although she could imagine throwing them away uneaten, there was nothing else she could think of to get as a substitute.

The butcher was looking at her cynically. 'Are you *quite* sure?'

She looked at him sharply. She took the white plastic bag from him and felt the coldness of the meat through it.

The thought of the butcher no longer troubled her. She was quite looking forward to the lamb chops.

As she walked home from the bus stop she recovered her optimism and was humming 'The King of Love my Shepherd is', when she saw that her gate was open. She knew she had shut it and yet – had she? She looked down the path and sitting on the doorstep was a plump young woman in black. Her hat was pulled down. It seemed to be covering her eyes.

The woman stood up and Edith felt her heart race.

'It's me,' the woman said.

For a moment Edith told herself she recognised neither the voice nor the figure; didn't want to.

The woman pulled off her velvet hat. Her hair, a red-blonde, was flattened to her head.

'Alicia,' Edith said.

'The prodigal daughter,' Alicia said slyly.

Edith hugged her butcher's bag. 'You've –' (got fat? Swollen? Gross? Obese?) '– filled out,' she said. She couldn't bring herself to rejoice. She felt resentment and fear. She wouldn't be bringing out the fatted calf. On the contrary.

But Alicia was waiting.

'I've got two lean lamb chops in my bag,' Edith said resignedly. 'Come on in.'

Chapter Six

Faye sat in front of her dressing-table thinking about what she should wear for the photograph that Nick had arranged to have done for Edith's sixtieth birthday present. She couldn't help wondering if it was a way of giving his mother a permanent reminder that his role as 'The Good Son' was and always had been Edith's present. Nice work if you could get it, she thought wryly. It seemed unfair that accidental virtues should be so appreciated.

She pulled her hair back tightly from her face and stared at herself in the mirror, looking for the signs of smoker's complexion as read in the *Daily Mail*, which were grey skin-tone and wrinkles around the lips. Grey skin-tone? Honestly, she'd *never* seen anyone with a grey skin-tone, and wrinkles around the lips were going to come if she lived long enough, smoker or not.

Nick had never smoked, not so much as a quick drag behind the science block. Why not? He'd never wanted to, that was his explanation. Even at thirteen he'd been sure of, and pleased with, himself. At the age when cynicism, fear and recklessness were put on frequently, tried for size and taken off again, in adolescence, when nothing really fitted, goodness fitted Nick.

It made him untouchable.

She released her hand and let her hair fall over her shoulders.

It was not always a comfortable quality to find in a husband.

She'd expected to marry someone like Richard Cross, in which case she would have been divorced by now, she thought hollowly. Richard Cross was a lad and always would be, no matter how old he got. He laughed too loud, drank a couple of drinks too many, stayed in places too long.

He used to lean on her in the office when she worked at Mahler Industries – and on Susie, too, there was nothing personal in it any more than there was in being bounded on by a labrador puppy. (She had told him that, once.) The three of them would go to the pub at lunchtime, the Queen Beatrice it was then, in the days before it became an Irish theme pub. Richard had told Susie he fancied Faye rotten and Susie had passed it on over a glass of Merlot, the three of them laughing at the fact through a veil of cigarette smoke.

She wondered now when it had become serious. For Richard, perhaps it never had. But knowing he liked her had made her see him differently. She'd gone with him to the Queen Beatrice quiz night and he had seemed so furtively funny, ringing the BBC in Langham Place to find out the motto on the front of the building. Even with outside help they hadn't won, but the laughter stayed with her as they'd left the pub. She had felt it like a bubble inside her as they'd walked back to his place for another drink.

He'd sung her a song from *Bugsy Malone* and made her sing it with him in his flat. She remembered thinking how tidy his room was.

Long time ago, she thought as Nick came in from the bathroom with a towel wrapped round his waist. He ducked down behind her to look in the mirror as he combed his wet hair, and she could smell the pine fragrance of the Badedas shower gel that Samuel had bought him for Christmas wafting over. 'Nick . . .'

'What?'

'I'm not wrinkly and grey, am I?'

'Not really. Should I wear a suit?' he asked, and followed on immediately with, 'I suppose I should.'

'What else did you have in mind?' Faye asked, winding her hair around her finger. It fell in tendrils around her face and clashed jarringly with her red silk kimono. Curly hair never looked smart, that was the problem. Casual suited it better. White shirt, red sweater, black trousers – but the photographer had said not to wear black. 'Why don't you wear a polo shirt and a blazer?' she suggested. 'We'd all be more comfortable that way, posed before the aspidistra.'

'Mother would probably prefer it if we made an effort.'

'Story of your life,' Faye muttered. 'I'll wear my green dress and jacket in that case.'

Nick didn't answer. He took a pair of underpants out of the drawer next to her and dropped his towel.

Faye looked at his bottom, which was permanently pale in contrast with the rest of his skin, which was always slightly tanned. She reached out and smoothed her hand around his buttock and he half-turned to

25

look at her, stretching his arms up and out with a blissful groan. 'Where are the children?'

'Watching television.' She got up off the chair. 'I'll tell them to go and get ready.' She winked at him. This was a prime weapon in her psychological armoury. Stay out of sight and they would come looking for her. Ask them to actually do something and they'd stay glued to the television until she lost patience.

She left the naked Nick and went up the stairs carefully, save tripping over the bottom of her kimono. 'Get dressed, chaps,' she said over the sound of the television. Two small faces looked at her blankly. 'We're going out soon.'

Samuel nodded but Isabel's attention was back on the screen. Her mouth was slightly open. Faye glanced at the TV. Pickling Jeff was pickling a birthday cake. 'We're having a photograph taken for Grandma's birthday and we'll have to look nice. Got that?'

They nodded and she left them and went back down to the bedroom. Nick was lying on the bed waiting for her and she took off her wrap and threw it on the end of the bed. She jumped on the bed and got under the duvet next to him but he grabbed her and pulled her on top of him. She looked down into his lazy-looking eyes, inches from hers. She kissed him on the mouth, and took his pouting lower lip between her teeth. His body still felt slightly damp from the shower and as she lifted herself briefly off him their skin separated with a slurping noise. She lay on him, smelling the Badedas again. Her hair tumbled forward, shrouding part of his face, adding the smell of shampoo to that of the bath gel. They smelt so clean.

'What are you thinking?' he asked softly.

It wasn't the first time he'd said it in recent weeks and once again, she wished she could come up with something impressive – something sexy, loving and a little profound instead of the relative merits of perfumed products. 'You smell good,' she said. 'That's all. What are you thinking?'

'Just wondering what you're thinking.' He smiled at her slowly, looking into her eyes as though searching for something.

She felt he wasn't finding it. 'What?' She smiled to mask her sudden anxiety.

'Nothing. Really.' He rolled over in a sudden single movement with her still in his arms until he was on top of her, heavy, warm, hard.

She thought he would kiss her but he put his head next to hers, cheek-to-cheek, his face in the pillow, holding her tightly, but as he moved with her the thoughts in her head fragmented in the face of the greater, more immediate sensation.

A rush of intense love for him hit her and the force, the heat, the love, the dampness of his body, was for a moment her only reality.

How long the moment would have lasted, she didn't know because she was quickly brought out of it by the sound of a small voice in the room.

'Mummy?'

Faye found herself struggling beneath Nick, but only briefly because he moved off her immediately and propped himself up on his elbow. 'What is it, Bel?' His voice was slightly unsteady.

'What are you doing?'

'Hugging,' Faye said quickly, her heart still racing. She pulled the duvet higher.

'Where are my socks?'

Socks? For a moment Faye couldn't think what they were, let alone where. She couldn't believe it. Isabel had actually listened and obeyed. 'Are there none in your sock drawer?'

'I don't know.'

Nick lay back on the bed and Faye jumped out, pulling her kimono back on. 'I'll get them for you,' she said, and turned to Nick. 'Don't go away.'

She hurried into the sugary sweetness of Isabel's pink bedroom and took vest, pants and socks out of the drawers and slammed them shut again. She took a dress out of the wardrobe and draped it on the bed. 'Here you are. Good girl,' she said, kissing her dark, soft hair and managing a smile before she went back to her own room.

'We'll have to put a lock on the door,' Nick said, watching her from the bed as she came back in.

'Or do it in the bathroom,' Faye said, taking off her kimono with a sense of *déjà vu*. The bathroom was the only room in the house with a lock. She got back into bed, pulling the duvet back over them both. The cool cotton was light on her skin and Nick was warm and strong, kissing her back into closeness. It felt so abandoned, making love in the daylight, but there was a new furtiveness about it now that Isabel was in the next room. Still, they finished what they'd begun and Nick seemed in good humour as he got out of bed and she stayed there in the warm sheets watching him as he dressed.

As he was buttoning his shirt, he turned to look at her. Pausing at the collar button, he smiled. 'Staying there all day?'

'I'm tempted,' she said.

'We'd better get a move on,' he said, turning away.

She wondered if all marriages were like that. For a brief moment they had – she couldn't think of a better word – connected. They'd made a circuit, created light and energy, and now the light was off again. She was pleased with the analogy, but it was a depressing thought. She shivered.

'Cold?' Nick asked.

'Something walked over my grave.' A shadow had fallen across her. When she'd first met him she'd thought her fear of the dark had gone, the fear of something lurking. Depression was what most people called it, she thought, reassuring herself. Nick had told her it was seasonal affective disorder, but her passion for light, colour, brightness, went deeper than that and not only because of her childhood spent in the dark. Oh no, Faye? she thought ruefully. Try telling that to a psychiatrist.

She brought her arms in under the duvet and hugged herself. Out of habit she mentally searched the important things in her life for threats of any kind, turning the characters over gingerly in her head like Tarot cards and laying them out in front of her.

See? There is nothing wrong.

She got out of bed and opened the wardrobe door to look for the green dress.

Everything was fine. And soon they'd have the picture to prove it.

Nick had cursed the traffic all the way to the photographer's studio in Baker Street and they'd arrived there on the dot, bundling in flushed and irritable while Nick put money in the meter.

They were told to wait. Faye knew it. She could have told Nick that. People made you wait for everything and even if you were late you had to wait. She sat with the children on a plush velvet bench in a waiting area-cum-gallery-cum reception room, and looked at the huge portraits on the wall. They gave her an odd feeling that she was being cold-shouldered. All the sitters were looking off-camera as though avoiding her. She wondered if it was the sign of a good photograph when the eyes didn't follow you around the room.

Samuel was holding his arms out anxiously in front of her. 'I've grown out of this jacket,' he said.

'You've already told me that.'

'I look funny. The sleeves are too short.'

'You'll have to keep your hands behind your back. I'll get you a new one, but I can't do anything about it right now, can I?' Thanks, Nick, she thought. He had made them all irritable.

Samuel went to sit down as far away from her as possible. Retired hurt, she thought. She glanced at Isabel who was looking enviously up at a picture of two dark-haired sisters wearing pink bridesmaid dresses. They had their heads together and their dark skin glowed in the studio lights and the satin of the dresses was highlighted to white against the pink of the shadows.

Looking at it she felt envious herself.

She loved pink. Pink was the colour of sugared almonds, sweetness. She remembered Christmas nights when she'd looked through creased pink Roses wrappers and seen a world changed for the better. Pink fireplace, dark pink sofa, pink carpets, pink chairs, pink mother, pink Eva, Faye holding out her pink hand to be pink herself. Then red, the colour of fire, devilishness, heat, excitement. Two colours so far away in emotion but so near in hue. Pink had been her favourite, then purple, cool and mysterious. Blue was the worst of the colours, cold and dead. Different wrappers, different colours, different moods. She'd known that even then.

Nick came in through the door and frowned to see them still there. He looked towards the reception desk and checked his watch.

A girl came out of a back door and greeted them. 'Five minutes,' she said, and slipped away again. Faye got to her feet to say something consoling to Nick, but he turned his frown on her. 'Eleven o'clock sharp,' he said. 'It's already five past.' He checked his watch again as though he suspected it of doing things behind his back.

'Will we get a copy?' Faye asked him.

'What's that?'

'Of the photograph?'

'We could do.' He buttoned up his jacket looking pleased, as though it hadn't occurred to him before.

Faye saw that, oddly, she had succeeded in distracting him.

'Would you like one?' he asked her curiously.

'Yes.' Her eyes wandered to the portraits hanging around them, the faces mellow, soft, gleaming, the eyes dreamy, their darkness lit by the reflection of the flash. 'Yes, actually I would.' She liked the thought of the four of them captured together for posterity, a permanent set.

The photographer came out of the back. He was wearing a suit, to Faye's surprise. She'd been expecting a leather jacket and jeans. And a t-shirt, definitely.

'Brian's the name,' he said, rubbing his hands together. 'Sorry for keeping you. Come this way, please.'

Nick looked mollified and they followed him into the studio in a line, with Samuel still tugging at his jacket sleeves.

The studio reminded Faye of the theatre. There was a mahogany armchair set against a mottled blue backdrop, and next to it a box draped in black velvet which Faye fancied she'd caught a glimpse of in the portrait of the sisters. There were lights grouped around in pairs.

'Right, Dad first,' Brian said, rubbing his hands again. 'Dad, you stand just behind the chair.'

Nick walked self-consciously to where he'd been told.

'Mum, you next, in the chair if you will.'

Faye obeyed and went and sat.

'Dad, you put your hand on Mum's shoulder. Not so far forward. Stop, that's fine. Now, young man, you go and stand next to your Dad. Not that side, the other side. Where's the young lady? A stool for you, I think.' He looked round and found one and placed it at Faye's feet. 'Come and sit on this. Get your skirt straight, that's it.'

He stood back and looked at them critically. 'Mum, take the young lady's hand. Good, I like that. Dad, put your spare hand on your son's shoulder. And you, young man, keep your hands down by your side.'

'My sleeves are too short,' Samuel protested.

'Pull your shirt cuffs down. That's right, they've got tucked up there, haven't they? Always show an inch of cuff. Happy now?'

Faye wondered why she hadn't thought of that.

He switched on the lights and took a couple of light readings. Then he picked up a Polaroid Land camera. 'Look at that light-switch on the wall,' he said, 'and ready.'

'Should we smile?' Faye asked, anxious to be told they should.

'Smile, by all means,' he said. 'And ready . . .'

Smile by all means, she thought. Had those portraits in the lobby been smiling? How hard it was to smile, cold. She made the effort as the flash went off. Too late? Or just in time?

Brian was pulling the print out of the back of the camera and shaking it.

'I want us to look happy,' she raised her voice to tell him. 'Could you tell us a joke or something?'

'*Mum!*' Samuel breathed in protest.

'I smiled,' Isabel said smugly.

'Good girl,' Faye replied, squeezing her hand, because Nick wouldn't have smiled, she was sure. To him this was not a picture to denote enjoyment, but achievement. This was a picture of the Good One of the family, who had adopted his mentally ill sister's baby, who had worked his way up in the same company from a graduate, who had married a slightly flakey, non-Catholic wife and put up with her infidelity. This was a portrait of a man who had worked for what he had got.

And she would smile. She would smile because this was a picture to show she was a happy and grateful wife, a wife who was toeing the line.

Isabel would smile because she knew that in front of a camera, smiling was what you did.

And Samuel . . .

'Once more, please. Look at the light-switch.'

She smiled again, a ridiculously big smile that she felt lifting the apples of her cheeks. Still, it wasn't for real yet. Samuel, he couldn't fake smiles. All right, come to that, neither could she, but Samuel would look uncertain rather than cheesy. Or he would look stern.

He was nine now, nearly ten, too young for adolescence but those growth hormones were buzzing, the ones that let you know the world was a big place and you were only a small, insignificant part of it. She knew he was detaching himself from them – but only in small ways and only for a short time. He detached himself and then he rushed back, demanding: How much do you love me? More than what?

She wasn't very good at that. The stars, the heavens, the universe . . . she'd had a stab at them all, and left him and herself dissatisfied by her imagination.

He always trumped her. The last time he'd said: I love you more than there are bacteria.

So no, he wouldn't smile in this family portrait. It was a serious thing.

'Mum, your hand's slipped,' Brian said.

It was a moment before Faye realised he meant her. She moved her hand. He went over to Samuel and moved his face, and told Nick to drop his chin, just a little.

'Ready!' he proclaimed. 'Look at the light-switch!'

Flash. Flash. Flash. She thought of the stern faces of her mother's family glowering in black-and-white from their frames. She smiled at the light-switch. She was not one of them. This was a different family, one which would glow on the walls. A unit with a sense of unity.

It was rather an anticlimax when many flashes later Brian called a halt.

She stretched stiffly and asked if she could see the Polaroids and Brian handed them to her and switched off the lights. She held the photographs up towards the overhead bulb. They looked an elegant group, but Nick looked tired, and Isabel had her eyes closed. Samuel had one hand on his jacket sleeve. She herself looked insanely happy in comparison, smiling at something that it seemed the others had missed. In the other photograph, her smile was even brighter.

She stared at her happy self, bemused.

'Let's go to Pizza Hut,' Nick was saying to her and she smiled him the picture smile.

He smiled uncertainly back.

Pizza Hut was busy and by the time they'd eaten and got back home she'd forgotten about the smile altogether. The feeling of unity was what remained with her.

She was changing into her jeans when the phone rang. She picked it up in the bedroom. 'Hello?'

'Faye, it's Edith. Could I speak to Nick?'

Faye knew that something was wrong. She put the phone on the bedside table and called up the stairs, 'Nick, it's your mother.'

She went back into the bedroom and waited for him to pick up.

'Hello, Mother.'

She was about to put it down but without preamble Edith said in a rush, 'Nick, I have to tell you. Alicia's back. She wants to see Sam.'

Chapter Seven

Alicia.

Such an uncomplicated name, Faye thought, replacing the receiver gently and sitting down on the white bed.

Alicia. Her son's natural mother.

She hated the jealousy that surged through her on hearing the name. I thought she was dead, she realised, surprised. Or perhaps she hadn't thought it, just hoped it. God, what an awful way to think of someone she'd never met and who hadn't done her any harm. On the contrary, without Alicia there would be no Samuel and she loved Samuel, sometimes more than she loved Isabel who was her own. She loved him because he found life hard and it was a feeling she knew well.

Envy niggled away at her and she reached for her remote control and switched on the citrus green lights above the bed. Green was the colour of envy, she thought, but didn't believe it. This green was the sexiest colour on earth, it appealed to all the senses; it was exciting, dimensional, cool and hot, jungle, swamp, moisture, sun, moss, shade, healing, and she lay back on the bed for a moment, bathed in it. She glanced at the remote and added more yellow but that was a mistake, it lost its freshness immediately. Like over-cooked sprouts, she thought, with a fading grin. She would stay with green.

Green had been the colour of her first light. It had been easy to make because pieces of green glass were easy to find, their edges often rubbed smooth with age.

She lifted her head as she heard the door open. Nick's footsteps as he came into the room made it seem as though it was his will and not his feet that had dragged him in.

He stood at the bottom of the bed looking at her critically. 'Your hair looks black,' he said. 'Maybe you should let the red grow out.' Perhaps hearing the dissatisfaction in his own voice, he added, 'You look as if you're underwater.'

Her senses rebelled more at this glaring mistake than at the criticism.

33

'No – totally wrong, this is not an underwater colour. Not enough blue. It's not cold enough for water, Nick, although algae, I suppose, can make a pond a pea-green –' she stopped herself as she saw him stifle a yawn inexpertly, his nostrils flared with effort.

Besides, white light was good enough for Nick. And wallpaper. Yes, when it came down to it Nick probably saw a lot less in colour than John-the-restaurateur, who she still hadn't heard from. In fact, her only appointment pending was to go back to a house she had done to replace a couple of light bulbs not easily come by.

'Can you put the light on?' Nick asked.

She smiled. 'It is on.'

'I want to see you.'

She got up off the bed and walked to the sofa at the end of it, out of the green and into the white where all things became normal again and her hair was red and not black. She put her hands into her pockets. 'You don't have to tell me, I heard Edith say. Alicia's back and she wants to see Sam.'

'We can't stop her,' Nick said. He was still wearing his dark suit and it gave the scene an awful gravity that it wouldn't have had, had he been in jeans.

The way he said it, she knew he'd considered trying to stop Alicia, which surprised her. Relaxed her, too, because it suddenly seemed impossible that there could be anything to fear on his part. It was she who had competition, not Nick. She stood up and went and hugged him. He relaxed a little in her arms.

'The weird thing is,' he said, 'it's like having a stranger come into our lives. I hardly know her. Families shouldn't feel like that.'

'But they do,' Faye said. She sometimes thought that he had an unrealistic view of family life. His elder brother Derek lived in Boston and they hardly ever wrote. And, being twelve years older than his sister, he'd left home while she was still quite young. Not that it would have made a difference from all that he'd said. She was out of control at ten and pregnant at fifteen with Sam.

She shook her head in disbelief that this . . . fictitious person was real, and back.

'I don't want Sam and Bel to feel like that,' Nick was saying.

'No. But they might,' she said, thinking of her own sister, Eva. She and Eva had pretty much, now she came to think of it, the same personality combination as Samuel and Isabel. Whereas she was fearful,

Eva had always seemed oblivious of the bad things. Eva hadn't worried about their father leaving them. She hadn't worried about the curtains being perpetually closed. After their mother's death she hadn't felt one way or the other about the furniture her mother had kept the house dark to preserve, on the grounds that now their father had gone they would never be able to replace it. Eva had wanted neither to keep it nor to destroy it – she just hadn't cared one way or the other.

Faye rested her head on the arm of the sofa. She felt tired and edgy. It was thinking of the past that did it. She felt her face burn, as though the heat from the fire had been resurrected by her memory.

At the funeral she had worn a yellow wool coat. Eva had worn black. Even with their men next to them, they had made a feeble procession as they had followed the six bearers who were carrying the coffin down the aisle. One would have been enough, she'd thought, to carry her mother's sparse body in its polished box. When she'd last seen her, at home, her collar bones had jutted through her grey blouse like wire coathangers.

At the end of the service she had seen her father standing straight but red-eyed at the back of the church. He hadn't followed them to the crematorium but at the time she wasn't to know, and in the car she'd looked out of the window rehearsing bitter phrases to confront him with, reproaching him for turning up when it was too late to save them.

But she couldn't forget Eva's betrayal. For in the church, Eva had stopped and hugged him.

Faye had heard the sob catch in her throat. She had heard it and felt envious.

'She must be all right,' Nick said.

Faye turned her head and gazed at the green light.

'Knowing her, she won't stay around for long,' he said. He sounded bitter rather than relieved. He took his shirt off and pulled a navy sweatshirt over his head. He stepped out of his suit trousers and hung them up. He picked up his jeans from the floor of the wardrobe and hopped around doing the trouser dance for a moment before buttoning the fly. Every so often he walked into the pool of green light and became momentarily transformed. 'She does what she wants. Always has.'

She wondered for the first time if he was jealous and was about to ask him when a pain suddenly lanced through the soft part of her shoulder. It was so unexpected that she tried to scream but the pain had taken her breath away. She felt sweat break out coldly on her face and her mouth was wide with a silent gasp as she tried to get Nick to look at her.

He had his head down. Fear and absurdity combined and popped into her head and out again. She was dying here in front of him as he laboriously found the right notch on which to fasten his brown leather belt. She could hear a high-pitched sound getting louder in her head which remained hardly audible, like a silent dog whistle. Dappling black shapes began to multiply in her eyes and she slumped forward, instinctively trying to get the blood back to her head.

'Faye?'

Nick had at last noticed her. For what seemed like a long time, he did nothing. Then he was bending in front her, pushing her shoulders up.

'No,' she said in a high hurt voice, but she was breathing again and despite Nick's hands fixing tightly on her shoulders the pain was easing. The black dots were turning white and she blinked but there was no need, her vision was already clearing. She had an overwhelming urge to cry. 'I think it was a heart attack,' she said, on the point of breaking down.

Nick looked at her, still crouched.

He bit his full, lower lip. 'Heart attack,' he said. Then he started to laugh.

He often called her a hypochondriac. It came from smoking, her worry that something was wrong. It was periodic and usually followed the same pattern; the medical checks, the subsequent reassurance, the knowledge that it was safe to carry on a little longer.

But this had been something new, something vicious and frightening. 'I've had such a pain – for ages, just here.' She pressed her fingers into her shoulder. 'That pulled muscle. It doesn't seem to be getting better. That was the worst it's been.'

'Have you tried Deep Heat?'

'No.' She flexed her shoulder a couple of times and was relieved to find the pain had subsided to a dull ache. Once she'd had the okay she would try to give up smoking. That was a promise. She managed a smile. It would put a bit of a damper on the portrait if she dropped dead now.

Chapter Eight

Nick was in his office, holding the purring telephone receiver with a combination of longing and foreboding, like an addict trying to stay on the wagon.

But he had no peace.

That was what he wanted to tell her.

He thought he might engineer a meeting to do just that; he saw himself walk down the same bit of road on the dusty, pale-grey pavement, repeating the journey step for step with increasing hope until she appeared.

He put the phone back and felt a swift flash of triumph which quickly passed. He was a man on a ledge, on a precipice. He was going to fall.

'Daydreaming again?' asked a woman's voice, Beverly's, light with flirtation as she came into his office tucking a strand of blonde hair behind her ears.

He leant back in the black vinyl chair and stroked both hands over his short, dark hair. 'Just thinking.'

'You shouldn't do too much of that,' she said with a smile, and sat on the edge of his desk. 'Trust me, I know. I'm going to the deli. Can I get you anything?'

'A cappuccino, thanks.'

'And a BLT?'

Ralph looked in just at that moment and caught the last sentence. 'I'll have a BLT, Bev,' he said, 'on white. Nick, how's the backlog?'

Nick glanced at Beverly as she slid off the desk with a look of exasperation on her face.

'Three quid,' she said to Ralph.

Nick pushed a chipped 'No More Mr Nice Guy' mug towards her. She picked through the coins in it.

'Take for Ralph's, too,' he said, as Ralph was patting his pockets aimlessly.

She didn't look at either of them as she left. Ralph watched her go through the door and shook his head. 'Doesn't she realise she's wasting it on you?' he said wistfully. 'Women have got no taste, I tell you.'

'You wanted to talk about the backlog,' Nick said, welcoming the distraction. It wouldn't last long, he knew that.

'Are you on top of it yet?'

'Getting there.'

'That's all I wanted to hear,' Ralph said, raising his hand as he ambled out.

'Ralph . . .' As soon as he'd called him, he knew it was a mistake. 'If you had the chance, with Beverly . . .'

A slow grin lifted his boss's mouth. 'Like a shot, mate,' he said.

And then Nick was back to wanting to ring.

He wanted to ring her so badly that speaking to her seemed the pinnacle of his desire, he just wanted to speak to her and be finished. That, though, wasn't how it would be. He would speak to her and they would be precisely where they were two weeks ago, with Susie wanting a physical relationship he couldn't give her.

He couldn't blame her for wanting him, she'd had little enough so far. Merely words, as if he hadn't noticed that something shimmering ominously between them like hot oil in a pan.

'Cappuccino,' Beverly said, coming in and putting the polystyrene cup on his desk.

He knew she was still annoyed at having been treated like a gofer by Ralph. 'Thank you,' he said. 'I'll get them tomorrow.'

She looked at him, her lips pressed in a thin line, a 'that'll be the day' expression on her face. 'I might hold you to that,' she said, but she gave him a smile after she'd said it. 'It would be more to the point if Ralph went.'

He took the lid off the coffee after she'd left and wiped off the chocolate froth with his finger, wondering why Ralph should go when Ralph was in charge. He wondered why it was a problem to get a sandwich for Ralph when she was going out anyway. He knew why she didn't mind getting something for him, why she was conferring favours, sitting on his desk.

The image of her doing just that came back to him, but the face was not Beverly's face but Faye's, and he was not a scrupulous executive but a man called Richard Cross, a man like Ralph, who would take her 'like a shot, mate'. It made him angry, still. He was glad she'd given up work to stay at home playing with her lights. He wondered if she missed him.

He felt an unease, a sort of tension. He pushed the cappuccino away from him, got up from his desk and hurried out of the building.

It was windy as he went round to the car park, jumped into his car and drove to Susie's office, the adrenaline inside him making him reckless enough to jump a red light.

Luck, because he called it luck now, hardly in the circumstances able to call it divine intervention, saw to it that he immediately found a parking space just where he'd wanted one. He went into the building, up to the girl at the desk. 'Nick Reading to see Susie Jacks.'

The girl at the desk looked at him coldly and inhaled through her nose as though she was insulted by the smell of his impatience. 'She expecting you?'

'No.'

'I'll have to check, then,' she said as though she had no doubt his presence would be undesirable.

Nick wondered if Susie had warned her about him, and the thought cut deep, that she had anticipated his calling there, and gone to these lengths to avoid seeing him.

The receptionist got out a list from under the desk and went down the names, pressing each one slowly with her thumb. 'Jacks, was it?'

'That's right.'

'Yeah, got it. And who are you again?'

He would make a complaint about her, about her attitude, he told himself, struggling to keep his temper, but he was desperate enough to go along with it peacefully, so he kept his patience. 'Nick Reading.'

She put the list down in front of her and dialled. 'Hello? I've got Nick Reading here for Susie Jacks?' She glanced at Nick, and then back at the phone. 'She's not at her desk?'

Nick squeezed his eyes to clear them.

The girl at the desk was looking up at him. 'She's coming down. Wait over there, please.'

Nick sat down in a black leather chair and picked up a newspaper from the table next to it. He held it, but he didn't attempt to read it. The lift doors opened and he looked up, his heart kicking with expectation, but it wasn't Susie. He looked at the girl who came out, nevertheless. What made one person so different from all the others one ever met? The doors closed and the lift clunked and hummed back up the shaft.

On its return journey it disgorged her and he felt the excitement well up inside him like a bubble as she walked towards him, her dark glossy hair swinging around her face as she walked. She was wearing a brown knitted dress and he wanted to hug her.

He dropped the newspaper on the table. 'I've got the car outside.'

'What are you doing here?' She was frowning. 'Where are we going?'

'Anywhere. Nowhere.' He pushed the revolving doors and Susie got in and he pushed in with her, forcing them both to have to shuffle round and out onto the windy pavement.

'I've only got five minutes,' she said, getting into the car. He waited for a break in the traffic before opening his door. He slammed it behind him and the car rocked gently under the force.

Susie was looking at him and her dark brown eyes were gleaming. She always gleamed, he thought. It was as if she was loved, and polished regularly.

'What is it you want?' she asked.

Nick tugged his lower lip. He screwed his eyes up in despair. 'Just this,' he said after a moment. 'Just to see you.'

Susie turned her head and looked out of the passenger window. As her hair spun around he could smell her perfume. He thought that that smell of spring flowers would for the rest of his life reduce him to tears.

'What's the point, Nick?' she said.

Nick looked at her. The bubble of excitement burst and felt like fear. He gripped the steering wheel and thudded his head against it. 'I had to see you.'

'Don't beat yourself around the head with it.' It was a rare flash of humour. She looked serious, leaning back against the headrest, her hair slipping back off her face, exposing her throat. 'Nothing can come of nothing. Which is all our relationship is.'

She glanced at him, bouncing him a look from the corners of her eyes, and away again.

He stared at her face, memorising it. What did she look like? Beautiful, probably. How could he tell? He loved her, she was beyond description.

Staring back through the windscreen Nick thought of divorce. He experienced something that was becoming more and more familiar; the feeling that he was existing on different levels of reality. Divorce. That mortal sin. He could almost feel his soul fly off and downwards, plummeting into the abyss, tossed there by his own hand as if it were worthless.

And maybe it was, if she was the alternative.

'I think Faye knows how I feel about you,' Susie said. 'She never rings me now.'

Nick folded his arms against the steering wheel. He didn't believe it, although he didn't doubt she did. He and Faye had knocked together a marriage bit by bit as most people do, without much planning, and it didn't make for a stable structure. But even if the foundations hadn't been that solid, there had been an upright shoring it up and the upright was his faith. He also knew his faith had been her upright, too.

A delivery truck pulled up behind him and pressed down on the horn. Nick jumped with the shock and realised he was obscuring a delivery bay. 'I'll have to move it,' he said, switching on the engine.

'I've got to get back, anyway. See you, Nick,' she said, opening the door and easing her legs out first. She smiled at him reassuringly. 'If you get over your scruples, ring me!' she shouted over the blare of the lorry's horn.

He heard her. She made it so, so simple.

He pulled out of the space. He felt like driving, anywhere. Work was a distant intrusion.

Everything was an intrusion. All that he knew and believed in meant little compared with the thought of pressing his face into the shoulder of the warm brown knitted dress.

That was reality.

PART TWO

Let me fall into your arms. It is all over.

Castlereagh

Chapter Nine

———————— ❧ ————————

Unravelling, sometimes, throws up a surprise. She shouldn't have met Nick, not at a cinema, because . . .

. . . Faye has always disliked cinemas, the waiting in the half-dark for the show to begin, the heavy crematorium curtains, the itchy seats, the smell of dust. The dimming lights, like approaching unconsciousness and the helpless passivity of being a spectator and sitting still despite thrumming heart and drying mouth.

There are times, though, when a quick trip into another world brings a temporary relief. She's a sucker for Walt Disney and the simplicity of the problems and the cleanness of the light. She knows the songs and the sentiments. She likes the voices and the colours. She takes her Walt Disney seriously.

A small boy comes into her row. Her heart sinks. He is no more than a toddler, too young to concentrate, too young to follow the story, too young to sit still. She looks around the red-tinted, filling auditorium for his family, frowning her disapproval in advance. With a struggle, the boy sits on top of the folded seat. He looks at the curtains.

She glances at them herself, hoping that they are opening. They are still hanging heavily, awash with red and blue light. She looks at the boy. He is alone and sits patiently looking towards the hidden screen. She knows he must have done this before. She looks round again but amongst the rows of seats dotted with people there is no-one obviously attached to him. Whoever he is with is showing the same curious self-possession. She stares at the boy, and when he doesn't notice her she leans slightly forward, hoping to talk. The instinct to befriend the young of any species is strong.

The lights go down, imperceptibly at first, drawing from her that primitive fear of blindness; blind panic. Her eyes strain to see. The curtains whisk open and sound like taffeta. Night glows on screen, and a fanfare of sound, and bright letters. She rests her head on the back of the seat and forgets the boy.

Later on, during a song, she remembers him. The film is colouring his face. His mouth is open, his jaw dropping heavily. She can see that he is not watching the film, he is in it.

The ending, when it comes, brings tears to her eyes. She waits, drained but satisfied, while the credits roll. The lights lift. There is a man leaning over the boy, fastening the buttons on his coat. From where she sits it looks a serious sort of coat, with a collar.

She wonders if the man does it regularly, brings the boy and leaves him, and the disapproval pulls at her face and it is this face that she is wearing when the man looks at her. She looks away, bends, feels on the floor for her handbag. She is cautious; the strap is hooked around her foot.

She straightens and the man has gone. She sidles out of the row. The stream of people is quite dense. There is no sign of them.

She remembers the man's face. She remembers a full lower lip, a thinner upper one. She remembers being looked at through round eyes partly obscured by lowered eyebrows. A cautious look.

She leaves the cinema, blinded by the daylight. She is happily surprised, having forgotten it is not yet dark. She tries to look round without moving her head, worried that she might catch his eye. Then she looks round in earnest. But they have gone, and she is disappointed.

Saturday again, and she is standing outside the cinema reading the billings as passing. Coincidentally, it is time for the matinée. She does not buy a ticket yet. The film is not the purpose of the visit.

Out of the corner of her eye she can see people go in through the double doors and she can see those at the very front of the line queuing at the ticket stand.

She is waiting for the father and his boy. It is not his round wary eyes half hidden by a frown that attract her, nor the full lower lip, nor the short hair, the colour of which she hasn't seen. What attracts her is the fact that he has an ex-wife and a Saturday son who won't sit with him; he is damaged goods and she goes by the ancient Ionian school: Like is only known by Like.

The Saturday father and son walk past her and her eyes register them seconds before her mind does. She is surprised and not surprised. The surprised part of her is the part of her that does not expect to win raffles, and perhaps she is disappointed – that the chase is so easily won and at the predictability of the man who has dark brown hair cut short-back-and-sides, longer on the top, lightly gelled; he is wearing a navy bomber jacket, dark t-shirt, faded jeans. The boy is wearing a brown coat with, probably, a velvet collar; anyway, it is darker than the coat itself. She can imagine the mother who put that on him. He has reddish-gold hair so bright that it leaves a shadow of green as she blinks, the same flash as that of the sun before it sets.

She watches them walk inside. She can see them indistinct as moving ghosts behind the reflection of the street on the glass.

She feels insubstantial herself, having imagined that they might have recognised her. She looks at the billings, but she knows the films now: *Die Hard*, *Snow White*, *Virgins on Top*. The adventure is over; she is aimless, restless, empty and ready to go home.

From where she is standing she can hear the raised voice of a speaker in the square. She walks in his direction, also the direction of the bus stop, smiling to herself at the thought of rebellion of any kind. 'And the mighty shall fall,' she hears him say. She glances at him. He is wearing a green puffa jacket and standing on a blue bread pallet. 'And the meek shall inherit,' he says. 'That's you, lady.'

Startled, she stops walking and grins, wondering whether to heckle back.

'Yes, you,' the speaker says.

She is both embarrassed and amused. 'Well, thanks.'

He takes off his woolly cap, and bows and continues. 'And there shall be crying in the wilderness, and where is that? It is here, ladies and gentlemen. It is here in Leicester Square, right here, right now.'

She tucks her hands in her pockets. Three youths are watching him as they eat fries out of red cartons. In the pedestrian turnover, one or two people hesitate, listen a moment and walk past. The speaker's voice is a little too light to add weight to his words . . .

She is preparing to walk on when she sees the Saturday father and son. The son has a hat on. Perhaps it is the prophet's promise that she will inherit that has given her a lift because she smiles widely and walks towards them.

'Oh, hello, weren't you watching *Snow White* last week in the Odeon?' She addresses this to the son, and looks up and smiles at the father. 'Your son was sitting by himself?'

He gives her a steady look through hazel eyes.

He can see right through her, through her and beyond, weighing, measuring and balancing the result.

47

She feels the blood pumping in her neck – flirt, you bastard – and feels the blood rushing to her face.

'And money is the root of all evil,' the speaker shouts.

The man looks at her, grins and turns. 'The love of money,' he says, loud enough for the speaker to hesitate. '*Proverbs*,' he adds, turning back to Faye.

'Same thing,' the speaker calls to him.

The three lads jeer.

He turns back to her and almost smiles; his upper lip, which was straight, is curved slightly upwards, the full lower lip still in a pout. 'He's not my son,' he says.

Damaged goods, the box says, the box she always rifles through. There is a filter over one end of her choice mechanism that keeps out the good stuff and lets the second-rate fall through. She's not sure where this filter comes from. At times she is tempted to find out whether she took it up of her own accord. For instance, why did she choose a plain straw boater with a red ribbon for her baby sister's christening when she could have had a white hat with imitation pastel flowers that looked real? Or one with peach flowers and hoops of pearls? 'Your choice.' Her mother's words. That was the first choice she remembered making; that was the first time the filter appeared, keeping out the good hats and letting the boater fall through.

So she eyes the Saturday father warily. 'He's not your son?'

'Not exactly.'

She glances from the man to the speaker. He is still proclaiming in his light voice. The spring wind grabs her wild hair and flings it across her eyes. She smooths it away and wipes the tear that had been drawn by the lash.

'He's my nephew,' the Saturday father says.

She looks back at him.

'And you're right, we did come here last week. He left his hat.'

She looks at the boy. His hat is on his head. It is knitted and white. Beneath it, his face is beautiful, the most beautiful face she has ever seen, smooth, translucent, the eyelashes and eyebrows fair, the eyes large. He is totally unblemished. He looks at her steadily and she smiles a bit and looks at the man again who is saying to her, 'What did you leave?'

She sees a lightness in the teasing. He is bright, uncomplicated, a man taking his nephew out for a treat.

She laughs at the question and although many answers come into her head she is not sure yet which of them, if any, might be true.

Chapter Ten

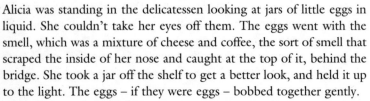

Alicia was standing in the delicatessen looking at jars of little eggs in liquid. She couldn't take her eyes off them. The eggs went with the smell, which was a mixture of cheese and coffee, the sort of smell that scraped the inside of her nose and caught at the top of it, behind the bridge. She took a jar off the shelf to get a better look, and held it up to the light. The eggs – if they were eggs – bobbed together gently.

'Do you need any help?'

She turned and looked at the person who had spoken. He was white, but had his brown hair in dreadlocks tied back from his face. He was wearing a white jacket and a white hat and a wide smile – she saw them in that order, the smile last, and she stayed with it and smiled back. 'This shop is dreamy,' she said. She wanted to live in it, to play with the jars on the shelves and open them and smell them and dip her fingers in and try them on her tongue. There were wine pitchers, the colour of tea stains, that she would have liked to have filled with water and poured from. 'It's not like a real shop. It's like a mystery.'

'Oh, it's like a real shop all right. There are no mysteries in it for me.' He adjusted his cap, pulling it lower on his forehead. 'Anything here you'd like to try?'

She looked down at the refrigerated display. She could see little fish curled around olives and speared onto long cocktail sticks. She moved her gaze from those to the meats. There was a great hunk of something that looked old and mummified. All the time the strange smells of spice and vinegar and brine and cheese wakened her, made something clearer in her mind, a sharpening of the olfactory nerve.

'Have a taste, go on. What do you fancy?' he urged her, amused. 'That's parma ham you're looking at. Want to try it?'

She shook her head. She still had the jar in her hand and she held it up to show him.

'Quails eggs,' he said. 'Over there by the milk there are fresh ones. Cheaper, too, there are only six in that jar. Hang on.'

He came around the counter and went over and showed her the box of fresh quails eggs. Inside the plastic bubbles she could see the eggs plainly, speckled with brown against a pale aqua background, and very small. 'They're nice,' she said, 'but . . .' There was still something fascinating about the white peeled eggs in the fluid bobbing around as though there was life in them.

'But those are the ones you want,' he finished off for her. He gave her a smile of understanding. 'Do you live round here?'

'Round the corner. With my mother. I'm trying to get a flat, I've been away and I've just come back recently to be with my son.' She smiled at the thought.

He was rearranging the cartons of quails eggs, bringing ones from the back to the front. 'How old's your boy?' he asked over his shoulder.

'He's nine.'

The man turned slowly to look at her, curiosity in his eyes. 'So how old are you?'

'Twenty-four.' She saw the disbelief in his eyes and it reminded her. 'There was a bit of a fuss.' She stroked one of her plump hands with the other.

'I bet there was.'

A bit of a fuss on her mother's side, she thought. None on Nick's. Nick could soothe the baby better than either of them and sometimes he was the *only* one who could soothe him. It made her sad at the time because she loved that baby, but sometimes she hated him, too. Sometimes it seemed one against one. Sometimes she knew the baby hated *her*. If she wanted to eat, he would cry; if she was in a hurry, he would cry; as if he knew and wanted to make things worse, so that sometimes her hand would fly up high as if it didn't belong to her and then come swooping down. Sometimes she would make herself miss him.

One against one, that was what it had seemed like every time he had chosen Nick over her. In the end she pretended it *was* Nick's, to herself, and that she was free, and because she was free she and a friend went to work in an hotel in Llandudno as chambermaids. 'Tanya,' she said, remembering.

'Tanya? I'm Adam.' He held out his hand and she shook it shyly.

A woman came into the shop and went to the window and put two croissants into a bag. Just after her came two schoolgirls. The small shop seemed to be getting crowded.

51

'Lunchtime,' Adam said, and called towards the back, 'Frank! Customers!'

Alicia followed him back to the delicatessen counter.

'Keep those eggs,' he said, 'and come out with me for a drink tonight?'

His eyebrows were raised at her, and she had a feeling that unless she said yes, he wouldn't let them down.

'Okay, thanks,' she said. 'Where?'

'White Lion. Eight o'clock?'

She nodded and turned her attention to the jar with the quails eggs. They were like blind eyes bobbing around, trying in vain to see. She'd felt like that at times but now she could see clearly.

Now she had plans.

Chapter Eleven

Faye sat in the pale-green hospital waiting room pressing her shoulder and trying to get the pain to come back.

It was always the same. You made an appointment and by the time the date arrived you were normal again. The secret was to anticipate the illness in advance. Book a date and try to catch a bug. Or more accurately, let a bug catch you.

Her GP had rung her to say that a consultant wanted to talk to her about her x-ray and the ache in her shoulder. Her appointment with the consultant was for one-thirty and she had got to the hospital early, a mistake, since she was now sitting in the waiting room with a cured shoulder and a copy of *Homes and Gardens* on her knee and nothing to do but wonder how the appointment system was supposed to work.

A woman who had come in ages after her had just gone in to see Mr Angkatell although it was now twenty minutes since her own appointment time. Each minute dragged.

She imagined going up to the receptionist and saying, 'What's going on? I'm not waiting here for the sake of my health, you know.' It was a feeble attempt to cheer herself up. Like schools, hospitals made her think of trouble.

I could do with a cigarette, she thought, swinging her leg. The orange plastic seat squeaked and the magazine began to slip. She caught it and put it on the seat next to her and began to look in her handbag for change for the drinks machine. She found twenty pence and carried on searching in the hope that there was a stray pound coin tucked into the corner of the lining. For once, there wasn't.

A scuffle in the doorway made her look up, hopeful of an interesting distraction. A man in a suit took a few unsteady steps towards the door, hesitated, and reversed out again.

Wise decision, she thought, zipping up her bag.

The retreat had apparently been a temporary one because she could hear him now make a run up. Picking up speed he galloped through the door, past the waiting room and down the corridor where he did a cumbersome three-point-turn before vanishing from view.

She tried to catch the eye of the middle-aged man opposite her in the hope of sharing a smile but he wasn't playing. She opened her handbag again and took her cigarettes out, debating whether or not she had time to go outside for a quick puff.

'Faye Reading?'

Just like school, she thought, jumping to her feet, pushing the packet back in her bag out of sight. 'Yes!'

'Room Five, please.'

She congratulated herself on not missing her turn. She went to door five and pushed it open and went in. The consultant was looking in a filing cabinet by the window with his back to her. 'Come on in and take a seat,' he said without turning.

She sat on the chair by his desk. She hated people who did that, acted as though what they were doing with inanimate objects was more important than responding to a person.

She stared at his back, hoping he would feel her eyes on him. Looking at him from here she could see that he was quite a tall man. He wasn't wearing a white coat. His suit was dark green. She would lay money on the fact that he was wearing a bow tie.

The phone rang. 'Could you get that?' he asked, as though he hadn't the inclination himself.

Shrugging, Faye picked it up. 'Mr Angkatell's room. Yes, he's here.' She held out the phone. 'It's for you,' she said, heavily ironic.

He turned, came towards her smiling and took it from her. 'Yes. Yes, yes,' he said into it, turning away while she studied him.

No bow tie after all. Was that just gynaecologists? His tie was a mix of green, purple and red; very lively. His shirt was a pale green – lighter than her own outfit. He was balding and had a few wrinkles around the eyes. Good-looking in an obvious way, like a TV doctor.

Good tactic, too, she thought, getting her to answer the phone, making her feel as though a consultant's life was no big deal and his phone calls no secret. She watched him nod at the phone. He put it down with no closing words – mid-sentence, it seemed to her.

'Faye Reading,' he announced.

'That's me,' she said. His lack of a white coat was making her feel flippant.

'Well, Faye, I've seen your x-rays and we've got a problem here. There's a shadow on top of your lung.'

That was the word he used. Shadow.

She heard the word and she thought, this is it. This is what I've always been waiting for.

And she'd never thought it would be in a clean room with the fluorescent light invalid against the cold daylight that clarified everything around her with its harsh glare. Opposite her, Angkatell looked like a snapshot. She could see every line of his taut face, and behind him books leaning on a shelf, and in front of him her red case-file askew on the desk.

'It will need to be checked out,' Angkatell was saying in a monotone, as though he wanted it to be reported at some future time that he had given nothing away.

'A shadow,' she said. She nearly laughed. She knew what a shadow was, hell yes she had been dogged by shadows. 'Fine,' she said. 'Check it out.'

Angkatell reclined in his chair, looking to the left of her. He put his hands round the back of it and clasped them. With his shoulders pushed back and his upright posture he looked like a hostage and the pose did not go well with the co-ordinating suit, shirt and bright tie.

She looked from him to the room again, at a green examination bed covered with a paper sheet, at the shelf with the few books, the last one of which had fallen on its side, at the window with a view of the dirty building opposite, and above it at the flat, white sky.

Other people had sat here, looking at these same things, hearing this same news.

'Have you ever had pleurisy, anything of that nature?' Angkatell asked.

Faye shook her head.

'And you're suffering shortness of breath?'

'Yes. Had to give up the gym. Can't walk to school without stopping to read the benches, although –' although she didn't have to stop for long, only until the ache passed and her lungs filled again.

'It could be old scar tissue,' he said. 'Any numbness in your fingers?'

'Yes,' she said, 'these three.' She hit them on the desk to demonstrate. 'They feel sort of dead at times. I thought it was to do with my shoulder.'

She could see him evaluating her words, measuring them against some sort of medical template that he'd cobbled together from his experience. He wouldn't share it with her of course. They never did.

'How long have you been smoking?'

The mention of it made her want one. Funny how it was only ever one. Not like with food when, if she was hungry she wanted masses. 'Since I was eleven. I was rebelling,' she added helpfully.

'All right. I'll spare you the lecture but you know what you're going to have to do about that.' He leant forward on the desk. 'The next step is to find out what exactly we're dealing with. I want you to come in on Monday for a bronchoscopy.'

'Oh.' She was startled by the distance of it. Three days away. She was startled by the nearness. Fear washed over her. What about the children? She watched Angkatell pick up the phone and dial. She listened to him make arrangements. She was amazed by the lack of drama in his voice, but then she thought, sick people were as common to him as insurance fiddles to Nick. It should have been comforting. She wanted a cigarette and thought, how do I become a non-smoker? How does that work?

He was putting the phone down again, and once more she hadn't heard a goodbye.

He closed her file and handed it over to her. 'Give this to the receptionist on the way out,' he said, 'and I'll see you next week. In the meantime, try not to worry.'

In her hands it felt light and flimsy. 'Am I –' she stopped and cleared her throat. She held up the file as though it had the answers. 'This . . . shadow.' She could hear the dismal hope in her voice. 'Is it curable?'

He met her eyes. 'That's what we're going to find out,' he said.

Standing outside the hospital she felt disorientated, as though days had passed since she'd gone in. She could see that getting home was going to be a problem.

It was so cold. People were hurrying past, collars up, faces closed against the wind. She felt raw and exposed.

She wanted to be home without getting there. The thought of talking to taxi drivers, or catching a bus or pushing onto a tube, the thought of people speaking to her, made her feel alarmed.

She turned her collar up and standing in the flow of the crowd she imagined going somewhere warm and real and sitting down to eat. Habitat was only a short distance from here.

She changed direction and walked away from the bus stops and towards the store. Two telephone kiosks loomed and one was empty. She ought to ring Nick. Feeling unreal she went inside and probed in her bag for the twenty-pence piece. Tucking the receiver under her chin she dialled Nick's number at work and while she waited she looked at the coloured cards that lined the walls: Busty Blondes, Masseuse New On Scene, Erotic Secrets, Blue Eyed Scandinavian. She stared at the accompanying drawings of women with Barbie doll figures, the receiver cold against her ear.

Finally Nick picked up. 'Faye? How did it go?'

Her breath came in a jerk. 'I've got a shadow on my lung.' The absurdity of the phrase hit her afresh, as if the absence of colour itself were the disease. And yet . . . it was so familiar.

'Oh shit,' he said harshly. There was a silence, then he asked, 'From smoking?'

She didn't answer. What did it matter what from? She became aware again of the roar of the traffic outside. She let her gaze drift back to the coloured cards. Bottom Marks For Naughty Boys. Welsh Dresser With Big Chest.

'So what's going to happen?'

'I've got to go back next week for a bronchoscopy. They want a better look.'

'A biopsy?' he said.

'No, bronchoscopy.'

'I love you. Oh, Faye . . .'

She knew he was crying. She, cold and clear-headed as she'd ever been, held the phone tightly and detachedly listened to the sounds of his grief.

'Forgive me,' he pleaded down the line, breathing in a shuddering breath.

'Yes,' she said. It seemed right that he was crying when she was so dried up. 'I've got to go, I've got to pick the children up.' She put the receiver down sharply. 'I'm ill,' she said to the cold bulk of the phone, and suddenly she wanted to be back with Angkatell, for whom this was everyday life, breaking news of one sort or another, the good and the bad. Like Angkatell she had just hung up and hadn't said goodbye. The connection made her feel better, yet as soon as she thought of it she felt worse.

The coin had dropped inside the pay phone and she slid her fingers into the cold metal mouth but it was empty. She pushed the door and stood outside on the pavement and saw a bus approaching. She remembered the children and began to hurry towards the bus stop, Habitat postponed until next time. Monday. Not far away, not nearly far enough.

She broke into a run and became aware of a heaviness in her chest, a new feeling, as though her lungs were two water-filled balloons, and she felt a creeping panic and slowed down. Gasping, she reached the tail end of the general push onto the bus and kept close to a woman in a purple mohair coat, shuffling behind her off the pavement and onto the road, and stepping up onto the platform inside the bus. When she reached the driver she realised she didn't have any change. She took a ten-pound note out of her wallet and slid it under the screen. 'One-fifty, please.'

He looked at her and shook his head.

'It's all I've got,' she said.

'Lady, I can't change it,' he said, looking past her at the people crowding up behind her and leaking in.

She still had her hand on it. 'Just give me five back,' she said.

He jerked his thumb, letting someone with a pass push past. 'You're blocking the aisle.'

'Keep it all,' she said angrily, jostled from behind, pushing the note towards him and feeling her throat tighten again, 'just give me my ticket.'

'I can't,' he said.

She stared at him. He was in his fifties, corpulent and benign, his face ordinary, skin folding slightly from nose to mouth, the face of the kind of man who knew where he was in life and how he'd got there, and how he liked spending his money and where he liked to take his caravan for holidays. An ordinary man.

But his eyes were sharp and he was spoiling for a fight and the fight was with her and he didn't care that behind her, people were getting on without paying and the bus was filling fast. 'I'm going to have to ask you to get off,' he said.

'I'm not moving. Just take the money.'

He was almost smirking. 'No can do.'

The ten-pound note was stirring in the black coin tray, disturbed by the movement in the bus. In theory they could stay there all day but of course she couldn't, she had the children to pick up and time was moving on.

She snatched back the note, crumpled it and stuffed it in her coat pocket. She felt like killing him.

The last man on was pressed up next to her, his leather coat new enough to still give off the smell of hide. 'Where are you going to, love?'

She glanced at him and it was an effort to get the words out. 'Belsize Park. Thank you.'

He winked at her and dropped the money on the tray and looked at the driver. 'Here you are, mate. Now, can you get this bus moving?'

Faye tore the ticket from the machine, jerking against the handrail as the bus lurched forward.

The driver was having the last word.

By the time she reached her stop she was already late in picking up the children from school.

Hurrying made her chest burn. She adopted a sort of scurrying run which was kicking up leaves in the alley when she heard a voice call out, 'Mum!'

She lifted her head automatically but she didn't expect to see Samuel. Yet there he was with Isabel by his side and although she was aware that someone was with them her thoughts moved slowly, setting up explanations in motion: a teacher was bringing them home because she was late. Ready to be annoyed, because being late was a rare event, she looked at the teacher and saw that it was actually Nick.

Breathless, she stood still and waited for them to get to her, ribs still heaving as they approached. She saw Samuel look quizzically at his father.

'What are you doing here?' she asked Nick angrily, folding her arms over her chest.

'I didn't know whether you were picking them up or not,' he said, pushing his hands into his overcoat pockets. 'You hung up on me,' he said with cosseting patience in his voice.

'And you thought I'd just leave the children in school?'

'I thought you'd got enough on your mind,' he said softly.

Samuel had slipped his hand into hers. It felt dry and cool as she held it. Their breath was mingling in clouds and breaking in the damp and woody air.

'Daddy says you're ill,' he said, looking up at her.

Faye looked at Nick. 'What have you told them?'

'That you're going into hospital for tests. They've got a right to know,' he said, pulling the collar of his raincoat higher around his ears. 'This involves all of us.'

'I don't want you to be ill,' Isabel said, the atmosphere between her parents pushing her to the brink of sudden tears.

'Do I look ill?' Faye asked.

They all looked at her. Isabel shook her head, smiling, relieved it was that simple. Faye looked at Samuel who was shaking his head too, slowly, his eyes locked onto hers. She could see tears brim in the lower lids of his eyes.

'Well then,' she said. 'Let's not talk about it, what do you say?' She turned and started walking back the way she'd come, leaving them behind.

Nick caught up with her. 'Faye . . .'

'What?' She looked away from his face, twisted with pity and remorse. 'You're making me feel worse,' she said.

Isabel ran past them, her dark hair bobbing around her navy coat collar, but Samuel was keeping close and she let it go with Nick and turned to him. 'Sam, it's that ache I've had in my shoulder.' As she said it she could feel a rumble in her chest like a low growl. Smoker's cough in the afternoon, now. 'I'm going into hospital on Monday for them to have a better look.'

'And will that cure it?' Samuel asked.

She reached for his hand and tucked it again into her pocket with her own. 'Hope so.'

'I'll miss you,' he said, leaning against her arm.

'And me,' Isabel said, running round them.

Only Nick said nothing.

Perhaps he hadn't heard.

Chapter Twelve

For Faye, the night seemed to last a lifetime, sleep torn apart by nightmares which jerked her wildly into wakefulness and momentary relief, soon broken by the remembrance that there was no relief to be had from this particular one.

The last time she woke, coughing, her heart echoing against her ribs, she checked the time on the luminous face of the clock and saw it was five a.m. The ache in her shoulder had returned, and she eased her arm round tentatively in its socket, put the clock back down and slid out of bed without waking Nick.

She went upstairs, made herself a coffee and switched on the lights: red, bloody and vulgar. She changed them to orange. It was like a tropical sunrise gilding her, and her heart lifted.

She heard the paper being pushed through the letterbox and went down to collect it. She glanced at the front page on the way back up the stairs. DATE WITH DEATH, ran the headline, and beneath it a woman's face stared out. The woman looked in her late thirties, with short, wavy hair. Faye sat down and skim-read the story, which was that the woman had been killed on the way home from a friend's party after saying she was meeting someone.

I'm not the only one, she thought. She folded the paper and looked carefully at the picture of the woman, Sheila Jones. Sheila Jones did not look like a woman who would arrange a date with death or anyone else. She looked unsure of herself, smiling stiffly into the lens as if unused to the attention. Faye looked closer and tried to detect a knowledge of the woman's fate in her eyes, but Sheila Jones seemed to be bothered only by the sun.

Faye balanced the paper on the arm of the chair, dissatisfied by Miss Jones's innocence.

I want to blame her, she thought, for her death; easier that way. It was such a – reassuring thing to do, to say she brought it on herself. It's only human, she thought, to apportion blame.

People would do the same with her; she remembered Nick asking, is it because of the smoking?, and knowing he was relieved it wasn't on his particular list of old enemies. It's your fault, was what he meant.

'Your fault,' she said aloud.

She felt a bond between herself and Sheila Jones. She had also courted a potential killer. Had invited him in.

Thinking of cigarettes made her want one with a sudden desperate need and she felt light-headed with the force of despair that washed over her.

She jumped at the roar from the boiler as the central heating kicked in.

'Mum?'

Another jump as Isabel appeared at the top of the stairs, blinking crossly in the artificial sunlight. 'There's a noise in my bed.'

'It's almost time to get up, in any case. Come and sit on my knee. I'll change your sheets before tonight, that will get rid of any squeaks still hanging around in there.'

Isabel giggled, always ready to be amused, and climbed up on her mother's knee. 'Who's that lady?' she asked, looking at the paper.

'Oh, no-one we know,' she said quickly. 'Just someone who got into trouble, that's all.' Standard line. Gloss over it. Hope it won't happen to us.

Seemed like it already had.

Nick got up shortly after Isabel. 'Didn't sleep a wink,' he said morosely, slumping on the sofa and reaching for the paper.

Faye stared at him. 'You were snoring most of the night.'

Nick opened his mouth to protest but then appeared to change his mind. He got up off the sofa and went into the kitchen with the exaggerated slouch of a weary man. He popped his head out. 'Coffee?'

'Yes, please,' she said, without enthusiasm. It was ridiculous, all she could think about was a smoke. Nicotine patches, they might help. She remembered Vicky, the mother from school whom she was friendly with, saying they'd given her nightmares. No, she didn't want nightmares. But Vicky had also seen a hypnotherapist.

'I might see a hypnotherapist about the smoking,' she called to Nick.

He came out of the kitchen with the coffees. 'I can't believe you need to. Hasn't it put you off?' he asked, puzzled, and shook his head as though to clear it. Some of the coffee dripped onto the floor. He handed her a mug. 'Look, I'm sorry, do what you want, whatever helps.' His voice was soft and warm. He glanced at orange lights overhead without comment, and gave her a gentle smile.

Faye took the mug. 'Thanks,' she said. She wondered when his solicitude would wear off. Soon, she hoped. It would drive her mad to have no-one to snap at, but perhaps people with shadows weren't supposed to snap.

The word brought the fear back sharply – of course it hadn't gone, how could she have believed that? It was merely lurking. Galvanised with fright she put down her mug and got to her feet so quickly that Nick looked at her in alarm. 'Got to get Sam up,' she said.

'Take it easy,' he said soothingly after her as she went down the stairs.

Shut up, she answered him in a whisper through gritted teeth, and went in to see Sam.

He had his face buried in the darkened nest of cloth.

At one time she'd taken a holiday job as a breakfast waitress in a small hotel and her first task had been to take wake-up trays of tea and coffee into the bedrooms of businessmen. Humans in their lairs in the morning smelt much like any other animal, she'd thought then, but Sam's room smelt of Sam: vanilla and butter and popcorn. She put her hand on his back. 'Samuel?'

He awoke in alarm, lifting his arm to defend himself.

'It's me,' she said quickly.

He sat up and looked confused. 'I had a dream . . .'

She stroked his smooth hand. 'Aw. What was it about?'

Frowning, he cocked his head as though listening for it. 'I can't remember now,' he said after a moment. 'Do you love me?'

Tears pricked her eyes. 'More than anything.' She leant over and hugged him. Sometimes he seemed so grown up, but sometimes he seemed so small her heart hurt for love of him. He always surprised her.

'When are you going to hospital?'

'Monday, but only for the day.'

'Good.' He got out of bed and looked at her sharply. 'Mum, it's not BSE or AIDS, is it?'

'Gosh no,' she said indignantly. 'What made you think that?'

'I was just checking,' he said.

The plus side of Nick's concern was that he hugged her so tightly in the kitchen as she got out the cereal that she thought her ribs would break.

But she was moved almost to tears. 'I love you,' she said seriously, looking into his heavy eyes.

'You do?'

'I do.'

'I love you too.'

'Funny words, aren't they?' she said with a laugh, trying to lighten the atmosphere. 'I *lerve* you,' she said, thinking of her favourite scene from *Home Alone* where the hall manager is on his knees.

He didn't laugh with her. 'I know you do,' he said.

She nodded. 'I think I'd better tell Edith about Monday,' she said. 'And I'll find out if Alicia really wants to see Sam. If she does, we'll have to tell him. And I'll see if I can get to a hypnotist this afternoon.'

'You're very organised,' he said, winding her hair around his finger. 'Do you want me to come with you on Monday?'

For the first time she realised she didn't have to go alone. 'Yes,' she said. 'I'll ask Edith to pick the children up from school.'

'She'll be glad to help,' he said gently.

Faye released herself from his arms. He was starting to sound like Oprah Winfrey at her most compassionate. 'Breakfast time,' she said.

One thing about having a Catholic mother-in-law was that to Edith suffering was common currency. She handled it with familiarity, welcomed it; Faye would go so far as to say she made a hobby of it. She spent much of her time visiting the sick and elderly and had a fondness for memorial services. Where there was suffering, so was Edith, Faye thought ruefully, amassing shares in the heavenly bonus scheme.

Knocking on her mother-in-law's door later that morning Faye realised with surprise that it was the first time she had ever visited Edith alone.

When the door opened and Edith saw her, she seemed struck by the same confusion. Her face creased with anxiety as though, without Nick by her side, she couldn't place her. But her good manners surfaced quickly. 'Come on in,' she said. 'It's lovely to see you.'

Faye did, and smelt lemon Pledge in the air. She could see that Edith was dressed up in a pink shirt with navy polka dots, and a wool skirt in the same shade of pink. Edith was always smart. Or perhaps she had plans. 'Am I disturbing you?'

'No,' Edith said, 'as a matter of fact I was going to call you, but the window-cleaner came.' She looked at the window. 'I don't know, those things that they have with the red plastic handles, they don't clean as well as a chammy although they're quick.'

Through the glass Faye could see the house opposite slightly over-laid with smear. It was a bad window-cleaning job, streaky. 'I use newspaper,' she said, checking to see how far the smear extended. 'Maybe it's inside.' A glance at Edith's face suggested it wasn't the most tactful answer she could have come up with. And why was she defending the window-cleaner, whom she didn't even know? 'You're right. Chammies are best.'

The older woman's eyes caught hers; brown eyes made brighter by the contrast of her cheeks which were permanently flushed with broken veins. Her red hair was turning non-descript by the greying process but the eyes made up for everything. There was nothing Edith didn't see.

'It would have mattered to me, once,' Edith said, self-mocking, 'but I don't know – things change. Sit down. I'll get us some tea.'

Faye sat, feeling that she ought to offer to help, but she was a guest and Edith would want a guest to sit and be patient. She was a guest and not a daughter-in-law and at times this saddened her. Edith would have liked Nick to have married a Catholic, she knew that.

Waiting like a stranger in Edith's parlour, Faye listened to the flat ring of cups being put on saucers. She sat on the wine-coloured velvet sofa and rested her arm on the armrest. The pose felt unnaturally stiff and she glanced at her hand to see whether it looked as odd as it felt.

She imagined going to join Edith in the kitchen and sitting on the edge of the table to keep her company while the water boiled to a domesticated roar in the kettle. It didn't seem such a good idea and she stayed where she was, stroking the wine-coloured velvet of the armrest and noticing the fabric had been combed or scratched. She felt along the indentations with her fingertips as Edith came back from the kitchen with a gently rattling tray, which she put down on the small table next to Faye. Faye looked at two china cups and saucers sprigged with forget-me-nots, a small plate holding four digestives on a doily, a milk jug and a sugar basin with a spoon in it. The tea had been poured in the kitchen.

Faye took her cup and put a teaspoon of sugar in it, mainly because she liked the delicate sound of the spoon ringing against the china as she stirred, a warm, encompassing sound she associated with her father, who in those good days would bring them tea in bed on a Saturday morning.

Edith was sitting forward in her chair opposite, knees together, cup held steady in both hands.

Faye sipped her tea and wondered how to start.

'As I said, I was going to ring,' Edith said, picking up where she'd left off. 'You know that Alicia wants to see Samuel.'

Faye could see the freckles scattered across her face, the freckles Samuel had inherited, making him a member of the tribe to which, for all her dyeing her hair red, she would never really belong. 'Yes. We haven't told him yet, just in case she went away again.'

'She's talking of getting a flat.'

Faye was surprised. 'It will be nice for you,' she said, rallying. 'I mean, having her back.'

Edith pursed her lips and didn't reply.

Faye was surprised at how calm she felt about it. Looking at it dispassionately, what would a twenty-four-year-old want with a nine-year-old boy?

'She's gone to a drop-in centre. For drop-outs. Mixing with the wrong sort again.' Edith stirred her spoon through her tea, not in a circular movement but back and forth as though mixing bathwater. 'You wouldn't recognise her, Faye,' she said.

'No,' Faye said, neglecting to add what Edith had forgotten, that she'd never met her. But Samuel had a photograph that she knew by heart. It was of a leggy, strawberry-blonde in a loose white cotton dress leaning against green railings in a park. 'How is she?' she asked curiously. Nick had always maintained that Alicia's illness had started with post-natal depression and that after Sam, she had gone into a psychiatric hospital but come out well enough to go away and be a waitress. That was Nick's version. Nice and simple.

Edith sighed and seemed to be wondering about what she wanted to say. 'You know she got pregnant because she had a Saturday job in Brinkley's chemist and, as a Catholic, saw herself called upon to put pinholes in the con –' she paused awkwardly, glancing at Faye, '– contraceptives? As it turned out they were the ones she used herself.'

Faye hadn't heard this story before. Was Edith saying she'd always been strange? Alicia, the Mad One. 'Bring her for supper tomorrow night,' she said. 'I'll tell Samuel this evening. I'm sure he'll be glad to see her.'

She felt shockingly tired all of a sudden. Finishing her tea, she remembered what she'd come for; even that seemed to have happened a long time ago. It was like a story only half-remembered. The fear was lying low. 'Edith, I'm going into hospital on Monday. It's only for the day, but I wondered if you could pick up the children from school?'

The sharp, dark eyes seemed to pierce her. 'Of course I will,' Edith said. 'What's wrong?' Her tone conveyed gravity and offered a tempting invitation to talk.

Faye hesitated for a moment and then said, 'I'm having a bronchoscopy – they've found a shadow on my lung.' She wondered whether it would become meaningless if she said it enough, but the look of utter distress that crossed Edith's face made her feel afraid for herself, and she wanted to cry.

'Oh, my dear,' Edith said, putting her hand to her throat. 'Oh, my dear.'

Faye was nodding. 'Oh my dear' summed it up. A slow sensation of strangulation began around the middle of her throat and as her eyes filled with tears Edith was up off the chair and right in front of her, taking the cup from her gently and putting it back on the tray. The cup rattled in the saucer and the spoon rang against the cup. 'I'm sorry,' she said.

'No, no. Of course I'll come,' Edith said. 'I'll keep an eye on them for you.' She paused. 'You're young and fit, that's the main thing.'

It's serious, Faye thought, as if she'd glimpsed it clearly for the first time. And she's wrong, I'm not fit at all, I'm not well.

She lifted her head to look at the cold light coming in through the smeared window.

It didn't help. The darkness had already crept in.

Early that afternoon she called in at Vicky's to ask about the hypnotherapist she had used.

Vicky opened the door wearing a grey tracksuit. She was brushing a fringe of damp, dark hair away from her eyes.

'Fighting the flab,' she said. 'Come on in and I'll finish my work-out while you talk to me. Too knackered to talk myself.'

Faye followed her into the kitchen and sat on a wooden pew which had been salvaged from a church that was now a recording studio. She leant on the table, which was covered with a piece of purple oilcloth, and watched Vicky get back on the bike, her high ponytail bobbing as she began to pedal.

'Don't you go to the gym any more?'

'It's not the same, going on my own,' Vicky said. 'No incentive to keep up the effort.'

'I gave up because I was unfit,' Faye said. 'You know how it is, you get out of the habit.'

Faye watched Vicky change the fitness level and her pedalling slowed. 'I love sitting here watching you though,' she said. 'I feel fitter already.'

Vicky laughed and blew her fringe out of her eyes. 'Why don't we start going together? Let's make a date and stick to it.'

Faye looked at the purple cloth, and up at the gothic windows through which the daylight arced. Talking of the gym made her think of Susie. Susie and she had grown apart, that was the truth. Working together had been the common denominator and without that, what did they have? Susie talking about men and clothes, she herself talking about Nick and the children, defensively in both cases it had seemed towards the end. Susie had talked about finding her clients for the interior lighting but they hadn't materialised. Perhaps that was down to the 'man trouble', too.

'What do you say? When are you free?'

Faye dragged her eyes from the light at the window and turned to her friend with a deep breath. 'Vicky, I'd better tell you why I'm not fit.'

The hypnotherapist's name was Frank Sindon. That same afternoon she was in his house, staring across at him in the chair. He looked vulnerable and the light of the sun shivered along the side of his face as she waited for him to speak.

'You have no head,' he said to her, keeping his voice soft.

She felt alarmed.

'You have no head for smoking, any more.'

His back was to the window. It felt very hot in the room.

'Find a spot on the ceiling,' he said, 'concentrate on a spot on the ceiling and when your eyes are heavy, very heavy, you will close them.'

The ceiling had a woodchip effect and no shortage of spots to choose from. She stared hard until the spot blurred and began to dance. Damn, she thought, lost it.

'You are staring at a point on the ceiling and your eyes are getting heavy.'

She'd found a better spot now, a more prominent one. She stared at it and waited for her eyes to get heavy. She knew that if she dropped her gaze and looked at the man she would be staring at him into the glare and his silhouette would shine around him, blood red, painful to the eye. But politeness kept her looking at the ceiling.

She could hear him breathe. She could imagine his wide chest rise slowly under the blue polyester shirt, rise, pause and fall. She shifted and sat up a little straighter in the armchair, an old, studded, begrimed Chesterfield. She felt her trousers slip against the leather and she let herself slump again. She could hear the grandfather clock ticking. It went with the Chesterfield suite, certainly, but what it reminded her of now was of a cabbie's meter ticking away, the ticking that carried on when the cab was stuck in traffic, when she was spending money on getting somewhere and not getting anywhere at all.

She thought she'd better close her eyes.

'You are free,' he said softly to her. 'You are free from the tyranny of smoking, from the anxiety of having cigarettes, from your trips to the garage at night. You are free to be yourself now and your time is your own. You can relax.'

It was certainly warm in the room. And she did feel relaxed. She was slumping further into the Chesterfield.

'Cigarettes are your enemy now. You want the best for yourself because you deserve the best. You breathe only fresh air into your lungs. Only fresh air.'

It was her own snoring that woke her up with a start. She closed her eyes again quickly and wondered how long she'd been asleep and worse, whether he'd noticed.

He began talking again, or perhaps he hadn't stopped. 'And as I count from one to ten, you will enjoy this feeling of freedom, and carry it with you to full awakening consciousness. I'm going to start with the count of one . . . two . . . three . . .'

She stirred slightly. 'Four . . . five, and you are beginning to feel refreshed and renewed, six and seven, eight . . .' Her eyelids were fluttering, 'and nine, your eyes are opening, and ten.'

She blinked and ducked into his long shadow, out of the sun. He gave her a slow, relaxed smile and she stretched, and heaved herself upright in the armchair. She looked around her, dazed and vaguely pleased, like someone who had unexpectedly slept well. Which she had.

'Well, Mr Sindon,' she said after a moment, and lapsed into silence again. Talking required more effort than she was willing to make. 'I want to believe it,' she said. 'No more trips to the garage.' To prove she'd been listening.

'If you want another session you can get me at the Heath Healing Centre. I'll give you a leaflet.' He went to fetch it and returned and handed it to her.

She looked at it. Maybe now was the time to be less cynical. As well as hypnotherapy, the Heath Healing Centre offered Sahaja Yoga, a flotation tank, reflexology, mountain air, aromatherapy, Shiatsu massage, polarity and spiritual healing. 'I'll see how it goes,' she said. 'I mean, do people –' hearing the tight wheeze in his chest, she wondered if it mightn't be a good idea for him to put the Heath Healing Centre to the test.

She looked at him as he sat back into the sun again. How to pay? She felt oddly furtive, picking her handbag up off the floor. 'Sixty pounds,' she said, getting her chequebook out. She could see the gleam of her cigarette packet inside and guiltily she brought it out and shook it near her ear. She could hear the cigarettes jostle around inside.

'I ought to give these to you,' she said, 'just in case.'

'Keep them,' he said lightly, 'you'll feel safer.'

She felt relief and smiled. 'Goodbye, Mr Sindon.'

He made a thumbs-up sign and closed the door behind him.

On the pavement she took out the packet. She flipped open the lid, hesitated, shut it and put the packet back in her bag.

Testing himself, she thought, and she glanced up at the window and saw him looking down at her.

Chapter Thirteen

Samuel was sitting on his bed holding a wooden box with brass hinges that could only be opened by a secret method.

He pushed his copper hair out of his eyes. Without knowing the secret, you could force the box all day and not manage to come up with a way of releasing the lock.

The box was from China, brought back by an old boyfriend of his mother's, in which she used to keep old love-letters, but now she had his dad she had thrown her old love-letters away. What she did with the ones from Dad, he didn't know.

But the box was his now. In it he kept details of the Spy Club and its members. He had done the forms himself on the computer and he kept them hidden because where he'd put 'Favourite Disguise', the members had all written 'hat', copying from each other he could tell because they'd written the same thing. His father had read them and laughed.

Since then he'd added a few things like Lorne Chamberlain, who was listed under 'Enemy'. That's why he hid the forms. Some things he couldn't tell his father. Adults could blow a thing up from some small worry to unbelievable proportions, touching teachers, parents and other children and causing worse trouble to everyone than ever it had to him.

Lorne Chamberlain was one of those people who knew everything. ('So does his mother,' Faye had said once when he'd mentioned it.) In the showers after gym, if you looked Lorne's way he would jut his head forward and come out with, 'Want a postcard, gay boy, bum bandit,' that kind of thing, and he could just imagine his father's face if he'd told him that. And his mother's. She took things much more seriously than he did. When he was fighting in judo and losing, he could sometimes see her pale face set still on purpose. He half expected her to leap out to help him and what a worry *that* was.

Another worry was the reappearance of his original mother who had left him when he was a baby because she was ill. She'd come back, only to see him his mother said, but she'd said it more than once as if it wasn't as simple as that.

Underneath the Spy Club files and a picture of the Blackbird, his favourite aircraft, he had a picture of her, right at the bottom of the box. To him she looked more like an au pair than a mother, but she had more or less his colour hair and he took their word for it that she was the mother because although adults lied about the strangest things, he didn't think they would lie about that. Still, he didn't feel in the slightest that he belonged to her when he looked at the picture.

He got off the bed and knelt on the red carpet, putting the box on the Rug Rats duvet cover and doing the secret movement that opened the box. Then he felt under the spy files and drawings and took out the photo.

She was laughing in the picture, his original mother, and she didn't look ill, not in the least. You couldn't always tell, though. His own mother was ill now, but she was acting the same as she always did.

He wouldn't think about that. Faye loved him, he knew she did, from big things and small. One of the big things was that one day, when Isabel had been a baby, he'd looked at her hair (dark) and at his father's (dark) and at his mother's (dark) and he'd said he wanted dark hair too, to be the same. And the next day, his mother had dyed her hair red, to be like him. She still did it. That was a big thing. The small thing was that she never tried to kiss him at the school gates like some mothers. He loved her for that.

So it was no big deal that his original mother was coming to his house tomorrow to take a look at him (and he hoped it was only a look) but on the other hand it was a very big deal indeed. What should he call her? Would she want to take him somewhere like the zoo (or was that awkwardness only with stepmothers, of which some of his friends had quite a few)? And the other question was, was she cured? He knew about diseases, about AIDS and stuff, that they were something you could catch easily like BSE, and die from, and it was something that he worried about a lot when it was mentioned on TV, but on the other hand he didn't know anyone who'd caught either. And he didn't want to.

The point was, was she better?

He hoped she was.

He hoped he would like her. And he hoped she would go away again, pretty soon.

He put the photograph back in the box with his written secrets.

The ones in his head he kept to himself.

Chapter Fourteen

The following morning, Saturday, they went shopping for food for Alicia and Edith's visit.

Faye was exhausted by the afternoon. Nick had thrown in delights she never bothered with – 'Mini Kievs? Why have we never had Mini Kievs?' – and Isabel had kept telling her about My Little Pony bubblebath and Samuel was stocking up with Jaffa Cakes and cans of Pepsi when she wasn't looking. She'd gone to get bin-liners and had come back unable to recognise the trolley as her own.

The ache in her shoulder was worse, much worse. She'd thrown in a tube of Deep Heat, thinking why not, everything else was in there, including cereal that they would never eat but which contained a free gift. And teabags with a pack of Penguin biscuits thrown in for nothing. A normal family doing a normal week's shopping.

Back at home she wondered if her tiredness was psychosomatic. They all seemed edgy with each other. 'Is Alicia vegetarian?' she asked Nick suddenly.

Nick hitched up the sleeves of his white shirt and took his eyes reluctantly off the TV and looked at her. 'I haven't seen her for eight years. I wouldn't know.'

'What if she is?'

'You can always do her an omelette. That's if she turns up.'

'Do you think she won't?'

'How would I know?'

She got out of her chair and stood looking at him. 'Why say it, then?'

He looked up. 'What?'

'Why are you in such a foul mood? Is it because of Alicia?'

'Yeah, that's it.' His eyes flickered back to the screen.

She left the room, and went downstairs to check what Samuel was doing. He was fixing a lighting circuit in a matchbox, to make a disguised torch. He lifted his head. 'Hi.'

74

'I'll be downstairs if you need me,' she said, listening to Nick move around overhead, probably to get another beer from the fridge while he watched the rugby, excluding her. Excluding all of them. Isabel was at a tea party and let's face it, Faye thought, out of all of us she has the best social life.

She went down to the basement. They had originally designated it to be a games room, but it was chilly and too far from the rest of the house for the children to want to play in by themselves. And it had no natural light. She'd claimed it for herself and called in a carpenter to fit some architraves. One day it would be her office. Would it though, now? she wondered fleetingly, and pushed the thought away.

Hidden above each of the architraves was a lighting bank and she could step into any colour she wanted, any colour. It gave a completely different effect from the ceiling lights, whose colour was diffused.

Her dream was to totally co-ordinate a room; say, blues and reds and as a living border, jars of Siamese fighting fish on a narrow shelf around the room. Given a free hand and a large house she would create Prince Prospero's palace with stained-glass windows of single colours lighting each suite by means of a brazier burning in the passageway behind: blue, purple, green, orange, white, violet. She'd omit the Red Death suite.

She shivered and switched on the white lights. The room looked pure and Arctic and made her feel clear-headed. One day she would section off a room with a fish tank. The problem was, it would have to be reasonably narrow but strong enough to take the weight of the volume of water.

She went over to the single fish tank she had down there. The fish inside were silver dollars, shiny bright, but they could catch any colour she chose or remain white. Some people were afraid of colour – Goethe had said that colour attracted savages, animals and the unrefined. Idiot.

She crouched to check the shoal and saw that one of the silver dollars was dying. It was being bothered by the other fish, who were making pecking motions at it. As they struck, small clouds of sand burst up off the bottom with the impact.

Faye turned away in disgust. She took a jar from the desk and went fishing. 'Gotcha,' she said, lifting out the fish in the dripping glass.

She checked the fish's gills, which were hardly moving. 'You'd better stay in the jar for now,' she said, and turned to see Samuel coming down the stairs.

'Dad was wondering where you were,' he said. 'He's in a foul mood.' He picked up the remote. 'England are losing. You know you told me about black light, how black light would make things invisible? Can you make me one?'

Faye laughed. 'Who are you trying to get rid of?'

'Oh, no-one in particular. What are you doing?'

'One of the fish is ill.'

He came over to look into the tank and the silver shoal turned with precision at the movement, heading for the far end of the tank. He picked up the jar from the table. 'What's the matter with its fin?'

'That happens when they're not well. Occupational hazard of keeping fish, you always lose one or two in the beginning.'

The hum of the filter was loud. Faye looked at the stream of bubbles, looking as tangible as mercury. The shoal swerved, catching the light. She heard Nick walking overhead and then his footsteps changed direction and he came down the stairs.

'What are you doing down here?' he asked, his hand on the stair-rail.

'Day dreaming,' she said.

'It's so cold,' he said, coming on down to look at the fish. He rubbed his thumb against the edge of the tank and didn't look at her. 'You should keep warm. You should be resting.' He carried on smoothing the glass.

She imagined it cutting into his thumb, deep red, a relief of colour against the monotone. 'Careful,' she said.

They were silent against the hum and bubble of the tank. The silver sand at the bottom rippled slightly. Flash; the body of fish turned and sailed slowly, meeting its reflection coming the other way.

It was almost seven and they weren't ready. 'So what *should* I wear?' Samuel asked, coming out of his bedroom and looking down at his navy tracksuit bottoms and dirty trainers.

'Wear some proper clothes,' Faye said sharply. 'Put your school shoes on, for a start.'

'Am I all right?' Isabel asked, twirling round in a red check dress that she'd worn all day. It had food in primary colours down the front.

'What does it matter what you look like?' Samuel said fiercely. 'She's not your mother. She's not going to be interested in you.'

'Sam!' Faye stopped herself from yelling as she saw the anxiety behind the scowl. 'You look fine, Isabel. Perhaps you could wear your red jumper over it.'

It was too late. Isabel was tugging at a strand of dark hair and looking at her tearfully. 'Why isn't she my mother, too, Mummy?'

'Because I am, you sausage,' Faye said. She could smell smoke. 'Back in a minute.'

She went upstairs to find the kitchen hazy and acrid. She opened the oven door and the smoke came out in a puff. Fanning it with her hand she looked at the chicken, which seemed about the right shade of tan – at least it wasn't burnt. She opened the windows but the smoke billowed back in.

The doorbell buzzed.

She took a can of furniture polish and sprayed it around quickly.

'I'll get it,' Isabel shouted. Faye hurried to look at herself in the mirror. She wanted to look cool, in control, the kind of woman Alicia could trust with her son. She smoothed her hair hurriedly but had to admit she looked like she felt. Tired, with more things on her mind than she could put right. She wanted to call for Nick, who was still in the downstairs bathroom, but Isabel had opened the door to the visitors and she could hear Edith's voice drifting up.

Forcing a smile to get her facial muscles working, she went down the stairs to greet them.

'Edith, come in.' Kiss. 'And Alicia.' Kiss, though she hadn't met her before. Faye smiled, trying to look as though she wasn't desperately scrutinising her. She was wearing a black dress and black sneakers on her feet. And she was plump – Faye hadn't expected that. 'Go straight up. Isabel, take their coats and give them to Daddy. Will you have a sherry, Edith?'

'I'll have a glass of white wine if you've got one open,' she said, shrugging out of her jacket.

Faye smiled. 'Alicia?'

Alicia was already going upstairs, looking up at the lights.

'Cool,' Faye heard her say as she caught up with her. She was like a child whose mother had forced her to come along but who had found something that would momentarily ease the boredom. She clasped her hands behind her back and her gaze wandered and came to rest on Faye.

'I'm glad you've come,' Faye said, thinking of Nick's warning. 'What would you like to drink?'

77

'Diet Coke, if you've got it. Anything, really. Where's Sammy?'

'Getting his shoes on.' He hates being called Sammy, Faye thought apprehensively. She glanced at the kitchen where the drinks were still chilling in the fridge. Diet Coke. She must be watching her weight. Who wasn't, Faye thought. 'I'll get the drinks and I'll see if he's ready.' She went into the kitchen, uncorked the wine and poured a glass for Edith and herself, and opened a can for Alicia. Edith had come silently up the stairs and was sitting next to her daughter, as though Alicia was Isabel's age, Faye thought, bemused. She put the tray on a table next to Alicia. 'I'll just see where they've got to.'

She found them in Sam's bedroom. Nick was talking to him in slow, reassuring tones. Samuel's freckles stood out on his pale face as he protested, 'But I don't want her to like me!'

'Nor me,' Isabel said cheerfully.

'Come on,' Faye said, taking Sam's hand, 'she's all right, honestly. She's drinking Diet Coke.'

'She hasn't come to see you,' he said with the bitterness of one who'd been singled out.

'Sammy,' came a voice from the door.

They all turned at once. Alicia was smiling and looking straight and solely at Samuel and Faye saw him colour.

'You're different from your photograph,' she said.

He tucked his hands in his back pockets and looked at her shyly. 'So are you.'

There were a couple of seconds of total silence, and then they both, to Faye's surprise, began to laugh.

Supper was a success, in so far as the vegetables were overcooked just as Edith liked them – she was a great believer in boiling the stiffness out of cabbages.

Samuel had loosened up and Alicia was funny, making them laugh. She also knew all about Game Gear because she knew someone who had one, and he was working up to getting a PlayStation.

Samuel was impressed by that.

She told him he could play with it any time he liked.

Faye and Nick exchanged glances, but Alicia changed the subject again and to Faye's relief she didn't treat him in what anyone could call a motherly fashion. She seemed to want nothing from him at all, and when after the pudding he asked, she said he could call her Allie.

She told them about her waitressing jobs and how she'd had to dress up in Welsh costume one hot summer until the sweat had poured off the ribbon holding her hat on and she'd come out in heat rash.

By the end of the evening they were all relaxed. Faye was glad to see that Nick had a smile on his face. Only Edith surprised her. She seemed to remain apart, her dark eyes alert.

It was Edith who decided it was time to leave, just after nine, as though she could stand it no longer. She kissed Isabel and Samuel and told them she'd see them on Monday.

Alicia went down and waved from the door, dodging goodbye kisses.

'Don't let Faye do too much,' Edith said, gripping Nick's arm before she left. 'Mind you look after her. Mind you pray for her. Has Samuel started confirmation classes yet?'

Nick looked startled, and blank.

Edith seemed vexed. 'The boy's nine,' she said.

'I know, Mum,' he said.

Faye was tired, but grateful that the evening had been happily uneventful; only Edith had struck a wrong note. She looked at Nick. As he glanced back at her, he looked hunted.

She hoped she'd remember to ask him why.

Chapter Fifteen

Monday morning came too quickly after another sleepless night. An unnameable horror had haunted her through the night.

'Is it going to be painful?' Nick asked as they got dressed on either side of their double bed, back to back.

Faye was pulling on a navy wool dress – so much easier to get into and out of than jeans, she thought. 'Doctors don't talk about pain, they talk about "discomfort",' she said. 'It's a code. When they tell you over the phone that someone is comfortable, they just mean the painkillers are working.'

'So, is it going to be uncomfortable?'

Faye zipped her dress up at the back. 'I don't want to think about it,' she said. More accurately, she didn't want to talk about it.

She remembered that Nick had been like this when she'd been pregnant with Isabel, coming to ante-natal classes and asking questions and worse, telling her that she was doing her exercises wrong. Must be the Edith in him, she thought wearily. He seemed inordinately interested in experiencing medical procedures by proxy.

She was putting her make-up on when Edith arrived absolutely on time. Faye could hear her in the bathroom, washing Isabel's hands and face and doing a running commentary at the same time. 'Grow potatoes in those ears . . .'

Sam was in the shower in the upstairs bathroom, keeping out of the way. She checked the time and looked in on him.

He opened the door of the shower stall. 'What?'

'I'm off now. Grandma will pick you and Isabel up from school. See you later.'

'See you.'

She picked up her handbag and went into Isabel's bedroom. Isabel was sitting on the bed and looked up as Faye entered. So did Edith, who was kneeling on the floor putting her socks on for her. 'I'm off.'

'Good luck,' Edith said. 'And don't worry.'

'Bye, Mum.'

Faye smiled and closed the door. She felt alone and dismissed. Should have had them waving me off at the door, clutching handkerchiefs, she thought.

Nick was coming down the stairs checking his watch with good humour. 'Ready?'

'Yes, I'm ready.'

Perhaps he picked up something of her emptiness, because he put his arm around her and squeezed. 'Don't worry, we'll be back before you know it,' he said.

Or there again, she thought, perhaps he hadn't.

He dropped her off by the main entrance and she went inside the hospital as he drove off to look for somewhere to park.

Waiting for him, her holdall over her good shoulder, she realised that although it was only her third visit the hospital was already beginning to feel familiar, as was the constant trickle of people, coming and going on business of their own, patients and visitors and workers alike. It was their world. She didn't want it to be hers, too, but it was getting to be. She could imagine it; a long round of doctors, radiologists, consultants, nursing staff, of endless waiting for her name to be called, of lying on beds and not being her own self any more, being theirs, to be cut, poked, tested, measured, stitched, drugged, taken over in a way that not even those closest to you ever get near to doing. The helplessness that went with it – it was the fear of that that she was experiencing now. I haven't got the time for a life-threatening illness, she thought plaintively, watching Nick stride through the door. I want to be free.

Nick smiled as he saw her, a 'nice' smile, a mixture of sympathy and comfort. Heaven help her, she'd given it herself in her time. She could even describe the muscles needed for it. She was never going to smile at anyone in that way again.

He was wearing a suit, ready to 'go on' afterwards to work, fitting her in, really, like the children fitted in their desultory goodbyes. She felt resentful, looking at the suit.

'What's up?' Nick asked.

She thought about it for a moment, and shook her head. 'I wouldn't know where to start,' she said, 'and you wouldn't want to hear it. Come on, we've got to go to the fourth floor.'

'Let me carry your bag.'

'I'm not helpless,' she said sharply, and immediately regretted it. 'Sorry. I'm just nervous. I'm glad you're here.'

Was she? I should have come alone, she thought, walking along the corridor with him to the lift. Alone and suffering in silence. Nick being here encourages me to worry aloud and worrying brings out the worst in me.

She checked in and was told to sit down until she was called to a cubicle. The waiting room was large, with grey plastic chairs arranged in two rows, which didn't encourage her to hope for a quick turnover. There were three Indian men sitting together talking, and a middle-aged husband and wife a few respectable seats away from them. She and Nick sat in the back row, befitting the fact that they were last to come in. Nick picked up an old copy of *Options* magazine that had been left on the chair next to him and flicked through it, stopping at the horoscopes.

Another man came in, alone, and one of the group of three was called. He stood up and looked at his companions without smiling. One of them made a joke and he grinned suddenly, and went just as his name was called again. The two men laughed together at something and that was it, Faye thought as she watched them, that was the difference between the patient and the guest. Neither could put themselves in the other's place. She would have given a lot to have been able to sit there looking at a glossy magazine, glancing at the horoscopes, enjoying the chance to do nothing. 'What's mine?'

'Sorry? Oh, right. Leo: "It is time to reassess your life. Pluto, the planet of transformation, is encouraging you towards a new start, while Jupiter and Uranus, the planets of growth and change, help you towards a more equal relationship with your partner that will help you both to develop as individuals. In addition, your ruler the sun sheds a light on deep emotions that have been threatening your sense of well-being."'

'Who says there's nothing in it?' Faye said. 'What's yours?'

'Fresh opportunities at work.'

'Is that all?' She went to take the magazine from him and he moved it away. 'Nick! Let me see it!' She reached for it again and reluctantly he let her take it. She read aloud: '"New romantic and creative opportunities are opening up for you. Work on them now, both for your personal growth and for your future happiness."'

'Load of rubbish,' Nick said heatedly. 'That applies to a few million people and I can assure you, there are no new opportunities at work. Nor the other bit.'

Faye closed the magazine and gave it back. 'I'm scared,' she said tiredly.

'I know that.' He turned towards her. 'Let's not talk about it.' He took her hand and squeezed it.

She squeezed back. It was nice to have her hand in his, being warmed up.

The two men stood up and ambled out. A couple of minutes later they were back.

'Faye Reading!' called a disembodied voice.

A plump nurse with bleached hair came into the waiting room with a file. 'Faye Reading!'

Faye stood up and stretched. 'Me,' she called, and picked up her bags. She bent and kissed Nick on the lips. She felt sick.

'I'll wait if you want me to,' he said.

'No, pick me up at five. That's what it said in the leaflet. There's no point in you waiting.'

'No, I suppose not.'

She went out of the waiting room and wondered why everything that she said contradicted her thoughts. What she wanted him to do was to stay, and watch with her and wait, be someone who was there for her, and on her side.

The blonde nurse was waiting. 'Faye? Go into the room at the end, on the left, and put this on. It ties up the back. You can wear your dressing-gown and slippers and we'll call you when we're ready for you. You can hang your clothes up here. You're not wearing any jewellery? Good. Put your handbag in the locker, it will be safer.'

Faye took the garment she was supposed to put on. It seemed to be made out of the same material as a disposable tablecloth. 'Is Mr Angkatell here?'

'No, you're seeing the physician, Dr Rees. He will be taking care of your procedure. He's very good.'

She went into a room lined with empty beds like a ward, all except one, on which the man who had gone in before her was lying, staring at the ceiling. His eyes flickered towards her as she went in and she nodded.

'Bed five,' the nurse said. 'I'll help you with the screens.'

Once the pale blue screens were in place she got undressed and put her clothes and bag in the locker. Then she put her slippers on her feet, her dressing-gown on, and sat on the bed.

How often did people sit in silence? It added to her sense of isolation. Presently she lay on the bed, too, and stared at the ceiling.

Her watch was in her locker. She lost track of time.

When they came to get her, she was almost glad.

The bronchoscopy showed nothing wrong, Dr Rees told her, but before she had time to feel relief he had her booked in for a CT scan.

Faye stared at the pale blue screens and waited for Nick to come and take her home.

Chapter Sixteen

At noon, Nick was waiting for Susie in Laing's café-bar. They had met before at Laing's. It was the one place they were known as a couple and it was nearer to Nick's office than to Susie's, which suited both of them. He sat at the blonde wood table in the corner with a small vase of flowers on it, his back to the wall, and stared at the bleached floorboards, thinking of Faye.

He'd left her there with the sorrow hardening in his chest, the same feeling he'd had when he'd taken his old dog Gimpy to be put down. He'd taken him in and said goodbye and that was it, job done, he'd had to leave with nothing but a solid lump where his heart had been.

He decided he would tell Susie the story, just as he'd thought it then. He hoped. He often rehearsed things to tell her, and in the end he never did. He used to put the radio on as he drove to and from work but now he talked to Susie in his head instead, telling her things, always telling her, perhaps because in real life there was little time to talk about trivialities. He pushed the thought aside.

Susie liked him for what he was. Not for being the Good One – she was trying her hardest to change *that*. Not for Samuel – she told him the children were the reason that she never visited at weekends. She liked him, Nick the man.

He reached out for the shiny cobalt-blue glass dish on the table, which was empty and probably an ashtray. He gave it a spin, which it did, briefly and reluctantly before rocking to a halt.

And Susie came in through the door just then, her beige mac flying loosely behind her, her dark hair swinging, her eyes bright and her heels banging on the bleached wood floor. She slid into the seat opposite him, her spring flowers scent settling around him as she leant towards him over the table. He kissed her carefully, not wanting to knock over the flowers.

'Hasn't this morning dragged?' she said, shrugging out of her coat. 'It just totally dragged after you rang.'

'Susie.' Nick tried to get a lot into that one word. He loaded it with warning, compassion and impending doom. He smoothed his hand over his short hair.

'I was never cut out to share an office,' she said, and looked at the counter. 'Hey, where's Mickey today? Juan, where's Mickey?'

She liked calling waiters by name. Juan said over his shoulder that he didn't know where Mickey was, he hadn't shown up. He sounded resentful.

'Hasn't shown up,' Susie repeated to Nick, making her mouth glum. 'Our waiter.'

'Yeah I heard. Susie –'

'Have you ordered?'

'No.'

'Two espressos. *Grande*,' Susie said, and smiled at the waiter.

Nick hated him.

But for a moment the waiter seemed to ignore both the smile and the order. 'Two espressos, *grande*,' he muttered presently.

Susie turned back to the table, to him, her smile warm and bright. She pulled the blue ashtray towards her and gave it a spin.

'Susie, you know I had something to tell you?'

Her smile dropped right off her face.

He was glad, because he knew what she was thinking; she was thinking he was going to talk about them, face to face, and she didn't like it. He watched the blue ashtray wobble to a halt and reached across the table, his hand palm upwards, his fingers curled, the table cold against his skin.

She put her hand out and brushed his fingertips with her own so lightly that the imperceptible touch tormented him.

He gripped her hand hard and looking into her eyes he thought about the story of old Gimpy, but after that, would Faye seem an anticlimax? Perhaps. He would leave the dog out, for now. 'Susie, Faye's in hospital, having tests,' he said carefully, his brown eyes brave beneath heavy eyelids.

Susie looked at him suspiciously for a moment and shrugged with her mouth. 'So?'

'So. I just wanted you to know.' He was keeping his voice low, grave.

'Tests – tests for what? Not another baby?'

'No, not a baby. Worse than that.' It wasn't what he'd meant, but he carried on. 'Susie, I think she's got lung cancer. Bronchial carcinoma. You know her cough? You should hear it in the morning. The doctor picked up on it, and the ache in her shoulder. It's all part of the same thing.'

Susie sat digesting this information for a moment, and then stood and picked her raincoat up from the back of her chair and gave it a shake and took it over to the coatstand near the door.

She looked confused when she came back. 'But she's having tests,' she said when she sat down again. 'What are the tests for if you know what it is?'

'To check her bronchii.' He was still keeping his voice low. It seemed more respectful. 'They found a shadow on her chest x-ray. They just want to be sure.'

She leant across the table to be nearer to him, her arms folded. He went to take her hand, but she didn't respond, she just sat looking confused and slightly sceptical with her glossy hair framing her face. 'Nick, it could be anything, couldn't it? It doesn't have to be this bronchial cancer thing. I mean, I wouldn't want that to happen to her. No-one deserves that.' She was still confused. 'I mean, what makes you think – have they told you that's what it is?'

He took his hand off the table and straightened up. 'No. But she's got this shadow on her lung and she smokes. You know how she smokes and I've tried to stop her but –' he shrugged '– Susie, I can't do it for her. I looked the symptoms up in a medical book I've got and I wouldn't be surprised, that's all I'm saying. I hope it isn't that, but Susie, I've got to be prepared. We've got to be prepared.'

'Which medical book?'

'What? Oh, the Reader's Digest one.'

'Nick,' she said, 'I've got the same book! A red one, right? I've got the red one.'

Nick wanted to marvel at this new coincidence but at the same time it was confusing the tone that he wanted to set.

'It's got some great diseases in it,' she said. 'That moon-eye syndrome?'

'Oh, hell,' Nick said, holding his head in his hands. He could see from her face that her mind had leapt forward too, leapt and landed at just about the same point as his. 'I prayed,' he said, and looked up at her, gauging her mood. He decided to go ahead with it. 'I prayed for some answer – so that we could be together,' he said. 'If I'd only known . . .'

Just then he felt the enormity of his belief for the first time. It was like a glimpse of evil. The feeling was like a punch to the solar plexus and he looked at her in shock.

Was he insane?

Susie was staring at him, her mouth slightly open. She recovered herself and tucked her chair further beneath her. 'That's crazy,' she said firmly. 'Nick, you mustn't think like that.'

'No,' he said, and wondered, did I really think it was an answer to my prayer? He felt grotesque and yet – and yet, he couldn't avoid it; it was. 'No,' he said, 'I don't want her to die.' At the same time, the thought of it brought him alive. Fear did that, even as it paralysed it made things sharp. He felt as though he'd been living in a half-slumber all his life.

'Shouldn't you be with her?' Susie said, touching the cobalt ashtray again with her delicately manicured fingers. She drew her hair back from her face. 'I know she likes to be independent but there's a time and place, Nick.'

He couldn't bear her disapproval. He wanted the warmth back. 'I'm going to pick her up. They wouldn't have let me in and I wanted to come and see you – I thought you should know, as her friend.'

'Two coffees,' the waiter said, forcing them to sit back in their seats. Even so, he slopped it into the saucers of both cups as he put them on the table.

'When's Mickey back?' Susie asked him, wiping a splash on the table with her napkin.

'Maybe tomorrow.' He seemed to resent her attempts to be friendly.

Nick stirred his coffee absently, marvelling that she could so easily revert to discussing the whereabouts of the missing waiter. He glanced at his watch. He had an appointment at two-thirty. If they didn't have lunch, and Juan didn't seem to be encouraging them to, he could walk her back through the park and all that that entailed: being near her, risking being seen.

Not by Faye of course, who would be lying on a table with a tube down her throat.

The day seemed sharp with life and death. He felt energy surge through him. 'Drink up, Susie,' he said.

PART THREE

More light.

Goethe

Chapter Seventeen

Unravelling, because here is another knot in her life, the darkness.

She is a child and she plays outside until the other children have been called in for tea and it's dark before she goes in to the greater darkness of the house. In the living room the television flickers with the suddenness of lightning and she tries to see her mother's features by its glare. 'Mum?'

'Put the kettle on, Faye,' comes her mother's voice, heavy as the atmosphere, and flat.

Faye misses the sharpness of her mother's voice. It left when their father did. She stopped shouting then, stopped doing most things except save. Faye misses everything about her father. She misses his smell, she misses his brightness, she misses the arguments when her mother's voice would be shrill and clear.

They are not better off without him.

Or perhaps her mother is, sunk in inactivity instead of being worked off her feet. She doesn't get dressed until the evening, as though the day begins briefly at seven and ends shortly afterwards.

Faye watches her struggle and is angry.

But she does as she's told. In the kitchen the forty-watt bulb is so dim it makes the mustard doors and the black-and-white tiles look shabby, and Faye feels as though the roof is lowering down onto her head. The lampshade is black and casts beyond the halo of light a huge black disc of darkness around it. As she moves, it sways slowly in the breath of her movements, sliding like an eclipse over the nicotined emulsion.

Eva comes into the kitchen and takes the biscuit box down and offers Faye two broken Peek Freans and whispers, 'Do you think Dad will come back?'

Faye shakes her head. 'He wouldn't like it here now. But he might come to get us.' It is her only hope.

She makes the tea and after putting it next to her mother she kisses her on her dry cheek and goes up to bed. Under the bedclothes she keeps a black rubber torch that smells of Caramac and a box of empty sweet wrappers that she's saved since Christmas. She undresses quickly and gets inside the cold sheets.

They will soon warm up. She pulls the covers over her head to make a cave and covers the light with a red cellophane wrapper. The cave of her cold bedclothes is bathed in warm, rosy light. She picks out the green. It is the colour of grass, slightly more blue than yellow, the colour of sympathy. Put it over red. The cave of her sheets is dulled into chaos and decay, like her life.

Why would anyone choose the dark, where there is no colour?

She puts the red paper over the light again and dreams, but not for too long, because of the battery. Then she folds the sweet wrappers carefully and puts them back in the box, and comes out of the warmth of the bedcovers and stares into the darkness.

She hates her mother.

The low-watt bulbs save on electricity.

But stunt the children.

Chapter Eighteen

Angkatell's room was also getting to feel familiar. Faye pulled up her chair and looked around the room, trying to spot the changes again. The books on the shelf had been straightened. Apart from Angkatell, everything else looked the same, but darker. Her life was looking darker all the time.

Angkatell came to sit down at his desk. He was wearing a navy, double-breasted suit with a white shirt and a tie splashed with brilliant yellow, red and navy. He put her file in front of him, aligning the bottom of it with the edge of his desk.

He looked at her and she prepared herself, her heartbeat quickening, for the latest verdict of Faye *v* Shadow. She'd already imagined hearing the worst, she'd played it out whilst vacuuming and walking home from school, going over the words he would use, and her reaction. Her reaction was little reaction at all because there was no knowing what she might feel, no knowing until she felt it and no wish to know. So she waited while Angkatell inhaled deeply and thoughtfully through his nostrils and leant back in his synthetic leather chair, smoothing his colour-splashed tie.

'As you know, we didn't find anything,' he said. 'As far as we're concerned from the bronchoscopy, your lungs are clear.'

Faye smiled warily before she allowed herself to feel a disbelieving wash of relief. Her emotions seemed to be one step behind her actions, like a badly dubbed film. She encouraged him slightly. 'That's good, isn't it?'

Angkatell inhaled deeply again and held it. Then he sighed it out. 'There's still the problem of the shadow,' he said. 'It's there, we've seen it and it's not going to go away. Faye, I'm going to send you for a CT scan. It's an x-ray taken in slices, if you like. We'll find the position of the tumour, and we'll get a much clearer idea of what the next step will be.'

'Tumour?' The word came as a shock. 'I've got a tumour?'

He looked surprised that she'd asked. 'You've got a mass in there of some sort,' he said.

Faye rubbed her forehead with her hand. Her fingers were icy cold. 'The grey area, the shadow . . .' she began, and thought, I imagined something intangible, dark, menacing. A tumour, a mass were very different words. They were solid, immovable. The fear bubbled drowsily in the pit of her stomach. 'You're feeding it to me slowly, aren't you?' she said, suddenly understanding. 'You're letting me get used to things a little at a time, as much as you think I can take.' She felt betrayal and anger, and she stood up and with a huge sweep of her arm she knocked the file off the desk. There was a slap as it hit the carpet. 'Can't you understand that I want to know what's happening to me now? I've got a right to know – and a right to deal with it in my own way, you condescending shit –'

He was on his feet too, leaning towards her, his hands flat on the desk, sounding as angry as she. 'Faye, just calm down!'

'Why should I? Why should I be calm? Don't you think I've got a right to be angry?' she asked. 'Fobbing me off . . .' and she was suddenly crying, her body heaving with wretched, ugly sobs that hurt her to cry them.

Angkatell opened a drawer and put a box of blue tissues on his desk, pushing them towards her. She sat down, the noise of her crying jerking out of her, and she pressed her hands to her shoulder. As the sobs subsided to a shudder she pushed the tissue box away and looked in her handbag for a handkerchief. She turned sideways on to him and blew her nose and pushed the damp handkerchief up her sleeve. 'Sod you,' she said, sniffing. 'I want to see some-one else.'

'You can do that,' he said softly.

'Someone who can be honest with me.'

He bent to pick up the file from the floor and sat down again, putting it to one side on the desk. 'Listen to me,' he said, 'a tumour can be benign, don't forget that. Yours might be benign or it might not. We don't know.' He paused. 'Are you listening to me?'

Faye glanced at him, and looked away again.

'I didn't mean to mislead you. A shadow, a grey area, that's how it shows up on the x-ray, they are just words.'

'They're not just words to me,' she said, taking her handkerchief out again. 'Do you think it's cancer?'

'I don't know and it's impossible to tell until we operate and do a biopsy.'

'Could it be?'

'Yes, it could.'

The tears came back into her eyes and she pressed the handkerchief hard against her lids to stop the flow. How many times had he sat here and said the same foul words? She screwed the damp cloth in her hand. 'Your job stinks,' she said.

'It's not the way I look at it.' He cleared his throat, and said in a slightly different tone, 'You've been booked in for the CT scan. The tumour's at the top of your lung and we may be able to remove it.'

'And if you can't?'

'We'll try to shrink it with radiotherapy.'

'And what about chemotherapy?'

'Faye, you're jumping ahead here,' he warned. 'Don't face it before you have to. It might prove to be a waste of energy.'

She ignored his outstretched hand. 'Listen, I want to know what to be prepared for. I want to know the worst that can happen. What's the worst thing that can come of it?' Her own voice surprised her, rising to a whine that she, a mother of two, had heard and was familiar with, the whine of a frustrated child in the face of a futile demand. Because of course, even if Angkatell's expression hadn't told her, she knew what the worst was. She'd been dodging around it for days.

And she knew what she was asking of him. She was asking him to tell her that she wasn't going to die. She looked into his eyes. They were brown, slightly bloodshot, but steady under her gaze.

They sat there for what seemed a long time, without speaking. 'I know what it is,' she said finally. 'I've been dreading it all my life.' Her voice, this time, was weak and lost. 'I've always been afraid of shadows,' she said.

Chapter Nineteen

Nick was avoiding his mother's shrewd, all-knowing look. She'd turned the central heating up and the room was warm and musty. The white lights were on, so it was too bright for the way he felt.

She went to sit next to him on the sofa. 'You should be sitting with Faye,' she said.

'I want to let her sleep.'

Summoned by his fraught-sounding wife, he had left work early that afternoon, not long after getting back from the walk through the park with Susie. He'd cancelled the meeting, citing Faye's illness as an excuse. Ralph had been embarrassed and sympathetic, sending him off with his good wishes and patting him on the back, man-to-man, out of the office door.

He'd gone home reluctantly and guiltily. Faye had been beside herself with grief and anger, most of it directed at the consultant, to his relief. He had felt helpless in the face of it. Now his mother was watching – him, more than them, he thought.

He couldn't stay in any longer, with Faye ill downstairs and the alien smell of his mother beside him. He wanted to get out. The air in the house was thick with foreboding. Faye had said it was getting dark and he too had felt that behind the white lights there were shadows everywhere, and for the first time in his life he could understand her obsession with them.

'I'm going to church,' he said suddenly.

Edith lifted her chin. The red strands in her hair caught the light but she looked reassured. 'I'm glad,' she said, and her eyes softened and filled with tears.

'Yes, well.'

He went down the stairs and pulled his coat on. He avoided saying goodnight to Faye. He walked briskly in the damp evening air to keep warm, and was panting when he crept into the back of the dim-lit church like a schoolboy trying to keep out of the gaze of the headmaster.

He sat on a chair and bowed his head. Then he got off his seat and knelt on the hard stone floor. 'O God, thank you,' he began, but a sense of futility overcame him and he didn't continue. He opened his eyes and stared at the altar. Four candles flickered on either side of it, not quite symmetrical. He stared at the flames and tried to feel God around him as he always had, as a warm and consoling presence. But he was aware only of emptiness and silence. A part of him wondered again whether his religion could all be a huge hoax and the thought brought with it a bleak feeling of abandonment and desolation.

'O God, our Heavenly Father, thank you for . . .' The words seemed to stick in his throat. He had nothing to say. He was praying into nothingness. He felt as though he had stepped out of the wide light of God's presence and was stumbling on all fours in the dark.

He was silent for a long time. When he came back to himself his knees were hurting and he rocked sideways, easing the pressure on them and thinking, with this small discomfort, of Faye. If she dies, he defended himself, it would be her smoking that was to blame, not he. She knew the risks attached to the cigarettes that she always had on hand, that she lit up so – so sexily, he'd thought once. He remembered pulling up once in his car, right behind hers at some traffic lights, and sticking his head out of the window to call her. He'd seen her hand upturned, resting on her windowledge, fingers arranged so gracefully around her cigarette she looked like someone doing a shadow of a goose against a wall.

The memory tore through him. If she died he would be devastated. He'd miss her, miss her moodiness, he'd miss her for the children's sake.

He would.

His protestation sounded lame.

His gaze wandered to the statue of the Virgin on the plinth to his right. She wasn't looking at him. Her eyes were lowered, as though she'd seen something that she didn't want to and was making sure she wouldn't see it again. My heartlessness, he thought. He'd prayed for an answer. Maybe he was being given a second chance in life. Why not? he thought stubbornly, staring at the perfect, expressionless plaster face. Why shouldn't I have a second chance? He'd prayed for the ability to resist her and he hadn't been given it, had he?

He'd never asked for Faye to die, not in words, not in so many words.

Not at all.

The thought might have come into his head unwittingly, unwilled, as being the perfect solution, but not one he wanted and not one he would ever have prayed for.

But he had it. He had it anyway. His unspoken prayer had been answered.

A tumour. It may be benign, she'd told him, but it wasn't. He could see it in her eyes that she didn't believe it any more than he did. He would stake his life on it. He could see her frightened, tear-sore eyes now as they kept shutting out the future, shutting out Angkatell and his grey shadows and his tumours. May be benign. Wasn't.

He shut his eyes again. 'Almighty God . . . help me to –'

But there was nothing.

He was on his own. He was glad to be on his own.

No sooner had he acknowledged it than he felt released. The cold of the stone was seeping through his knees and there was blackness on his lids and silence in his ears.

Liberation in his heart.

Chapter Twenty

The following morning, Faye woke early, just as the sky was lightening. Nick was snoring gently beside her. She eased herself out of bed so as not to wake him and went upstairs to the kitchen. Through the window she could see the cold turquoise light of dawn streak the sky, burning away the violet, colour of piety.

She was saddened by the sight. I'm not up to this, she thought, leaning her forearms on the cold windowsill. It was the fear that she couldn't tolerate, the fear that brought the chaos and destruction.

The previous evening, with the curtains closed and the lights bright she'd talked to Edith about it at some length, ranting at times, the anxiety and fears flowing out and still she hadn't stopped. And Edith had waited, saying little, merely making noises of agreement or encouragement. Edith had not offered any false promises. On the other hand, wasn't that what she wanted? Reassurance that it would all be all right? Eventually she had got tired of her own voice. 'Pray for me, Edith,' she'd said in desperation.

Edith's calm words came back to her this cold morning. 'I already do.'

'But what good is it?' she asked aloud. She turned as she heard footsteps coming up the stairs. Nick was looking for her, his eyes squinting from sleep, his short hair fanned at an angle.

'What are you doing up so early?' he asked, tying the cord of his bathrobe.

'I just woke up.'

'Is the kettle on?'

'No, I was just going to do it. Nick . . .'

He was heading to the bathroom, but stopped and turned. 'What is it?'

'I was wondering, will you take me to church with you?'

The squint made him look querulous. He put his hands into the pockets of the bathrobe, shoulders slouched. 'I don't go any more, Faye.'

'You said you went yesterday and I thought . . .'

'And you're not a Catholic.'

'Yeah. I was put off it at a young age,' she said ruefully. 'Christopher Pemberton said Catholics drank blood.' She was pushing her arms up each opposite sleeve of her kimono for warmth. Her forearms still retained the chill of the windowsill and she rubbed them.

He looked at her now, eyes round and lazy, the squint gone. 'Is that meant to be funny?'

'Not really. But that's what he said. If you don't want to take me, I'll go with your mother.'

'Religion, the great panacea,' he said, half sorrowfully, and then he smiled ironically at her. 'All those years I asked you to come with me. Well, I've finished with it.'

'Because of me?' she asked, rather touched. All those Sunday mornings when he'd got up early to go to mass and had left her in bed to have a lie-in with Sam and Isabel when a lie-in with him was what she really wanted.

He smiled at her and she found herself smiling back. She hadn't realised how rare the sight had become until now, and she looked at him with sudden, hungry interest. She undid the cord of her dressing-gown. The front fell open; as the cool air hit her she felt her skin contract into goosebumps.

He came towards her and slid his warm hands into the red silk wrap, pulling her closer. She lifted her face up to his and he stared at her blankly for a moment, his eyes glazed, before shutting them and kissing her lips.

Against hers, his were full and hot and dry and the texture of them excited her. She dipped her tongue into his mouth and he groaned loudly, his lips vibrating against hers, his breath filling her chest. They staggered backwards until the wall caught them with a thump. One hand was holding her, the other was making its way up her thigh, a cool crawl, the culmination of which she awaited with a frustrated agony. His penetration of her was quick, frantic and the shock made her bite on his lower lip and as sex, the seventh sense, heightened every sensation she tasted his blood as it mixed with her saliva and he tore his mouth from hers as he came, his breath raw and harsh near her ear. For a moment he slumped against her. She braced herself until he pressed his hands against the wall and took his own weight, standing upright, staring at her. He took one hand off the wall and wiped her mouth carefully.

'It's yours,' she said, and watched him touch his lower lip and look at his fingers.

Her voice seemed to bring him back to reality. He looked round, as though expecting to find things subtly changed. 'The heating hasn't come on yet, has it?' he said. 'I'm going for a shower.' He hesitated, seemed to see her again and pulled her towards him.

He loves me, she thought as he carefully closed her dressing-gown over her naked body. He does love me. She marvelled at the careful way he tied her belt, his fingers steady and sure.

Afterwards though, she couldn't get rid of the feeling that she was being wrapped up again and put away, like something that would not be used again for a while; perhaps not ever.

She was eating porridge at the dining room table when he came out of the bathroom pink with the heat, his hair wet and a white towel around his shoulders. 'Tea,' she said, turning the radio down. 'Do you want porridge? I can do it in the microwave.'

'No, no porridge, sit down, Faye, we've got to talk.'

'The most dreaded words inside a marriage,' she said. 'No porridge. Joke,' she added as he looked at her. From that show of lust there was nothing wrong between them. Suddenly she wasn't even sure there was anything wrong with her. Sexual healing had cured her.

'Faye . . .'

She looked at him. There was a red mark on his lip. Seeing it made her want to do it all again. 'Nick . . .' she responded in similar drawl.

He frowned in what she thought of as a don't-make-it-hard-for-me way that made her grin slowly at him. Not for long, though. 'Go on,' she said, 'get it over and done with.'

'Who have you told about the tumour?' he asked her, pulling a red mug towards him from across the table. 'Have you told the school?'

It was the last thing she'd expected and the porridge she was swallowing suddenly felt hard to get down. The mood was shattered. She drank some of her luke-warm tea to help the porridge on its way, and put her spoon down on top of the rest of the oats in the bowl. 'I've only told Edith,' she said. 'Anyway, what's there to tell?'

He wasn't looking at her. First the mug and now the milk. He pulled

101

the small glass jug across and poured carefully as though precision was the key. 'I think we should start – preparing people,' he said. 'And the children. If they're distracted in school then I think it's best if the teacher knows why. And you were so upset yesterday that the children were very disturbed. Isabel woke up twice in the night.'

'Because she had two glasses of milk before she went to bed,' Faye said. 'I don't want anyone to know because I don't want to have to fend off constant questions about my progress. And the word tumour,' she knew perfectly well what effect the word could have, 'alarms people when they might have no reason to be alarmed.'

'And that's what you think, is it?' He picked up the teapot and poured from such a height that the tea frothed on the surface like a milkshake. He put the pot down and looked at her intently. 'You think you're going to be all right?'

Faye put her hand over her forehead. 'Hell, Nick, I don't know what I feel. Sometimes it feels – like a joke. And other times . . .' The low-level fear was back in an instant. 'Have you been speaking to someone? Angkatell?'

She could see the impatience in his face as he shook his head. 'No, no,' he said. 'But your sister should know. And the children's teachers.'

'All right. I'll tell them.'

'When?'

'I'll tell them soon, okay? After I've had the CT scan. I'll tell them then. And I'll ring Eva, although I can't see the point.'

'I think you should tell your friends. You'll need all the support you can get.'

Now it made sense. To absolve you from giving it, she thought; yes, that was it, that was something she could understand and sympathise with. She wasn't too brilliant around sick people herself, and he would be wondering how he would cope. 'Don't worry,' she said, 'I won't ask too much of you.'

'You never do,' he said. He sounded sad. 'I do love you, you won't forget that, will you?'

'You can keep reminding me,' she said, but that didn't seem to be what he meant. He ignored the nuance and she watched him, aware of a new, unidentified fear as he finished his mug of tea.

It was eleven o'clock that morning when she rang to break the news to her sister, Eva. Eva lived twenty miles and a lifestyle away in what had been three workmen's cottages knocked into one in Bedfordshire. She had five children, all by the same man, Frank, who called on them frequently and proposed to Eva constantly. Eva had an excitement for life that often led Faye to wonder whether their childhood had left her completely untouched. Certainly she had not developed their mother's obsession with the dark, nor hers with light.

They got together infrequently. Nick laid claim to the religious festivals, and most evenings Eva worked, inviting people round to her house for demonstrations of origami or Tupperware – a reversal of the usual way of direct selling but one that she made work brilliantly. Faye had been to a couple of her soirées and had found herself buying things she wouldn't think of in a department store, simply because Eva made them seem so appealing.

Eva sounded so pleased to hear from her that she was ashamed of what she had to say. She came straight out with it. 'I've got a tumour on my lung.'

'A lump?' she heard Eva say.

Not a shadow, not a grey area, not a tumour. A lump. Faye Reading, the Lady with the Lump. 'Yes, almost by my shoulder,' Faye said. 'I'm going in for a CT scan and thought I'd let you know.'

Her sister instantly began to cry. 'It runs in the family,' she said between sobs.

'What does? Lumps?'

'Smoking.'

'You've never smoked.'

'I did when I was young.'

This was followed by jerky intakes of breath. I should have told her in person, Faye thought in dismay, clutching the phone tightly. 'Look, there's no need to worry,' she said. 'It's probably nothing.'

'Are you still smoking now?'

'Hell, no. I've given up.'

'Oh, Faye.' There was something of a silence.

Faye waited. She could hear a drone which she thought was coming from the phone but then identified it as being from an aeroplane overhead.

'I'll come and stay, look after the children,' Eva said, her voice unsteady.

'Well, Edith's going to come. She volunteered.'

'Oh, that's kind of her. Faye, are you going to tell Dad?'

'Dad?' Faye asked, genuinely puzzled. 'What do you mean?'

Eva gave a short, light laugh, not quite hitting the right note. 'I've been in touch with him since Mum's funeral and he talks about you a lot.'

'I knew this was a bad idea,' Faye said. 'Why should illness suddenly make me public property? Why is it important for him to see me now I'm ill, when it wasn't when I was well?' In the background she could hear the sound of a child laughing; a long, spontaneous giggle. She heard Eva clear her throat.

'I know you blame him, Faye, for leaving.'

Do I? Faye thought. No, she didn't blame him for that. It was understandable. Eva had left as soon as she could, and then their own mother had left; thanks, guys, she thought bitterly. 'I blame him for not taking me with him. Do you see him regularly?'

'Now and then. He's changed, Faye, and under the circumstances I think you ought to make up. It's not a matter of being public property, as you put it. You might find you need him. You might find you need me.'

'Neither of you have been much use to me so far,' Faye said, 'so I hope I don't.'

There was a longer silence this time. The television was still on in the background.

'That's a cruel thing to say,' Eva said. 'I invited you here for Christmas and you were going to Edith's.'

'I go where Nick goes.'

'Yes, and in the circumstances I think we ought to stop this pointless bickering.'

'In the circumstances I'll think about it.'

'Oh,' Eva said in a small voice.

Faye was sorry she'd said it. She pressed her fingers against her forehead. She had a headache coming on. She had to find a way to finish the call on a good note but she wasn't going to say she'd meet her father – she'd rather hang up now. 'Eva, listen.'

'What?' The same small voice.

'Could you come with me to the hospital for the scan? I need someone with me and Nick's going to be working.' This was going to have to be something she would square with Nick, who had booked time off to take her. A silence followed.

'Of course I'll come. Everything's all right between you and Nick, isn't it?'

Resisting the urge to say, I'm doing this for you, she replied, 'More or less. He's taking an optimistic view of it at the moment.'

'And you?'

'It comes and goes. Anyway, if you can't come, he'll take time off. I just thought – it would be nice.' The conversation was now ringing hollow; what could be nice about going for an x-ray even if one were being accompanied to hospital by a sister who had spent her life being busy?

'Oh Faye,' Eva said, and went quiet.

Faye realised that during these periods of silence she was crying. Her own despair had cleared and crying seemed somehow inappropriate. She felt almost annoyed, as if the only valid emotions were her own.

'Who else knows?'

'Apart from Edith, you're the first person I've spoken to.'

'Apart from Edith.'

'Does it matter who knew first? Edith wanted to see me about something else.' (Fudging the truth a bit.) 'Alicia's back.'

'Oh, I am sorry. You keep a good eye on Samuel. Don't trust her. And let me know when you want me. And have a think about Dad.'

'Right.' This was followed by a little silence of her own. After a respectful pause to denote the change of subject, she said, 'The appointment's at ten. Do you want to come to the house or will you meet me there?'

'I'll come to the house. The last time I was at the Royal . . .' There was a pause. Faye, though still listening, felt her mind drift. Her sister finally picked up the end of what she was trying to say, and ended with some embarrassment, '. . . was when Mum died.'

'Damn.' Faye was looking at herself in the mirror, the one in the bedroom. There was a crease across the bridge of her nose from frowning that she could swear was new. Her sister had unsettled her. Her emotions were all over the place again, and she still had to go to school to see the head teacher to explain. Get it over and done with, she thought.

It was feeling real again, real and serious, and the fear and the anger were settling heavily upon her. Damn Eva. She needed to be buoyed up, not pulled down.

She brushed her hair. The roots, she could see, were growing out dark. Perhaps she could have it done that afternoon – it was worth asking, on the way home from school.

She put her coat on and got her bag. She felt nervous. Kill the messenger, yes, she could see why.

The head mistress's room was like a board room: oak-panelled, freesias on a table, smelling sweet, Mrs Lloyd herself getting up from her desk looking relaxed, open, welcoming; indicating the seat.

'Good morning, Mrs Lloyd,' Faye said, and felt she'd shrunk to ten years of age as she sat down, although Mrs Lloyd was, at most, in her late forties and almost her contemporary. She remembered the time when Samuel's mission in life was to shake Mrs Lloyd's hand. The school was big on handshakes.

Too late now to reach for Mrs Lloyd's.

'How can I help you, Mrs Reading?'

She felt the prickling reflex of tears about to come and held them back by staring and inhaling through her nostrils. 'I'm going into hospital shortly, just for the day, so if the children are upset – well, perhaps the school could bear it in mind.'

'Nothing serious, I hope.'

'A tumour on my lung.'

'Oh, I am sorry. The children know, do they?'

'Samuel does. We've told Isabel too, of course, but she sees it in terms of dressing up in a nurse's uniform and putting dolls to bed.'

Mrs Lloyd smiled at the mention. 'She's a lovely little girl,' she said. 'She's always so happy.'

'I know. Not like Samuel.'

Mrs Lloyd smiled. 'It's often the same at that age. They're so good in school, they have to let off steam somewhere and the parents get it.'

'It's not that he lets off steam, he's very well behaved. It's just that he takes life so seriously.'

'Very wise. You haven't done so badly, Mrs Reading.'

Faye looked up at her in surprise.

'He's got your courage.'

Faye pushed her seat back. Aye aye aye. She wished he didn't need it. Had to get out of there before the storm broke. 'It hasn't been tested yet,' she said. 'In either of us.'

PART FOUR

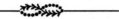

It came with a lass and it will go with a lass.

James V

Chapter Twenty-One

Unravelling her father's departure, she remembers, half-dreaming, that it was they who left. She'd forgotten that. They'd stayed with their mother at Grammy's, but not for long. Her mother and Grammy irritated each other and had a shrill row and the bags were packed again.

And so they return home. He meets them at the door – opens it before they reach it so she knows he has been looking out for them through the window. He picks Eva up first and Eva sobs, and he laughs, but gently, and he turns to Faye and lifts her up and holds her in the air and she looks down and sees that his hair is damp and flat and grooved with the lines of the comb he has run through it. His face as he kisses her is smooth and strangely soft and he smells of Old Spice. He puts her down and looks at Eva. 'Well,' he says. 'Cheer up.'

They go into the kitchen, which is clean and neat. He stands back so as not to spoil the effect. The wooden table has a cloth on it. The radio, red and white, is on low and she can hear the theme music for *The Archers*. Her father looks sheepish. 'It's company,' he says, and she feels sorry for him. Not so her mother, who has averted her head and is rolling her eyes.

'Go and play outside,' she says, looking meaningfully at Faye and Eva. 'Go and pick some gooseberries.'

'What shall I put them in?' Faye asks. She is reluctant to leave, feeling sorry for her father; also, on the shelf next to the radio she can see doll's legs, and the dolls she knows are meant for them.

'Put them in the colander,' her mother says, taking it off the hook with a tinny clank. Faye can see she is anxious to be rid of them. She goes out reluctantly, the colander in her hand, and as soon as she and Eva are out of the door it is closed behind her.

Eva sits on the step, still crying quietly, but Faye goes straight to the gooseberry bush. She knows which gooseberries are the sweetest; the big, fat, almost translucent ones with veins that show clearly. These are the ones she eats, dusting them off on her dress to get rid of the insects caught in the hairs. She likes the smell of the wood, the leaves, the grass. A broken bucket has been placed over a crop of rhubarb. At the bottom of the garden is a blue trellis, in need of a coat of paint, and beyond the trellis is an oak tree which is easy to climb. She leaves the colander with three gooseberries in it and climbs the tree. The moss stains her knees.

Up here she can hear her father shouting, shouting so loud that it floats over the garden. Her mother is silent. She sits in the tree without moving, straining to hear her mother, but her father's voice drowns everything out, the insects, the birdsong, the day.

The door slams. She sits motionless in the tree, waiting to be blamed. She can hear Eva crying helplessly.

She waits to see who has done the walking out.

She sees her father by the gooseberry bush, turning, coming down the path past the rhubarb, past the trellis. She hears him kick the colander and swear and she is caught now, caught up the tree.

'Faye? Come down a minute, will you?'

She climbs down, leaden with guilt, and afraid. He plucks her from the lowest branch and sets her down, and sits by the tree root.

'Faye, you're old enough now to understand – about your mother and me. She wants me to move away from here or else she'll take you both to stay in that little house of your grammy's – and it hasn't got a garden, has it? Not like this one. Answer me, Faye.'

'No.'

'She says you're happier there.' He shakes his head, bemused. His hair is drying out in the breeze, and crinkling up. 'Are you happier there? Be honest, now.'

She stares at the gooseberries that have spilled onto the ground. Her father's words are a trap, one she has fallen into before; she has been honest, and been punished for it. It seems so easy to be bad and so very hard to be good, impossibly hard.

'Faye, come on now, tell the truth,' he urges, his voice getting a little rougher now.

He frightens her when he's cross. She wonders where her mother is.

He jerks her arm. 'What happens to people who don't tell the truth?'

Faye looks up at him in alarm. That, she doesn't know, although she is supposed to. 'I want to stay here,' she says.

'I'm sorry?'

'I want to stay here.'

'You want to stay here with me, don't you?'

She nods, expecting, any minute, to be caught out in the lie (and we know what happens to people who lie, don't we).

'Righty-o.' He moves, shifting his position to a crouch, and bounces slightly on his heels. She can smell cigarettes on his breath. 'I want you to do something for me. I want you to tell your mother, and your grammy, that you and Eva want to live here with me, and tell your mum you want to come back where you belong. She'll listen to you. She loves you. Tell them – tell your mum – that I said I was sorry. Only don't tell her that I said to say that, all right? Just tell her, Daddy said he was sorry. You can do that, can't you?' He gives her a little shake. 'You're bright enough.'

She looks at a strand of his hair which is no longer lying flat. 'What did you do, Daddy?'

He looks at her intently. 'Nothing to deserve this,' he said, 'being told to leave my own home. Faye,' spacing the words so she doesn't mistake them, 'you can save the family.'

She looks at her father, and beyond the fear she feels a sense of outrage that blots out the fear. I shouldn't be asked to do this, she thinks, I'm not even the oldest, but he is looking in her eyes and nodding and she knows he thinks she will.

She will save the family.

She will save the family.

She will save the family.

She will, won't she?

Chapter Twenty-Two

Nick was at work, ignoring the messages on his desk and ringing Susie instead. He had to talk to her. He had to reassure her that it was going to be all right. He watched the rain warp the view from the window as the receptionist answered.

'She's not in today,' came the reply from down the line. 'She's off sick.'

Nick was just about paranoid enough to disbelieve her. He stood up, as though this would intimidate her into putting him through. 'Are you saying she's at home?'

'She's off sick, that's all I know.'

Nick replaced the phone and stared at it. Then he picked it up again and dialled Susie's home number. After a few rings, he started counting. He had reached ten when she answered.

'Hello?'

Her voice was hoarse and a wave of sympathy for her weakened him. He sank down onto his chair. 'Susie, it's me. How are you?'

'What's the time?'

'It's one-thirty. Can I come and see you?'

He thought he heard her groan. 'Is it urgent?' she asked, and started to yawn.

It was now. He wanted to look after her, make her better, see her. 'Shall I get you anything on the way? Day Nurse? Night Nurse?'

'You could get me some Alka Seltzer.'

'It's a hangover?' he asked, his sympathy fading.

'You haven't been in touch for a week. What am I supposed to do, stagnate?'

'I'll be there in ten minutes.' He hung up before she could argue. He hoped she would stay in her bed.

'Won't be long,' he called across the office to no-one in particular, and he took his raincoat from the peg and hurried out to his car before Ralph could commiserate.

The traffic was heavy because of the rain. He switched the radio on because if he didn't he would be rehearsing what he was going to say to her and he didn't want to rehearse it this time.

He looked out for the signs. Although he'd never gone into her flat, he knew where it was. He'd looked it up in the A-Z just to feel near her, as he had her name in the telephone book.

It was nearer thirty minutes later that he pulled into her street and drove into the residents' parking bay, taking a ticket out of his wallet and sticking it on the windscreen.

He jumped out of his car, leaving his raincoat behind, and ran to the door, sheltering under the concrete canopy above it. He pressed the buzzer, heard the door unlatch and pushed it open.

The hallway was carpeted with rather worn red Wilton. Straight ahead of him, past a dried flower arrangement, was the lift, and he opened the elaborate brass doors and went inside the jaws, jabbing his finger at floor five. With a grind the lift moved slowly upwards and lurched to a halt.

He got out, closed the doors behind him and looked round. Susie was at the door waiting for him, her hair tangled round her face.

She let him in and closed the door behind him and he followed her into the sitting room where he took a good look at her. The most surprising thing was that she had mascara smudged under her eyes and that she was wearing pale yellow pyjamas.

'Did you bring the Alka Seltzer?'

'Damn! I forgot all about it,' he said, snapping his fingers. He could tell she was annoyed. 'Do you want me to go back out?' he asked, not to cure her hangover but to put her in a better mood.

'No, I'll suffer without it,' she said, looking at her nails. 'What was so urgent that you had to keep ringing?'

Her matter-of-factness was disconcerting but she was demanding something of him and he had something to give. 'I think we ought to just stop seeing each other while Faye is ill,' he said. 'I don't know how you feel about it but I thought we should talk it over.'

Susie flopped back in the chair and winced as her head jerked. 'Oh, that's great,' she said, shutting her eyes as though to blot him out. She felt for a cream cushion and hugged it against her. She opened her eyes, just a little. 'How do you expect me to feel about it? You come here after not seeing me to say you're still not seeing me? Where's the sense in that?'

Nick passed his hand over his face. 'If you felt like that you could have called me,' he said, glad that she was bitter.

'Sure. And risk Faye or one of the kids finding out?'

'I've been at work. I don't want to take time off, not yet. I know I should have rung you and I'm sorry.' He saw the relief in her eyes and he went over to her and took her hand. He felt claustrophobic in her sitting room. It was like sitting in a conservatory; there was patterned foliage everywhere, curtains, carpet, walls, all in shades of green and brown. 'Susie, we will be together,' he said. 'We just have to wait . . .' He found he couldn't think of a way to put it.

He glanced at her and saw that it was all right, she'd picked up immediately on what he'd meant, and he was surprised to see her eyes fill with tears.

'Poor Faye,' she said.

'I thought that if we,' he wondered how to put it delicately, 'if we cooled off now, until . . .'

She nodded. She knew what 'until' meant.

'Then at some time, afterwards, we would be free to get married. That's what I'm trying to say. We'll have to wait, but it won't be forever.' He could see he'd said the right thing.

She smiled a watery smile. 'I'll feel like a born-again virgin. Actually, I already do.' She paused and her expression changed. 'I must see her,' she said. 'We got on well, especially at work. We had fun, I bet she didn't tell you the half of it. I always said she shouldn't have given up her job just because Isabel was ill.'

Nick stopped swinging his leg. 'It wasn't just because of that,' he said.

She looked at him. 'Oh, you mean Richard. That was because you were acting so holier-than-thou.'

'I *was* holier-than-thou,' he said, and she laughed.

'I suppose that's why we both fell for you. You can laugh at yourself.' She edged her index finger inside his cuff.

He raised her hand and sucked her finger, aware of the time passing and the fact that he had an appointment at three. He had to visit a two-bedroomed flat which had apparently been robbed of three television sets and three video cameras. It had taken him half an hour to get to Susie's and unless the traffic had cleared miraculously it was going to be much the same going back. And he liked to turn up early, before people had a chance to hide anything, and in this case see if the three tellies had ever existed.

He didn't want to break the moving moment by looking at his watch, but he thought he'd seen a clock on the mantelpiece, a little floral thing, Portmeirion. He glanced at it. Two-fifteen. He let her hand go and got to his feet. 'That's all I wanted to say,' he said softly, as though she had already died.

Susie wiped her nose with the back of her hand and raised her face to be kissed. 'I know I look a wreck,' she said. 'I'll miss you. But I understand. I really do understand.'

He kissed her lightly on her salty lips. 'You look beautiful,' he said, stroking her tangled hair. 'And we're doing the right thing, Susie.'

She stood back as though to get a better view of him, looking at him strangely. 'I can't see what makes it right,' she said. 'It's awful. I know she and I haven't seen much of each other for a while, but it doesn't mean I'm not upset.' She pressed her trembling lips together. 'I never wanted this. Yours is a weird religion, Nick, when a divorce is worse than wanting a person dead.'

He shook his head. He couldn't tell her how little she understood of anything – of him, of the Catholic Church, of the glorious resurrection. But one day he would. When . . .

He turned his mind away from it but a phrase popped into his head: Do you ask for bread and I give you a stone?

'It'll be all right, Susie,' he said quickly. 'I've got to believe that.'

'If it makes you feel better,' she said.

Chapter Twenty-Three

The night before the CT scan, Nick appeared at the door of his house with flowers. Heaps of them. 'Come and look at the car,' he said, and Faye went outside and even in the dark she could see the car was stuffed with them, their forms cracked and misshapen under the gleam of cellophane. The back seat had been pulled down and they were spread right across the rear of the car. He opened the door. The heady, sickly smell of forced blooms rose thickly into the thin, cold air.

She felt the anger come back, full force. 'What are they for? The funeral?'

Nick winced, his thin face jerked into a spasm of hurt. 'They're for you.'

'Why?' She was shivering, holding her elbows with her hands. She could feel the cold tapping of rain against her face. 'You never get me flowers. And I haven't enough vases. It looks like a hearse in there.'

'But you like flowers,' Nick said, feeling she needed reminding. He brushed a speckle of pollen off his suit as he followed her inside with an armful of flowers. Faye was still shivering and on the verge of tears of frustration. Samuel was standing behind her in the hall in his pyjamas and she nearly fell over him. 'What are you doing still up?' she asked, adding him to her list of annoyances.

'I heard you shouting,' he said. 'Who are the flowers for?' As he spoke, one of the bouquets that Nick had brought in was slowly sliding down the stairs. It nudged another and the pile was off, crackling as it moved, coming to rest on the mat by the door.

Nick pushed the door with his foot and gently tossed another two in. 'They're for me,' she said, looking at Nick. 'Your father's gone mad.'

Nick caught her eyes. His own looked lazy, hooded, intense, and he was shaking his head almost imperceptibly. 'I was mad,' he said, 'but I've gone sane.'

'Not on current evidence.'

'Are you going to leave them in the paper?' Samuel asked, picking up a bouquet and nestling it in his arms like a baby.

'We're going to sleep on them,' Nick said.

Samuel smoothed the cellophane above the yellow bow. 'What if they've got thorns?' He looked at her, alarmed. 'Mum?'

She'd turned away too late.

'Mum, don't cry.'

Nick's arms were outstretched. She didn't move into them, riveted to the spot in the hall as the cold air blew in through the open door. He got hold of her then and tried to rock her. Struggling for balance, she pushed him away. 'It's all right,' she said to him. And to Samuel, standing by, 'It's all right. You go to bed.'

Keeper of the house, he didn't want to. He stood defiantly, looking absurd in his red pyjamas – why hadn't she noticed before that they were too small for him? The sleeves revealed his bony wrists, the legs finished way above his bony ankles. The vividness of his hair drained the colour from his skin and his pale face was like a narrow moon. Her face screwed up again, ugly with grief.

Uncertain as to what to do, Nick went back outside to bring the rest of the flowers in from the car.

She recovered herself and wiped her face with her palms. 'Jump into bed, Sam. I'll just wash my face, then I'll come in to talk.'

'Okay.'

In the light of the bathroom mirror she looked hideous. The bulb was situated above the mirror and it cast strong shadows down the face giving the viewer a strange, lugubrious look. Perhaps there was something to be said for subdued light. She looked best in the bedroom, where the mirror hung with the light behind it; the small make-up mirror on the kitchen windowsill was the one for honesty, and the one to make her want to take to wearing a veil. She looked at her lugubrious self, saw the beginnings of jowls and put a white flannel under the cold tap, wrung it out and pressed it against her eyes. 'Oh God. Oh help me,' she said into the cold cotton, her hot breath warming, stinging her skin. She took the flannel away and sighed deeply. She folded it and hung it on the edge of the basin, dried her hands on a towel and patted her face. Then she went to Sam's room.

Samuel, out of reach of the pool of light cast by his bedside lamp, was facing away from her, facing the wall.

She waited in the doorway for a moment.

117

'Mum?'

'Yes. I thought you were asleep.'

Samuel turned over and she sat on the edge of his bed. 'Kiss me,' he said. She did, on his mouth, on his nose, on his forehead. Stroked his hair. He didn't take his eyes off her, but just kept looking.

She gave a little laugh. 'I am coming back, you know. I'll be back tomorrow night.'

'You read my mind,' he said. 'Why did Daddy buy all those flowers? It must have cost a lot.'

The flowers. She wanted to cry again. Such a pointless, pointless gesture, so pointless and so achingly pathetic. They could put nothing right. Had he expected them to? Had he imagined her laughing with joy at the sheer quantity of them? At his bravado? At their beauty? Had he really thought that they would sleep on them and make things good?

Samuel was still waiting for her reply.

'Well, he bought them to cheer me up,' she said, and, oh please no, the tears started again even as she said it.

'Are you upset because you don't feel well?'

'I feel all right,' she said, 'but yes, I suppose that's it.' She could hear rustling and footsteps as Nick scooped up the flowers and took them up the stairs. 'When you're ill you sometimes feel tearful, even if it's only a cold. Your mind starts to feel upset as well.'

Samuel just looked at her. She looked at him back. It was easy to look into a child's eyes; effortless, painless.

Nothing in there to hide from.

'Does that mean that when your body gets ill, your mind gets ill as well?'

'I suppose, in a way,' she said, still thinking of him, of a couple of days of unexpected tears before she found he had a sore throat.

'And does it work the other way around? Can your mind get ill just by itself or is it always the two of them?'

'Well . . . your mind can get ill when the body seems all right, but sometimes it's a chemical imbalance in the brain.' Her thoughts leapt to Alicia. 'And so yes, it is the two of them, isn't it.' She put her head to one side and mirrored her face with his. 'Any more questions?'

He shook his head.

'Right. *Sleep*.'

'Will the flowers still be here in the morning?'

She was surprised by the question. 'Of course they will. The problem is, how we're going to get rid of them. Goodnight.'

'Goodnight,' he said, and turned over. There was a gap between his pyjama trousers and his top, and a wedge of skin showed. She tucked his Rug Rats bedcover over him and backed silently out of the room.

Faye went quietly into Isabel's room. Her nightlight was still on. In its dim glow Faye could see the pale half of her daughter's face which was not pressed into the pillow. She watched her daughter's face as she slept. It was smooth, beautiful, untroubled.

What had she brought down on them? A catastrophe. Why hadn't she seen it before? Faye knelt by the bed and stroked her hair. She didn't move. It was such a deep sleep, Faye thought with envy. The kind of sleep that sucked you down and let you bob awake from it in the morning like a cork out of a bottle of fizz. Nothing like the restless nights she'd spent of late, images and fears treading the surface of her consciousness so that she could never feel the join between wakefulness and sleep.

She shut the door behind her. Let her sleep her untroubled sleep, she thought, while she can.

Upstairs, the flowers were propped up against the wall. Now they looked as if they were marking the spot of a road accident. Truly, she would have liked to have got rid of them all and would have had no qualms about it, either.

Nick was looking pleased in a boyish sort of way. 'You should have seen their faces,' he said, grinning. 'I bought the shop.'

'Must have made their day,' Faye said quietly, flopping down in the armchair. 'But you shouldn't have. I just want things to seem normal while they can. It's all so – wobbly, you know?'

Nick looked away from her. 'Do you want to start putting the flowers in water?' he asked after a moment.

They were still propped up against the wall. 'Not really,' she said. 'Unless we fill the bath.'

He came and knelt in front of her, his warm arms resting on her knees, his face scrutinising her own. She looked at him, her mouth clamped shut. 'It's going to be all right, Faye,' he said.

She stared at him. She loved the heaviness of his eyes, always had. And his mouth, the lower lip well-formed, almost pouting, the upper lip narrow. It could be a cruel face, but she'd never known him to be cruel, he'd had the cruelty beaten out of him, ha ha, by his religion.

119

So, looking at him now, she didn't doubt that it was the truth; that he wanted to make it right, that he wanted to believe it would be all right.

'Maybe,' she said.

'Believe me,' he said, giving her a little shake. 'I'm going to be here for you.'

'I know that. I do believe you.'

I'd have been stupid not to, Faye thought, you're lovely, you're a lovely man. Then why did I, for that brief time when Isabel was small, stop loving you? It was that old innate ability to self-destruct. She'd done it properly now.

But no, nothing was ever that simple. She'd liked Richard Cross for his dark side. His, oh never was there a more apt word, irreverence. With him she never had to worry about coming up to scratch. Kindred spirits, they were; there was a glamour in being with him and there was a glamour in the sex and there was a glamour in what she had to hide, the love-bites and the secrets. For a short while, she lived a life that was a veneer, with the real ugly her hidden below the surface. But the hiding of something always showed, strange how that could be. She'd come across it in homosexuals – a reserve. Secrets, kept, built up a wall between people. Was that why she'd told Nick? To knock down the wall? Or was it so that he would absolve her? It was a confession which would have been better kept to herself.

Faye looked at him, still leaning warmly against her knees, his eyes dark, three creases shortening the space between his eyebrows. The thought struck her then that she had never been aware of him hiding anything.

His light had not overcome her dark. 'What's that verse from John, about light?' she asked him suddenly.

'"In Him was light; and the light was the life of men, and the light shineth in the darkness; and the darkness comprehended it not."'

'I'm scared,' she said.

'Don't be. I'll be with you. They can do – you know – miracles.'

'You'd know more about that than I would,' she said, with a bit of a grin. It faded. 'So much for the hypnotherapist, all of a sudden I feel like a cigarette,' she said. 'Stupid, isn't it? Just the one.'

'Faye –'

'Don't worry, I won't, I'm just despairing of myself. That reminds me, I should ring Vicky, to tell her I'm going in. She'll feel hurt if she doesn't know. And Eva will come with me tomorrow. She'll come to the hospital with –' she stopped, wondering just what her sister would bring. Lucozade? DK water in a special holder? 'Cigarettes.' Yeah. 'That's what they're like in my family. When my aunt was first sent to a psychiatric hospital because she was an alcoholic, my mother smuggled her in assorted miniatures. One was Tequila, with a worm. My aunt got it in her mouth, spat it into her hand, saw a nurse coming and swallowed it, to save being caught. It was enough to put her off, she said.'

'Did it?' Nick asked, interested.

'No.'

Nick took hold of her hand. 'Eva will bring grapes.'

Faye's tears started again with that. Her limbic system seemed to be hearing things she'd missed.

'Er,' Nick said suddenly, 'cramp.' He got to his feet, held onto the arm of the chair and hobbled. He took hold of his foot and pressed it, wincing. 'Damn, damn.'

She could feel her knees prickle as the blood came back into them, prickle and get cold.

'Remember the Mayor's Bed?' she asked as he hopped gingerly on the spot.

A slow grin of response.

She smiled, blew her nose and picked up a couple of the bouquets. She took them into the kitchen, using scissors to open the wrapping, and cut through the ribbon. She cut through the string at the bottom and the stems shifted apart. There were those giant vivid pink daisies, white carnations, pink roses, pink something-elses that looked like daisies too but with smaller centres and little flowers, a cross between a sweet-pea and a bluebell. Carefully, she snipped the crisp heads from them all.

No thorns, here, just soft petals and the spring of the yellow cushions that held the pollen.

The smell of sap was strong. She looked for a carrier bag to sweep the heads into, a nice beige and orange Sainsbury's one.

Nick wasn't in the living room – she could hear him brushing his teeth in the bathroom. She went downstairs and scattered the flower-heads on the bed. They rolled off the pillow. The heat from the electric blanket lifted their combined fragrance to her. Not ready for bed, but ready to try them, she took her clothes off and lay on them. She could feel them hard against her skin, cool oases in the heat of the bed. She smiled at the sensation, and then . . .

. . . sorrow came down heavy on her, darkening the room. Was this how it was going to be, now? Everything relegated to 'an experience' in case it was the last time?

The last time.

Chapter Twenty-Four

After the flower-bed business, surprisingly, next morning Faye awoke and found herself looking round for her despair. It had gone. She didn't doubt that it would come crawling back over her, static with bad vibrations, but the fact she could lose it at all was a cause for celebration and she felt her heart leap.

It was just getting light.

She could see the detail develop on the wardrobes as they grew increasingly visible with the dawn. Aware of something under the small of her back, she lifted her bottom off the bed and swept some crumpled vegetable matter from underneath her. She breathed in a slightly sickly scent of crushed petals, and a more astringent smell of sap. She reached her arm out to Nick and touched his warm back. He didn't stir.

She moved up closer to him and, thinking of the night before, realised she was smiling. No, actually it was a smirk. Identifying it made it instantly fade. There was very little in her life to feel smug about:

> (except the sex . . .)
> she was ill,
> (but perhaps not very)
> and she was going for a CT scan
> (which made her nervous)
> and what did that matter?

'Nick?'

'Yeah?' Groan. 'What time is it?'

She switched the bedside light on. 'Er, ten past seven.'

He sat up. Stuck onto his arm and the right side of his shoulder were crumpled rose-heads. He squinted at her, his skin creasing up like a fan at the outer corners of his eyes. 'How're you?'

She smiled and nodded. 'Happy.'

'You're –' he frowned, staring at her shoulder. He rubbed her with the flat of his palm and held out his hand to show her a nicotine-yellow stain. 'You've been pollinated.'

They both laughed softly and it occurred to her suddenly how easy it was to share happiness. Misery, now, that was just as easily spread, but it couldn't be shared in the same way. Perhaps he was thinking the same thing; he was looking at her carefully, not squinting now, his hazel eyes half-hidden by his heavy lids.

She put out her hand to rub his bristles and wondered why those people nearest to you never looked familiar. He looked crumpled. She traced the bristles around his jawline, concentrating on the slight cleft in his chin.

He put his arm around her and pulled her close. 'Is Eva still taking you today?' he asked.

'Yes. Which reminds me, I must look for a book. There's always so much waiting around. I want something funny.'

'But you won't need a book if Eva's coming to keep you company,' he said.

She paused. 'You don't know Eva,' she said after a moment.

The bedroom door opened and Samuel came in, switching the main light on. His cheek was flushed from the warmth of the bed and a diagonal crease from the pillow that he'd lain on was fading slowly. He looked at them, then lifted his foot quickly off the floor. He bent to pick up the withered pink carnation that he'd just stepped on. 'What happened to the flowers?'

'We slept on them.'

'Did you?' Signs of a smile. 'All night?'

'Yeah.'

'What about insects?'

She wrinkled her nose. 'Squished.'

He came up to her side of the bed and turned back the duvet, checked the sheet was clear and got into bed beside her. 'What's happening today?'

Today she was happy. That was what she thought. 'Okay,' she said, 'today I'm going for a scan so that they can see where the lump is. That's it.'

'That's not much,' he said.

Not much at all.

*   *   *

Eva turned up early. Faye was touched by the effort she'd made and said so. She felt it was a good start.

Eva followed her sister upstairs and sat on the edge of the white sofa. Her fair hair was pinned up securely and her red coat was buttoned up to the neck.

Faye thought she looked as if she'd come for a job interview. 'You can relax, you know,' she said, glancing over the top of the make-up mirror as she put on her mascara. 'The covers are washable.'

'I should hope so. *I* wouldn't dare.'

'Sit back, or have white covers?'

'Not with children around.'

'Who's looking after the children?'

'Frank is. He stayed the night specially,' Eva said, and blushed.

The doorbell rang and Nick answered it. Faye could hear Edith's clear voice enunciating greetings as she wiped her feet on the doormat.

While Faye excused herself to get the children ready for school, the two women sat on opposite sofas sipping tea out of mugs and looking sober. It was the appropriate expression to wear in front of someone going into hospital, Faye thought.

When the children were dressed and back upstairs, Edith had taken off her coat. She was wearing loose camel-coloured trousers (slacks, she called them) and a white blouse. Work wear.

Eva had taken two packages wrapped in glossy red paper from her bag. Isabel ate her breakfast and nonchalantly buzzed past a couple of times, her eyes on the red presents.

Samuel was still at the table.

'Eat up,' Faye said, getting impatient.

'I can't,' he whispered.

'You know what I'm going in for, don't you? So they can decide on the best cure?'

He latched onto the last word. 'Cure? Can they do it straightaway?'

'Well, healing takes a bit of time.'

'How long?' he asked, his eyes intense. 'A long time?'

'Not long.'

'And what if they can't heal you?'

'Well they can.' It came out sharply and she saw him look up at her, shocked. He was on the brink of tears, but the truth was, she wasn't feeling so great herself now, with Edith and Eva conversing out of sight in hushed tones. All those negative vibrations. 'It's not a big deal, Samuel. I'll be home this evening. Lay the table for me, that would be nice.'

His eyes glazed pink with tears. 'I'm worried,' he said and she took him in her arms.

'Don't be.'

A few sniffs. He asked, 'How long is Edith going to be here?'

'Until I come home.'

From the living room Isobel's voice rose, her curiosity having got the better of her. 'Who's that present for?'

'It's for you.'

'Why?'

'Because you're a good girl.'

A bit of a pause for thought. Then, 'I am a good girl, am'nt I.'

Faye released Sam and kissed the top of his head. 'I love you. It'll be all right.'

Eva was saying, '"Aren't I". Here you are. And one for Samuel.'

Isabel came in with a small package in red, and a bag of gold chocolate coins. 'Here's yours,' she said, putting it on the table and waiting whilst he opened it to check that he had got the same.

Samuel opened it. 'Chocolate coins,' he said, and looked up as Eva appeared in the doorway. 'Thank you.' He picked up the gold mesh by the drawstring and weighed the bag in his hand. 'They're –'

'Yes. Don't tell.'

Faye could see pounds glinting amongst the foil. 'Keep them until after school,' she said brusquely, 'or you'll get messy. Go and brush your teeth now, you'll be late if you don't hurry.'

'Are you taking us?'

'No, Granny is.'

'I'll help you with your teeth,' Edith said, getting to her feet. 'Let Mum get ready.'

Faye was ready. The holdall was zipped up on the bed containing slippers, a book, and babywipes for her face.

Her children were being compensated with gifts and her family was being kind.

Looking at them, she experienced a leaden feeling, the kind one felt when something came to an end.

In the taxi, Eva did all the talking, about the children and a cookery book she was thinking of writing. 'It's going to be about romance,' she said. 'The recipes are going to be simple.'

126

That's for my benefit, Faye thought.

'For instance, if you cut the edges from a red pepper and fill them with cream cheese, they look like hearts, really pretty on a plate.'

Faye stopped listening. She was in this alone, that was the truth, and why would anyone want to suffer with her?

They reached the hospital and Eva insisted on paying. Faye let her, grateful at not having to bother with the mundane.

She gave her name at reception and they followed the directions to the department. She checked herself in and was told to wait.

One thing she'd noticed was how little they gave away in advance. Patients were only told what they needed to do right then: go for a blood test, room nine, for instance.

She and Eva sat in the waiting area with pale green walls and magazines on a table, next to the notice, *Please return magazines after use*. Eva put her bag on her knee and began to look through it. She brought out a rectangular gift wrapped in the same glossy red paper as the children's had been, and handed it to Faye.

'You want me to open it now?' Faye asked, taking it and weighing it in her hand. It was about the size of a box of chocolates.

She looked at her sister. Something about her at that moment reminded her of their mother; the quick, bird-like movements, the uncertainty that was almost fear. Faye looked at the red package in her hand and tried to muster up some enthusiasm before opening it.

The glossy red wrapping paper made her think of Christmas. She always preferred to open presents in private, mainly because she wasn't too good at feigning pleasure on the spot. She glanced at her sister and saw her forehead pull together, anxious in case she'd got it wrong. Faye's early disillusionment in Father Christmas had mainly stemmed from the fact that the things he brought were always too big, whether it was a bike, roller-skates or a nurse's uniform. It had been weird to think that the benevolent old man should have the 'she'll grow into it' mentality that was so much like her mother's.

Well, there was no point in dragging it out. Faye carefully unpicked the Sellotape on one neat flap, slid her finger along the seam and opened the paper just enough to take out a black box. The tension continues, she thought, taking the lid off the box. Inside was a red padlocked book with 'Five Year Diary' helpfully embossed in gold. It smelt strongly of new leather.

For a moment she stared at it, but the writing blurred. She knew she ought to say something but the on-rush of conflicting responses came out as a squeak in the back of her throat. She looked at her sister and raised her arms. They hugged awkwardly, Faye leaning the side of her head against her sister's soft, wool-clad chest. They let each other go and her sister turned away, her hand sliding up the inside of her coat-sleeve in search of a tissue.

Faye opened the diary, flicking through the gilt-edged pages thinking of five years' worth of blank spaces to be filled and Eva's encouraging show of faith. Five years. It was a faith Eva's tears belied.

Eva turned back to her, pinching her nose carefully between a white folded Kleenex.

'February the twentieth,' Faye said brightly. 'Dear Diary . . .' She smiled. 'Just what I've always wanted,' she said to break the silence.

'I didn't know how you'd take it. I know you're difficult to buy for.'

Difficult to buy for? Something she'd liked, in the right size, would always have been welcome. Was that how she came over to her elder sister? She looked at the five-year diary and touched the small, gilt keys. 'I can write my hospital appointments down in it.'

'Not just those, I hope.'

Faye raked her fingers through her thick red hair which she knew was dark at the roots because she still hadn't got round to doing anything about it. 'No, not just those.'

'I hoped it wouldn't upset you; I wasn't sure.'

'It's great.' She gave a little laugh. 'I was thinking of Mum's presents.' She smoothed her fingers over the soft leather. 'It never bothered you, did it, having the curtains closed all that time?'

Eva put her bag on the floor slowly, as though her mind wasn't on what she was doing. 'I associated it more with not having new furniture if you didn't have a man. That was the worse part, for me, that depressed pessimism. And I know it's rubbed off. I never want to be as helpless as that. That's why I'll never say yes to Frank.'

A nurse called out, 'Faye Reading!'

It was ill-timed, Faye thought as she got to her feet, feeling that there was still so much to say. She stared at her sister with sudden rare compassion and said softly, 'Now why couldn't I work that out for myself?'

'Faye Reading?'

'Coming.' A last wordless glance and she followed the nurse, thinking not of her sister's strained gaze but of the festive, shouting red of her sister's coat.

All the serious rooms had a bluish light, Faye thought, as, after changing, she was taken to the area that housed the scanner. The room seemed breathy with the hum of machinery.

'You have to lie quite still while we scan,' the radiologist said. 'It's just an advanced x-ray machine. It sends out a series of fan-shaped beams of radiation, each one passing through the body at a slightly different angle, and when it's been right round, then we have a "slice".'

'Are you going to do my whole body?' Faye asked.

'Just to your waist.'

Faye shut her eyes. Fear made her self-centred. Eva vanished from her thoughts. The radiologist could have been on another planet.

What she felt was: I'm on my own again.

Chapter Twenty-Five

A few days later Faye was resting her hands on her knees, avoiding her husband's eyes. They were in a different room, this time. It reminded her of the medical room in her senior school in that it was small, bare and painted white. Angkatell had just told her that the tumour was operable and that they wanted to do it quickly.

There was a knock, and a man in a tweed jacket came in, leaning his weight on his forward foot as he entered as though ready for flight. 'Have you seen my chest of drawers?'

Faye looked at him in surprise.

'No, sorry,' Angkatell said, half rising from his chair in response.

'It's got all my files in.' He looked around the consulting room and seemed to see Faye and Nick for the first time. 'Someone's taken my drawers,' he said.

Faye couldn't help but laugh. 'Bad luck.'

'Oh, well,' he said and went out.

They all looked at the door as he closed it behind him.

'What's the next step?' Faye asked.

'We want to test your lung capacity, which will mean removing about two thirds of your lung altogether, but people can manage quite well with only one,' Angkatell said, his voice calm and reassuring.

Nick made some movement next to her. 'And do you think that will cure it?' he asked, his voice pitched high.

She looked at him and laughed from disbelief. 'Oh, Nick. They don't know.'

'We'll do a biopsy on the tumour after the operation,' Angkatell said unemotionally.

Faye turned her attention back to the consultant. Anyone listening to the conversation without understanding the language would have been hard pressed to guess the subject matter. 'When are you going to do it?' she asked, moving her hand to her midriff and up over her right breast. 'Hospital waiting lists and all that.'

'Going to surprise you,' Angkatell said, grinning slightly. 'Monday.'
'That's better,' she said. 'I get worried when you look serious.'
The grin faded. Shame, she thought.
'How long will I be in for?'
'About a week. It depends on how soon you're up and about. You'll have to take it easy afterwards,' he said, looking at Nick.
'Sure, sure, I understand that,' Nick said. 'And what if it is – you know? What will happen then?'
'One step at a time, Nick,' Faye said softly.
There was a long sigh from Nick and she turned and saw that he was crying. Angkatell lifted his phone and called for two cups of tea to be brought in.
Is tea the best they can do? she thought bitterly, aware of the anger beneath the surface. She heard Nick swallow a sob. She was half a metre away from him, close enough to comfort him.
She felt as though she was sliding slowly, inexorably down some slope with black wings chasing her. Not yet gathering speed, but that would come.
She twitched her shoulder towards him in partial apology.
A nurse brought in the tea, and put a cup in front of her. 'Not for me, thanks,' she said.
Angkatell didn't laugh. He jerked his head. 'Drink it.'
Next to her, Nick was sniffing deeply. Angkatell passed him the box of Kleenex. Man-Sized. The tissues scraped hoarsely against the box, once, twice, a third time, and Nick blew his nose so hard she knew it must have made his ears pop.
The door opened again. Faye looked up. It was the man in the tweed jacket. 'I've found my chest of drawers,' he said. 'Randolph's been using it as a desk.' He paused, waiting for a response. No-one moved. He made a 'so-what' face and went out again.
Angkatell was the only one to look at the closing door this time. He stared at it for a moment and rubbed his ear vigorously. 'I'll get you fitted in. The sooner the better, really,' he said. 'Are you having much pain?'
'Some.'
'Fever?'
A shake of the head. She heard Nick sigh again.
'All right,' Angkatell said, adding a couple of lines of scrawled comment to her file.

Faye lifted up the teacup and smelt the tannin in the steam. She sipped and put the cup back in the saucer and glanced at Angkatell, who was looking at her as though somewhere inside him he hurt. She pushed the cup towards him, eyebrows raised, in the hope that he would grin again, but he didn't. He picked up the phone and arranged for her to have her lung capacity tested.

'Take this to the reception desk,' he said, 'and they'll give you a card.'

Nick's cup rattled in its saucer as he put it back on the desk.

She got up and walked to the door carefully, taking it easy. Nick opened it for her.

'Hey,' she said, turning, 'soon you'll know me inside out.'

He'd been standing as they left, but now he looked tired and he sat down.

She was rewarded with the trace of a grin.

'Maybe I already do,' he said.

Chapter Twenty-Six

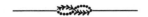

On Friday evening Edith came in from mass and as she opened the back door she was hit by a stifling wave of heat. Alicia was sitting in the kitchen with a backpack by her feet. She had her coat on and all the rings of the gas cooker were flickering with blue flame. Her face was red and slick with perspiration.

'I'm leaving,' she said to Edith.

Edith felt a wave of relief, followed by a greater wave of doubt. 'Where are you going to go?' she asked, going over to the cooker and turning the gas off briskly, ring by ring. 'I thought you were going to settle.'

'I'm moving in with Adam. I've got an evening job as a waitress in Slim Jim's six nights a week. We won't see much of each other. He says it might be better like that.' She giggled suddenly, putting her hand over her mouth.

'This man –' I don't know him from Adam, she thought. 'Does he work?'

'Yes, he works at the deli. Aren't you glad?'

'I'm –' (ecstatic, overjoyed, thrilled, alarmed, frightened) '– pleased,' Edith said slowly, 'that you've got a job. But I'm not sure about you moving in with, um . . .'

'Adam. He's lovely. Really normal.'

Edith looked at her and smiled weakly at that. 'I feel you're safer here,' she said, pleading.

'Safer?'

Edith took off her coat and went to hang it up. It had always been a source of surprise to her that Alicia could keep a job, but the fact was, Alicia had never been unemployed for long. Of course, many things that were strange to her, Edith, were not at all strange to the young. Perhaps to others, Alicia wasn't strange at all.

She felt her heart leap at this obvious explanation and how very obvious it was; how strange that she had not seen it that way before.

She glanced at her reflection in the hall mirror, checking it for self-deception, perhaps. She looked old. She was old, she thought. 'I'll be sixty soon,' she said under her breath and longed for the peace of the old days and for freedom from her suspicions. She was tired of looking for sense behind Alicia's gestures when there might be none to see.

For eight years Alicia had survived without help from any of them, and had come back none the worse. She'd obviously been feeding herself well. Edith went back into the kitchen, feeling troubled. It was still very warm in there, but Alicia had ceased to sweat. She was fanning herself with a plump hand and seemed rosy but utterly calm.

'Perhaps I should meet this Adam,' Edith said, 'before you move.'

'Come and meet him now,' Alicia said. She jumped off her seat and tugged at Edith's hand. 'He'd be glad to see you.'

'But I've only just come in,' Edith said. She wanted a cup of tea. She wanted to sit by the fire and have a biscuit, a shortbread, on a plate. Not out of the packet, as Alicia ate them. No wonder she was plump. A nice night in. 'When does your job start?'

'Tuesday. I have Monday nights off every week so I thought I'd make the most of it.'

Edith nodded; even she couldn't fault that reasoning. Still, it didn't seem *right*. 'Have you got his address?'

'Yes, I've written it out for you, and the phone number,' Alicia said, getting up and going to the kettle against which a piece of paper was propped. '103, Highgrove Mansions, NW1.'

'A proper address,' Edith said aloud, talking herself into it. Alicia was an adult, she could do what she chose whether Edith wanted her to or not. The dilemma was whether she was doing the right thing in letting her go. But how could she stop her?

Alicia had hoisted the strap of her backpack over one shoulder. She was ready to go. Carefully she put the piece of paper back against the kettle and turned to her mother. 'The phone number's at the bottom,' she said. 'I'll come and see you soon.'

So there was no stopping her.

Edith followed her to the door, where Alicia turned and gave her a big hug that squeezed the breath out of her. Then she opened the door. Outlined in the dark of the night she turned to leave. 'And if you ring,' she said, 'call me Tanya. That's what he calls me.'

Edith stared. Alicia went down the path, opened the gate and closed it carefully.

Shortbread and tea, Edith thought without enthusiasm, shutting the door, her appetite lost.

Chapter Twenty-Seven

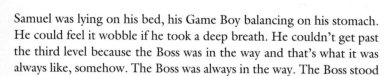

Samuel was lying on his bed, his Game Boy balancing on his stomach. He could feel it wobble if he took a deep breath. He couldn't get past the third level because the Boss was in the way and that's what it was always like, somehow. The Boss was always in the way. The Boss stood for worries.

Transition. It was a word he liked, along with interchangeable, for which he'd got a house point in school. Transition meant changing from one thing to the next and that's what he was worried was taking place here, a transition from one mother to another. Again. They got ill and then they passed you on.

Or was it a coincidence? Another good word. His real mother had got ill and his original mother had come back from wherever she'd been, Bristol, he'd heard his Dad say, and she'd wanted to see him again, understandably, he supposed, but his real mother had let her. She'd even invited her to the house. He'd felt at any minute as though she was going to walk away with him, or at least ask for him back. He'd felt that everyone at the table had been waiting for that to happen, including his Granny who had looked worried.

But she hadn't asked.

Where did that leave him?

There was a tap on the door. 'Come in,' he said, but he knew it was his mother and that after tapping she would come in anyway.

She came in, her hair tied up away from her face. Her hair had gone dark at the roots, as though she was growing him out. She sat on the edge of his bed and lifted his Game Boy off his stomach. 'I wondered what you were doing,' she said.

'Worrying,' he replied.

'About Monday? I'll only be in a week. Daddy'll bring you to visit. Don't bring me any chocolates, though, I'm going to diet while I'm there.'

Samuel turned on his side to see her better. 'Will you still be able to cope with me when you come out?' He saw a funny look on her face and wished he hadn't asked.

'Cope with you? What's there to cope with? You're a smashing boy,' she said. 'Come here.'

He put his arms around her and felt hers going round him, all the way round, it felt like, wrapping him up in warmth.

She held him still for a moment and then said, 'You're thinking of Alicia, aren't you?'

He wasn't surprised, she often seemed to read his thoughts. He nodded his head against her slowly.

'Because she got ill and couldn't cope.'

He nodded again.

She pushed him away from her, not unkindly, but to have a good look at him. She ducked her head so that she could see his face. 'Different thing altogether,' she said. 'Alicia was very young, that was part of it. Am I very young?'

He grinned and didn't answer.

'There you go! Alicia was young and couldn't cope. She's back, she wanted to see you and now she has. And she may do again. But you belong here and that's never going to change.'

'What if she wants me to live with her? I wouldn't have to go, would I?'

'I don't think she'll want you to leave us,' Faye said.

'But *if*?'

'We wouldn't let you go.' She made a face and said in a cartoon voice, 'Hey, buddy, what do you think we are, crazy?' And she tickled him in the ribs.

He loved being tickled but she didn't carry on. 'Anything else on your mind, Sam?' she asked, stroking his hair. He didn't answer and she carried on, 'I know it seems like a lot of upheaval.'

'I like that word,' he said. 'Upheaval. Like being sick.'

'Oh, you!'

He smiled. 'No. There's nothing else.' He paused and said, 'Is there anything on your mind?'

'Nah. It's a total playground.' They both laughed at that.

'Are you scared of it hurting?'

'There's a new policy in hospitals, they're not allowed to let you hurt. They feed you painkillers till you rattle, that's what I've been told. The worst thing is, I'll miss you and Isabel.'

'I'll miss you too.'

'But the point is, you can visit me any time, but I can't visit you.'

'I'll visit. I'll think of you all the time.'

'I know you will.' She kissed his cheek.

He could see the love in her eyes and for a moment he thought he could see tears, but it was just the shine in them.

'Goodnight.'

Chapter Twenty-Eight

It was drizzling. The fine, thorough rain seemed to blur just above their heads. Faye held her multi-coloured umbrella in one hand and Isabel's hand with the other. Samuel was somewhere behind them, complacent for once, kicking at puddles with his newly polished shoes.

Faye felt the anger building up in her and tried to calm it. She'd been ratty so often lately she wondered if the tumour had a personality. She stopped and turned. Sam was kicking at the path as though he had a grudge against it. He lifted his head and saw she was watching him.

'What?' His navy raincoat was sodden around his shoulders and his hair clung wet and dark to his head like seaweed on stones.

'Look at you!'

'What?'

She turned away, speechless, angry with herself for being angry. She couldn't bear to see him like that, dejected and poor. Being ill made her feel poor enough, everything snatched away from her, her future, her self-sufficiency, her peace of mind. She'd had enough of that.

She tightened her grip on Isabel's hand, reaching the end of the path where it met the pavement and where they crossed the slick, wet road.

There was a break in the traffic and she hurried across. They'd reached the other side when the drawn-out yelp of brakes on wet tarmac froze her. She span round, her heart swelling with fear.

A van window was sliding down. 'You could have got yourself killed,' a man shouted through it at Samuel, his face ugly with fright.

White-faced, and now on the pavement with them, Samuel glanced at Faye. 'Sorry,' he said to her.

She could see his mouth trembling. 'Come here,' she said. She glanced crossly at the van, which was pulling away. 'Stupid man.' She hugged her son awkwardly, pressing his wet head to her lips as the umbrella sent a cascade of rain down the back of her coat. 'We're so wet,' she said despairingly, but with a laugh of slightly hysterical relief. 'I hate this weather,' she said loudly, blaming it. 'I'll be glad when the spring comes. Bring on the sun.'

'And we'll go away,' Sam said.

'Yes. Somewhere warm.' They'd reached the school gates.

'Do I have to go?' Samuel asked, his green eyes pleading.

She looked at him. 'I know how you feel, but –'

'No, you don't,' he said. He turned abruptly and walked swiftly through the gates and into the school.

She was coming out of Isabel's classroom when she saw Vicky waiting on the pavement. She picked up her umbrella from the stand by the door.

Vicky was walking towards her, her raincoat collar up, her dark hair kinking in the rain. 'How did it go with the hypnotherapist?' she asked.

Faye put up her umbrella and held it over them both. 'I was convinced it hadn't worked. On the other hand, I haven't smoked since. I think about it, though, and I miss it, that's the worse thing, knowing I can never have another.'

'It's a sod, isn't it. But it gets better.'

'Does it?'

They started to walk up the road. 'Look,' Vicky said awkwardly, 'if there's anything I can do . . .'

Faye turned her head sharply to look at her. 'About what?'

'About the –' Vicky tapped her chest, '– the tumour.'

Faye listened to the rain bounce off the nylon. 'Who told you?'

'Mrs Lloyd had a word with the class. Nothing awful, no cautionary tales about the dangers of smoking or anything. She just told them that Samuel would need their support. I expect she'll do a toned-down version for Isabel. Done in the best possible taste, lovey,' she said appeasingly, and squeezed Faye's arm.

Faye felt a flush of humiliation rise inside herself. 'She had no right,' she said, her voice low with anger. 'I told her that in confidence.'

'Faye, it's nothing to be ashamed of. You should have told me about the tumour.'

'Yes,' she said, but she *was* ashamed. It was a weakness and no-one wanted to admit to a weakness, tangled up with old ideas of illness and sin. It was the antithesis of strength and she was disgusted by her vulnerability and the fact that her body was doing something without

140

her collusion. And she was ashamed that the school had thought her children needed support from their peers. 'They've got all the support they need,' she said. 'And love.'

'I know that.'

No wonder Samuel hadn't wanted to go to school, she thought.

'We can't stand on this street corner all day getting splashed,' Vicky said. 'Come back with me for a coffee.'

'I don't want . . .' What was the matter with her? 'I'm not very good company,' she said lamely.

'Great. Let's have a moan.'

Faye's arms were aching from holding the umbrella. A moan would be nice, she thought. A good, girly moan, preferably about Vicky's love-life and how difficult it was to diet. She would give anything for life to be that simple again. 'Everyone knows, don't they,' she said wearily. 'All of them thinking, thank goodness it isn't me.'

'And all wishing it wasn't you. You're all strung up. When was the last time you relaxed? You need a good soak in a flotation tank, that's what you need. You have to give your body a chance to heal itself. Don't worry about it, *do* something! You can give the health club a ring from my place.'

Faye looked at Vicky. She nodded thankfully. Sometimes, she thought, it really was easier to agree.

Ten minutes of whale noises and she was ready to get out. The tank was a tiled room like a flooded public lavatory. A crack of light shone through the door.

Let your imagination break through, the beautician had said, and Faye could feel her imagination telling her that the beautician had forgotten all about her.

You'll lose all track of time, she'd said, and will lose touch with all senses.

I have lost my common sense, Faye thought. She kept floating into the wall, an interesting phenomenon. It wasn't as if the tide was taking her there. She must make the effort to lose herself. What if she fell asleep? She could feel the water around her face, leaving just her features untouched, like a Balaclava helmet. The salts were crystallising on her skin. She pulled a face and felt her forehead crackle.

The whale sounds stopped and simultaneously the light shining through the crack in the door went out.

She felt a sudden panic and opened her eyes wider, to see. She waited for her eyes to become accustomed to the dark but she could no longer make out the shape of the door. She was in total blackness. She'd stopped floating towards the wall. She could feel the water, not so warm, now. She had the sensation that she was getting smaller, smaller and less significant, and the room, the tank, was getting bigger. It was not inanimate. The room seemed to be a huge presence growing around her. She could feel the smallness of herself and the water she was in was harbouring . . . It was like an ocean, harbouring . . .

She swallowed. Black shadows of manta rays skimmed the ocean bed.

They touched her cheek. She brushed them away frantically, splashing her face. It was the air cushion and she felt the right size again, but her eyes were stinging.

The beautician had forgotten her. She'd forgotten her and gone home. She'd soaked, de-cuticled, emeried, undercoated, painted the nails of her last client and said goodbye and put on her coat, her mind on whether she had any milk in the fridge at home.

Faye felt for the bottom of the tank. It was slippery. She stood up carefully and felt for the door. Now that she'd found it and opened it, she could make out a few things in the dark: a folded white bathrobe on a bench, the lockers to the left. The other door was straight ahead framed by a narrow strip of light. Her towel was hanging on a hook next to her raincoat and she reached for it, dried her hands and felt for the light-switch. With a click the world was normal again and she gave a big sigh of relief that started her coughing.

She stepped into the shower to wash the salts off herself, towelled herself dry and got dressed.

The beautician looked up in surprise as she emerged. 'Was it all right?' she asked.

'Actually I'm claustrophobic,' Faye said.

'Oh. Would you like your nails done instead?'

'I'm having an operation on Monday. I'm not allowed to wear nail varnish.'

'Another time, then.'

'Yes, thanks.'

She gave Vicky a modified version of her flotation experience because she could see Samuel coming out of the school building and looking for her from the top of the steps.

She raised her hand to him. 'I know what Mrs Lloyd told the class,' she said as he approached her.

'You should have told me it was a tumour,' he said. 'Whatever that is.'

'A tumour fish,' Isabel said.

'It's just a lump,' Faye said.

A knot of mothers was chatting by the gate. She saw the sympathetic glances they gave her and managed a brief smile.

'. . . left it too late,' one was saying.

Faye knew it didn't mean they were talking about her, but she couldn't shake off the impression that they were.

She took her children's hands and hurried away.

Chapter Twenty-Nine

It was a lonely trip, that final visit to the hospital, lonely although the children and Edith this time waved her off on a sunny morning, three small figures watching with brave smiles as they drove away. It was lonely even though Nick was solicitous, driving with care, keeping the conversation light and turning the volume of the radio down. And it was a lonely walk to the ward.

Her first impression of it was that the colour had been drained out of it. The screens and the bed covers were a sage green, a colour that reminded her of lichen. She looked out of the window at the bright blue sky.

She put her bag on the bed and turned to Nick and caught hold of his hand. 'Bring me –' Bring me a box of Cadbury's Roses and a torch, she thought. 'Bring me something bright,' she said fretfully. 'Oh, Nick, I wish I'd brought something bright to look at.'

'It's the least of your worries,' he said gently, smoothing her hair.

'No, no. I should have thought.' The lichen-coloured room made her feel blind. She sat on the bed and put her head in her hands. 'It's only for a week,' she said and took her hands away to look up at Nick.

'Only a week,' he said, and his eyes flickered away. 'Let me put your things in the locker.'

'It's all right, I'll –' She got off the bed and busied herself with putting her clothes neatly into the bottom of the locker, and her spongebag, underwear and hairbrush in one drawer and her coin purse, paperbacks, the five-year diary and some babywipes in the drawer above it.

Nick was standing by watching her, as though if he looked long enough he would find just the right thing to say.

The putting away didn't last long. She slammed the drawer shut and sat on the bed again, her legs dangling, her arms rigid, shoulders pressed upwards. The pain was irritating her. 'You can go now, Nick,' she said.

She could feel his relief from across the bed. 'Sure?' he asked.

'Really. I'm going to have a sleep. I didn't sleep much last night.'

Nick smoothed the cover of her bed and straightened the chair next to it. 'And you've got everything?' he said in his new, gentle voice.

'Yes, I've got everything.'

He kissed her briefly, his lips skimming her hair. 'See you later. Anything you want me to bring, just ring and I'll bring it tonight.'

'I'll do that.'

It was a relief for her, to see him go. She could concentrate on herself, on the rumbling cough and on the constant ache. After he'd gone she rather distractedly watched daytime TV on a small set by the window, losing herself in the drama before periodically coming back to her own with a sharp intake of fear.

During the afternoon she had to have blood taken, her blood pressure checked, her temperature noted. She was reading the *Daily Telegraph*, which had been brought round with other newspapers, when Angkatell turned up with a short, grey-haired man he introduced as Mr Williams. They were wearing white coats, for once.

'You look like butchers,' she said, not really joking. She put her paper down.

'The mechanics are the same but the intention is different.'

'Can I ask you something? Why did I get this thing now?' she asked Angkatell.

He unclipped the chart at the end of her bed without looking at her. 'Why did you get it now,' he said after a moment, to show he was listening. 'Try me with another – something I can answer.'

Faye folded her newspaper and looked at him reproachfully through a coiling strand of red hair which she brushed aside. 'Call yourself a doctor,' she said. 'Do you think it's in the mind?' she asked. 'Actually, what I was wondering was, did I bring it on myself?' It was almost easier to think of oneself as the instigator rather than the victim.

He added something to her chart. She could see the skin on top of his head shine in the sunlight. It made him look fragile, human. As he replaced the chart the sound of metal on metal rang around the enamel bedframe, one of the hospital noises that she knew would become familiar only too soon.

'Faye, at the risk of sounding preachy, cigarettes are the most common cause of lung disease. If you want to blame anything, blame smoking.'

'I didn't always inhale deeply.'

'Shallow inhalers seem to be more likely to get lung cancer. Deep inhalers are more likely to get heart problems, thromboses, hardening of the arteries. Both contribute to cancer of the mouth, larynx, bladder, kidney, pancreas. And no, there has not been a study yet that can prove any link between unhappiness and cancer, so you can strike that off your list.'

'But you don't know it's cancer,' she said.

Angkatell put her chart back again. 'No, we don't,' he said. 'And your lunch has arrived. We'll let you enjoy it in peace.'

Surprisingly, she did enjoy it. It tasted like airline food, and the big plus was that she hadn't had to cook it herself. She fell asleep, happy to escape her thoughts for a while.

When she awoke it was visiting time, and Nick, Samuel and Isabel were whispering by the bed.

'It's all right,' she said, opening her eyes. 'I was whiling away the time until you came.'

Isabel pushed a tubular parcel at her, wrapped in brown paper, and jumped on the spot several times after handing it over.

'I chose it,' Samuel said. He was still in his school uniform and his black-and-grey tie was askew.

'Thanks,' she said, smiling at him. She shook it. It rattled alarmingly and she widened her eyes. Isabel giggled. Faye took the paper off carefully. 'It's a telescope, no it isn't, it's a – a –'

'A kaleidoscope!' Samuel said eagerly. 'Isabel chose the colours.'

Faye lifted it to her eye and turned it, watching the myriad jewel shades mingle and fall with a clatter into a technicolour snowflake. 'It's lovely,' she said. 'Really lovely.' She lowered it and the ward looked more drained of colour than ever. Samuel was smiling, pleased at his choice. She looked into the tube again. Oh, the relief. Colour memory was an ill-developed sense, what a regret that had always been to her, to always have to remember a colour with words. But here were colours that there was no need to remember. Like uncut gems the pieces tumbled into a new harmony. 'Here,' she said to Isabel, 'have a look.'

They looked at it in turn, even Nick, although he adopted the brief courtesy of the unimpressed.

'I got it from the toy shop,' Samuel said, handing it back. 'I was looking for a torch, the kind with red and green filters on, but they

146

didn't have it and then I thought of that. Because there is enough light in here, isn't there? It's nice and bright.'

She looked towards the window again and nodded.

'Why are you in bed?' Isabel asked, taking her hand. 'Are you really ill now?'

'No, they just need somewhere to put me to save me being in the way. I'll come for a walk with you if you like.' She got out of bed and they did a small tour of the bathrooms, the WCs, the dayroom and the two adjoining wards.

Then she walked them to the lift. Nick kissed the top of her head and she lifted her face. He kissed her briefly on the lips.

'It's not catching,' she said.

He gave an uncomfortable laugh.

Did illness, she wondered, make one seem asexual?

She kissed Sam and Isabel, eventually unclasping her daughter's hands from her neck. 'I'll be home soon, good as new,' she told her. 'Be good for Granny, won't you.'

She watched the lift doors close on them. And felt very lonely indeed.

After they'd gone she tried to read a book but found herself watching the words dance on the page.

By eight-thirty the ward was quiet, all visitors gone. Someone came round with a trolley of hot drinks.

Sipping her hot chocolate, she looked at the other women in the beds around her and exchanged a brief smile with the woman opposite whose white hair fluffed around her face. She realised that her shoulder ached more. She finished her drink and lay back on the pillows.

The lights were dimmed soon after.

Lying in the dark ward she was acutely conscious of the people around her. Someone was coughing, a sharp prolonged bark that was worse than her own. Another woman sighed periodically. Faye turned over and lay still. It was a long time since she'd lain alone in a single bed and it had never been something she'd missed. After a while she gave up trying to sleep and got out of bed. The nurses did not look up from their station as she passed. She went into the day room and switched on the light, glad to be alone. The smell of cigarette smoke hung in the air and she went over to the window and cupped her hands around her face, looking out at the lights of the surrounding buildings burning in the dark. All looked normal. She'd expected to see fighting in the streets, stabbings in the office blocks – the world had seemed to be coming to an end, but of course that was just her world. She wiped away the condensation her breath had made.

There was a sound at the door and she turned round sharply. A man, in his forties, with dark hair, was coming in. He was wearing a navy towelling dressing-gown, and looked as if he was at a health farm rather than a hospital.

Something new to resent, she thought – his presence and his health. Status didn't count here, but illness did. It was easy to be dismissive, very dismissive of the odd ingrowing toenail.

'Hello,' he said to her, putting his hands in his pockets. 'Anything of interest happening in the real world?'

'No,' she said shortly. She turned back to the window and hoped he'd take the hint.

He came alongside her. If she looked up she could see his reflection in the glass as he looked at the street below.

There was no peace, she thought, even to get maudlin soberly. Why didn't he switch the television on, if that was what he was there for? And she glanced at his reflection again.

She couldn't tell what his eyes were seeing, but it wasn't the buildings.

'We've all got to go through it,' he said softly. To her? Or to himself?

She glanced at him, wondering what it was he meant.

He saw her looking and he smiled slightly. 'I wasn't at Dunkirk. I wasn't at Goose Green.' He turned away again to look at the city.

He's a good-looking man, used to laughing, she thought, thinking of the lines around his eyes. 'Are you in the army?' she asked, more out of curiosity than politeness.

He laughed, quietly, but it turned into a cough and he shook his head in reply. 'I'm an engineer,' he said, when he was able. 'The name's Phil.'

'You –' she tried to think of a suitable way of putting it, '– going under the knife tomorrow?' As soon as she'd said it she thought it sounded flippant compared with his own words, but she saw him nod.

'Thursday,' he said. 'And you?'

'Tomorrow. I'm having a tumour taken off my lung.'

He looked at her, his head tilted, and she looked at him back,

148

scrutinising his face for that limpid smile of sympathy she kept being given.

'Good for you,' he said after a moment, and sounded as if he meant it. Somehow it didn't seem odd.

'Did you smoke?' she asked wistfully, and with the words her breath clouded the window, making the reflections opaque.

'Yeah,' he said with a wry grin. He gave a short laugh. 'I still dream about it. Hate waking up. I dreamt I was going to eat a green apple, and the top came off and inside I found tobacco and a packet of Rizla papers.' He laughed at himself, but it turned into a cough again and he tapped his chest with his fingers.

Faye wiped the glass with her hand and smeared the mist into droplets. She was beginning to feel tired, tired enough, probably, to sleep. Her hand was damp and cold as she wiped it with the other. 'I think I'll go back to bed now,' she said. She thought he might agree with her and walk back along the corridor but he nodded and stayed where he was. 'Goodnight,' she said, turning to him.

He turned to her, his head tilted again as though to see her better. 'Good luck tomorrow,' he said.

'Thanks.'

When she took a last look he had turned back to the window and his reflection seemed to be looking beyond it, beyond the city, beyond the lights.

In his face she seemed to see the wistful hopelessness of an animal for whom captivity had become a way of life.

PART FIVE

Hold your tongue!

Malesherbes

Chapter Thirty

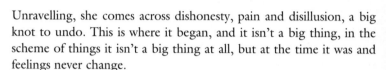

Unravelling, she comes across dishonesty, pain and disillusion, a big knot to undo. This is where it began, and it isn't a big thing, in the scheme of things it isn't a big thing at all, but at the time it was and feelings never change.

The kitchen always smells sweet, of sweet baking. It's jam tarts today. She is leaning over the table watching her grandmother spoon out the jam and slide it into the pastry cases with the back of a teaspoon. It just takes a blob. There is no need to level it out, the heat does that. She is not allowed to touch them before they go in or just after they come out – too hot.

It is one of the rules she is meant to keep.

There are lots of rules, some she forgets, some seem pulled out of nowhere for the occasion because there is a rule for everything. She doesn't argue. She knows her place, and it is quite a small place. She watches her grandmother put the tarts in the oven and feels the puff of heat that escapes as she shuts the oven door.

'I am going to peg out the clothes,' her grandmother says, putting the bag of dollypegs on the damp linen in the basket, 'it's a good drying day.'

She nods and makes to follow, but her eyes go back to the small white tube on the dresser. The tube is small but so big that it takes up all her attention. It holds tiny sweet tablets for her grandmother's tea.

She imagines what they are like; tiny and sweeter than sweet, the sweetest things imaginable. She is not allowed to have one – she has asked and no, the answer comes back, they are not for children.

This strikes her as odd because they are so small and child-sized. Smaller than child-sized; they are doll-sized, fairy-sized. Tiny and sweet. Sweeter than a spoonful of sugar, Grammy says.

She has imagined trying one. Many times she has felt her tongue holding the little tablet set comfortable as a ladybird on a blanket. She imagines the sweetness spreading across her tongue, into the top of the cavern of her mouth, sweetening her breath, her saliva, her throat, all sweet, sweeter than jam tarts, sweeter than sugar, sweeter than dreams.

And her grandmother has gone out, hasn't she, with the washing? Hasn't waited for her to come, hasn't called her to help and pass her the pegs. She is down the garden without her, pegging in the quiet drone of bees, with the sawing of the occasional fly the only thing to startle her thoughts.

The little white tube has rolled over and she goes to straighten it, to stand it on its end. She picks it up and holds it and even on her small hand it is very small.

She opens it and shakes a tablet out but a lot of them come out together and she puts them back in, one by one, until only one is left and she can put that in too, just as easily. But it is not easy, is it? That last one can go easier into her mouth. There are so many tablets in the little tube that just this one won't be missed.

I'm not missed, am I? she thinks, not by my mother nor my father at work nor my sister at school and not by my grandmother, still out there in the good drying day.

She holds up her palm and touches it with the tip of her tongue and takes the tablet into her mouth. It is sweet, very sweet, and bitter and foul. She makes a face like a gargoyle and here is her grandmother coming through the door with the basket and the peg bag inside it. So she closes her mouth and the bitterness mocks the end of her tongue and seeps down her throat.

She swallows the tablet.

Perhaps she'll die.

'Where did you get to? I was hoping you'd help me with the pegs. How are those tarts getting along?'

'All right,' she says, and even the air makes her words taste bitter and it's on her tongue, her gums, her lips.

The tarts are taken out of the oven and put on a wire tray to cool.

She wants to make up for it, for not going in the garden to hand over the pegs, and she reaches for the patty tin that the tarts have come out of and shocked, she burns her finger. She watches as it goes red and forms a white blister like a sucked Glacier mint. Hurts? Yes it hurts, and she gets brusque sympathy from her grandmother, who coats her finger with butter.

Pain and bitterness and disappointment cloud her mind. Not because of the saccharins, but because of herself.

Chapter Thirty-One

I am only young, Faye thought when she was woken up by the nurse next morning. Her mouth tasted dry and foul. The coughing in the ward sounded like liquid barking. And she couldn't leave because she was in their hands now, a dodgy bit of machinery.

A nurse with a pretty face and a Scottish accent came over and told her what to do. She had to shower and put on the gown provided, which closed down the back but was a reasonably decent length, and put on some thick, white stockings with holes in the toes.

Obediently she did so.

It tired her and she got back under the covers.

Annie, introducing herself from the bed opposite, was very admiring of the stockings. Annie told her she was seventy-seven and this morning in the sunlight she looked to Faye like a dandelion clock. Her white hair was perfectly fluffed and without a dent, and her body was so small that she hardly made a lump in the bedclothes.

The woman in the bed next to her made a joke about getting ready for the theatre for them all to hear. Faye laughed at this hospital joke. She imagined trying it out on Nick. Then she imagined trying it out on Phil. She felt better – the general atmosphere of the patients was merry, a cover-up for nerves.

The nurses were preoccupied, but then they would get their peace when the patients were still slumbering, post-anaesthetic.

The merriment died a little when the porter came for the first patient.

'See you later,' the woman managed to say to them. Faye too found herself saying it back; saying it, yes, it was all in the mouth, this merriment, and not at all in the heart.

See you later? There wasn't a 'later'. Her time stretched as far as them coming for her, which they did, after a long, trying while, and there was only Annie left to promise to see her later and no-one at all to say it to Annie in her turn.

The porter was jovial but Faye took in nothing he said. Lying on her fast-wheeled bed she watched the lights overhead go past, and if she thought she had been in their hands before, well it was nothing compared with now.

She would like to have walked to the theatre under her own steam, reading the signs on the doors. Authorised personnel. Radiology. Pathology Lab, past each in turn, until she reached the theatre.

Instead, she stared at the ceiling. They were picking up quite a speed.

Ordinary faces looked at her.

'Nearly there.'

'Feeling all right?'

'Left hand turn now.'

'The team,' said Angkatell when the bed came to a halt. He was surrounded by people. 'We'll be working on you.'

'Hi,' she said to them all. To him she wanted to say, let me go home now. 'Do you know a Phil?' she asked as they fixed a valve to her hand. 'He's having a biopsy on Thursday.'

'Yes, I know him.'

'Is that a smaller operation?'

Angkatell inhaled through his nose, slowly and deeply and said, 'No, it's pretty well the same op.'

'Am I having a biopsy?'

'We'll do a biopsy, yes. Any more questions before we start?'

She could stall him forever. She stared at him until her eyes began to get heavy, and then she shut them.

'Count backwards from ninety-nine,' one of the voices said.

'Ninety . . .'

Later she drifted . . .

. . . in and out through layers of sleep, bobbing, tilting like a bottle half-full of water in ever-lightening layers of grey sea, touching the surface and sinking back down, taking herself down to that calm darkness she had been fighting for such a long time.

When she finally broke the surface she opened her eyes and saw tubes stretching up from her body. She stayed still. She could hear groans coming from the next bed, and the sound of retching, but she lay still and quiet. They were all on their own now.

Her eyes wouldn't open properly. They felt puffy. Tubes were coming out of her side, she could feel them warm against the inside of her arm.

Not happy, she thought. Broken. She felt herself sinking again.

Later she opened her eyes and tried to lift her head.

The dandelion lady was curled in the bed opposite.

All was quiet.

The next time she woke up it was dark and she was hungry. She waited patiently, and when the nurse came to check her chart she told her so. 'And thirsty,' she added.

'I'll see what I can do,' the nurse said, helping her up into a sort of sideways sitting position.

'How can I sit properly?' Faye asked querulously. 'It's hurting on my back and my side.'

The nurse showed her a bar attached to the end of the bed that she could use to pull herself up.

She felt tears running down her cheeks. 'Can I have some tea?'

'I'll go and check.'

The waiting tired her so that she forgot about the tea which had briefly seemed so important, and went back to sleep.

The next day Angkatell came round with his team and drew the curtains round her bed. Williams looked efficient and impassive and got straight to the point. 'The tumour was malignant,' he said.

She didn't hear anything else. She felt the blood draining from her face.

'Raise the foot of the bed,' Angkatell said sharply.

She felt the bed move. The helplessness of being tilted backwards brought with it a cold despair. The fear, for all her readiness, settled inside her, a dark vacuity. She looked away from them. The only sound was of someone retching not far from her in long, harsh hoots.

'Faye,' Angkatell said.

'I don't want to talk,' she said, and every word was heavy.

'You don't have to do anything,' he said softly, 'that's our job. We've taken the tumour away. There's no sign at the moment of it having spread to the lymph glands but we'll keep an eye on you, I promise you that. How is the pain?'

She nodded. The effort of not crying was hurting her.

'You see this? You can press this for morphine when you need it. You can't overdose. Use it when you need it. Faye? Good girl. I'll check on you later.'

And the team moved off to the next bed, keeping the screens around her shut. She hadn't wanted to know. Let it be a fear and nothing else.

She thought she'd faced it but her fear had been of knowing.

Now it was of dying.

She wanted a rest from it. I didn't want to know, she thought. Too late now, she told herself, turning her face into the damp pillow. Now it was a fact that she was going to have to live with.

It couldn't ever be unknown.

Chapter Thirty-Two

Nick had bought a blue glass bowl for Faye and filled it with cherries. The bowl was cold and heavy, frosty in his hands, and the cherries glowed dark like blood and seemed to melt into it.

Life was just a bowl of them, wasn't it, he thought, pushing into the hospital lift with visitors, doctors, cleaners, people who seemed to have sprung from nowhere.

In the lift, the bowl got in the way, digging into his ribs as more people pressed in. He had been so sure the cherries were right when he bought them. Now, though, they looked showy and corrupt with their superficial shine, a gesture that was too much, too embarrassing, the kind of thing a stranger might buy, afraid of being thought cheap.

I should have bought her peonies, he thought. Something that means something to her. He pushed his way out of the lift and walked to the ward. He could see her in her bed, lying on her side, towards him.

She was curled up and the blanket was like a yashmak hiding her face.

He moved a space on the locker for the bowl and put it down. It's a beautiful shape, he thought, consoled, and he looked at his wife, the part of her he could see. She was still and pale and her eyes seemed swollen. There were tubes coming out of her and going into her and this surprised and slightly nauseated him. He was a fastidious person. It seemed to him more hygienic to plug the leak.

He looked around the ward uneasily. He was the only visitor, the only person conscious, it seemed to him. He pulled up a chair, and tugged gently at the blanket over her nose. 'Faye?'

Her eyes opened slowly and she looked at him.

He expected a smile, but there was no smile, and he could see that all the energy had left her face. She looked shiny and swollen and for a moment he wondered if it wasn't her at all. 'What have they done to you?' he whispered.

She gave a travesty of a smile, hardly moving her dry and flaking lips.

159

'All these tubes,' he said, marvelling and alarmed, following them with his gaze. 'Does it hurt?'

For a moment she didn't move. Then she shook her head. 'Morphine.' She moved her hand up from the white bedclothes. 'In the pump.'

She lapsed into silence and shut her eyes, and in the magnitude of her isolation he could think of nothing to say that didn't sound trivial. Even the thought of Susie seemed trivial now, and he was fiercely glad of it, blessedly clean as she was of illness and corruption.

'It was malignant,' Faye said, looking at him through her puffy eyes. Her hair was tangled around her cheek.

'Yes,' he said. He was surprised at the jolt it gave him, as solid as a blow even though he had always known it would be cancer. The blow made him feel querulous and started off a weakly hectoring voice inside him: she brought it on herself with her smoking and her lack of belief and who knows what else she has on her conscience. He was determined not to take it, this blow she'd just delivered. It was her own fault. Nothing to do with him.

How much simpler anger was than guilt. He could see why she'd opted for it, these last couple of weeks.

He was breathing heavily.

'I'm scared,' she said, her eyes still closed.

Don't drag me into the dark, he thought, feeling his heart-rate increase. 'I brought you some cherries.'

'Yes,' she said, although how could she know through that small, restricted field of vision taken in by those bleary eyes?

'And the children are fine. Fine and dandy, Faye.' Oh, it was a word he had never used before in his life. 'Fine and dandy,' he said heartily.

'And you?' A ghost of a smile. 'Are you fine and dandy?'

'Sure am. Missing you.' He wondered what the hot things were that were landing on his hand feeling like blood-bloated bugs, and he looked and they were tears. 'Going to find the nurse, to ask,' he said and got up off the chair.

Not one of the still, curled, sheet-wound bodies stirred as he hurried back, beyond the nurses' station and along the corridor, the breeze from his passing stirring the posters as he ran.

He was on his way down another corridor when he realised he had missed the stairs. A sense of panic engulfed him. Turning again, he found

160

a second set of stairs and ran down them, surprising two white-coated men on their way up who dodged to avoid him.

At the bottom of the stairs another corridor stretched ahead of him, the floor gleaming brightly so that he could not read the signs. It was like a nightmare. His eyes were dazzled. He was alone and lost.

He ran along it and was sobbing when he turned again. This corridor too was endless but shaded from the light. He stopped and bent over to catch his breath, head down, his hands on his knees, panting. As he straightened he saw above him white-printed words on a brown card: Chapel.

He pushed open the door quietly but there was no-one inside the small room. He listened for the emptiness and looked towards the altar. Behind it a length of purple cloth hung from the ceiling, and on a lectern was a large, open Bible. The familiar props steadied him.

Clutching one of the chairs, he sat down and bowed his head.

'I'm sorry,' he said in a whisper.

He'd seen the darkness, he'd stepped out in it. All this time Faye had hidden from it and he'd still not understood. Bulbs, yeah, that was the cure, folks, get rid of your fear with a light bulb. Not one, hundreds. Give me the light.

He could stand in front of searchlights and not escape this darkness and he might never escape it and she, Faye, was lost in it, lost to him. 'I need a drink,' he said aloud, looking round the small room. It felt so pure, the air in there.

He got up off the chair. On a table by the entrance was an open book like a visitor's book and he glanced at it. Prayer requests, it said at the top of the page. He flicked through it. Oh, there were requests there, lines of them, pages of them, leaves of them; the futility of the hoping made him despair.

He picked up the pen and flicked forward again to the last used page. What he wanted to write was an expletive, big, in capitals, hard, scoring the page. He pressed the pen down on the paper. That was what he wanted to write.

He sobbed.

An expletive.

Or a prayer.

Chapter Thirty-Three

Nick was back at home watching *Jaws 2* that night when, after the children had gone to bed, he thought he heard knocking.

He had a glass of Scotch in his hand and was swirling it round so the ice hit the glass, wondering if that was what he'd heard.

He wasn't inclined to get up. He felt comfortable and slightly numb. Happily numb, he corrected himself, losing track of the plot. Happily numb, and he didn't care about the knocking.

But it persisted, which was strange, because anyone coming to the door would press the buzzer, 'And if they don't,' he said to his drink, 'then I don't want to know.'

But he put down his drink and went downstairs, one hand on the wall for balance.

Through the glass in the door he could see a shape, broken up, but he knew it was Susie. He could see her hand wave at him through the glass in a little wave of greeting.

He opened the door and the cold night air rushed in around him, making him gasp. He blocked the doorway with his body. He suddenly felt very sober indeed. 'Susie,' he said. 'What's up?'

She lifted her weight from one foot to the other. Her hair was blowing wild around her face. '"What's up?"' she mimicked him, making a face. 'Nothing's up. I thought you might like company, you miserable bugger. I've had a bloody awful day and if you let me in you can give me a drink and I'll tell you all about it. Otherwise I'm going home.'

'I think that's a good idea,' he said, stepping back from the door and letting her in even as he said it. He felt alert, ready, wary, and touched her hand to balance her as she kicked off her shoes. She let him go and went upstairs in her bare feet and stopped dead at the top with her hand on the banister, taking in the lights above her. She sat on the sofa, her head flung back.

Nick rescued his Scotch and stood looking at her. Underneath her trenchcoat she was wearing a short black dress.

She smiled at him and stretched out her tanned legs, wriggling her toes which were the pearly pink of the insides of shells. She looked at the gentle flood of blue light that softened the height of the ceiling like mist. 'Effective, Nick. The girl has talent, I've always told her so.'

Nick backed into the television. Static crackled. He took a gulp of Scotch to blur the sharpened edge of his anxiety. 'Could you keep your voice down?' he asked. 'You'll wake the children.' And that wouldn't do because he wanted to see what happened next.

Susie lifted her hair with her fingers and let it drop. 'I just came to see how she was,' she said. 'I've been so worried for her.'

It occurred to Nick for the first time that she too had been drinking. He wondered with whom, and bearing in mind the weather, where her tights had got to.

He thought that Faye was amply able to worry for herself. 'She's fine,' he said.

'But how can she be? You said lung cancer, didn't you? She must be scared to death.' She put her fingers over her mouth in apology. 'Well, you know what I mean. What do you really think, Nick? Didn't she have her op today?' Susie asked, and seeing the direction of his gaze she tucked her legs together primly.

'She's how you would expect her to be,' Nick said shortly, hugging his glass for comfort. He didn't want to talk about Faye. That was something that he wanted to forget.

He sipped his whisky, looking at Susie's face because her attention now was on the TV and while she was distracted he could see that she was wearing make-up.

Dressed to seduce.

A shiver of desire ran through him. He should ask her to go, of course he should, oh yeah, but he could feel in himself the temptation to hand it all over to her; hand himself over. Here you are, look after me, lay me down on the floor and hold my head. I'm your responsibility now.

Seductive as the thought was, it was also in a way laughable. He tried to grip the thought.

The children might get up. They would come upstairs quietly, to save being sent back before they'd even stepped into the calm, dreamy light of the living room, their bare, soft feet noiseless on the stairs and breath held to be released, jerkily . . .

. . . his own breath was being held, he realised, and he let it out. It made a sigh.

163

'What?' Susie asked, looking up from the screen. 'You seem restless.'

'I don't think this is a good idea,' he said again, scratching his head. He had been scratching his head since he'd got in. Sam had brought a letter home about nits. Nits prefer clean hair, it said. Well, it was good to know that nits had preferences, options, like the rest of us, he thought, looking away from the tanned legs and the pink toes. 'I mean . . . how about I make us a coffee?'

'I'll have a Scotch, if you don't mind.' She was challenging him with her made-up eyes. No sideways glances any more. He was half afraid of her, and wholly afraid of himself.

As he went to fetch a glass he realised that her whole presence here was a challenge and that wine, Scotch, anything would do – even coffee. She'd intended it to be so. And she'd chosen her night well. She was there to offer comfort and something else he needed more – destruction.

He'd never destroyed anything in his life, hand on heart he could say that. He was the good son. He built, he worked, he put things right, no matter how long it took. He repaired laboriously. Things, people, Sam.

And why?

It was suddenly all clear. It's played with me, he thought, fetching a tumbler. The cut-crystal edges gleamed a rainbow of light as he poured in Scotch of palest amber. Religion, he thought, has played with me all my life and I haven't seen it. It's let me feel secure, at a price. As long as I build up, make good, be the nice son, the forgiving husband . . .

. . . and a voice inside was most insistent, saying: when it's a lot more fun and takes a lot less effort to smash things.

'What's played with you?' Susie asked lightly, coming up behind him.

He felt her arms slide round his waist, her head rest on his back. How much of it had he said aloud?

'Poor Nick,' she said, and he felt the words vibrate through his ribcage, through his lungs and heart.

He turned around to face her. She was looking up at him and she moved her hands to his face. They were cold against his cheeks and he shivered and hugged her tightly, drawing his breath in with a hiss over his teeth.

'Where shall we go?' she asked, as though there was no question. Her voice was soft, almost a whisper.

He rubbed his face in her thick, shambolic, wind-blown hair. They didn't have locks anywhere. They didn't have locks anywhere except for the bathroom. All he had to do was to keep her hidden in there and send the children back to bed if they woke up. That was all he had to do. He was frowning, angry at the imagined disturbance.

He put his arm defensively around her narrow shoulders, taking her, that was the intention, but she didn't need taking, she was walking with him through the living room and into the hall and into the bathroom.

It smelt faintly soapy. It echoed, bathrooms always echoed. He shut the door behind them, locked it and put his arms around her, hiding his face for a moment in her hair. He caught a glimpse of movement behind her and he lifted his head and looked up at himself in the large mirror above the washbasin. He moved his hands down the back of her dress and cupped them around her bottom, stroking, letting the fabric ride up slowly, slowly, until his fingers touched her warm skin. As soon as they did, he felt goosebumps firm up on her flesh under his fingers. He breathed in over clenched teeth, shutting his eyes.

He felt the tickle of his t-shirt being pulled slowly out of his trousers, and her cold hands flatten on his back. His skin crawled with pleasure. Kissing her, he slid his hand around her thigh, sick with longing. He moved his hands up under her dress. No bra. Her nipples hardened under his touch and his trousers, the belt rattling under her hands, loosened and fell at his feet. With a neat little jump she was sitting on the edge of the washbasin, her bare legs outstretched.

She wrapped them around his waist and pulled him to her, smiling as he shuffled forwards. She lifted the t-shirt away from him as he had her dress and lowered herself onto him in a silky rush of heat, a sensation so intense that for a moment he stayed motionless, afraid to move.

When the edge wore off, she moved, tentatively. It was unbearably near. Every slightest movement was magnified. She was leaning away from him and he wanted her close. With a sudden cry she threw her arms around him and he staggered under the weight and the weightlessness, dizzied by the rush of colour and consoled by the heat of her clinging to him.

With a great effort, he steadied himself, his head swimming. She lowered her legs and her dress fell over her bottom and over his hands, but held up at the front still. He opened his eyes and saw himself in the mirror, slightly flushed. He bowed his head.

165

She was looking up at him at close range, elated. Her mascara was smudged slightly beneath one eye, her lipstick had gone. He kissed her on the lips.

She was smiling. 'Wow! Just like I imagined,' she said.

If, for a moment, it struck a wrong note, the feeling didn't last.

He got dressed, his hands shaking as he fastened his belt, wondering whether she would want a shower.

'I'll have a quick dip,' she said, turning on the bath taps.

He watched her pour in his children's Matey. They seemed worlds away from him now, their presence unimaginable. He watched the water foam. The steam lifted, stifling. She turned round for him to undo the zip on her dress, holding her hair back. As he lowered the fastener, he could see the curve of her sharp vertebrae and felt a stab of desire. She let the dress fall and knelt over the bath to mix the cold water into the hot.

He reached out and stroked his hand down her back. She stopped moving, as though to concentrate on it. He took his hand away and she stood and stepped into the bath with the taps still running. It was so shallow that when she lay down the water was only halfway up her body. Her small breasts and her belly rose out like arid islands against the fertility of her pubic mound. She looked at him. That was what had changed, her glances which had been quick and shy were now long and brazen. What was she looking for in his face? Was she finding it?

She washed herself like no-one he had ever known, as scrupulously as an animal, in a preoccupied way, but she didn't stay in the water long, and after squeezing the sponge over her shoulders a couple of times she stood up and held out her hands for him to pass her a towel.

He would like to have dried her but she rubbed herself briskly and still steaming, though dry, she stepped into her dress and turned for him to do up the back.

'And now let's have that drink,' she said, matter-of-factly.

They drank their whisky together on the sofa, she leaning slightly against him. He was surprised to see that *Jaws* was still on and they watched it, or she did, commenting occasionally, snuggling up nearer as the children in their dinghies got lost in the fog.

When it finished he saw that her glass was empty. She moved away from him, making a show of stretching. 'Oh, you didn't tell me who was playing with you,' she said, teasing him.

'Didn't I?' He looked at her without expression. 'I don't remember now what I was thinking.'

'I'd better be going,' she said softly, regretfully, 'unless you want me to stay?'

He got to his feet. 'I don't think –'

'Shh,' she said, putting her hand over his mouth and smiling, 'it's okay, you don't have to say it.' She took hold of his t-shirt, bunching it in her hand as she pulled him towards her. 'And to save you worrying, I'm on the pill.' She raised her eyebrows. 'Two sins for the price of one. Tell Faye I'm asking after her, won't you?'

He wouldn't.

He followed her down the stairs. She held onto him while she put her shoes on, straightened and took her raincoat from him.

'I'll ring you,' she said, opening the door. For a moment he watched her legs move away, to the tap of her shoes, before the darkness absorbed her into itself.

His legs were heavy as he went upstairs. His calves ached as though he'd been walking in deep soft sand. At the top of the stairs he stopped and looked at her glass, smeared and empty on the floor. He felt as though he was standing in the ruins of a sandcastle that had been laboriously built with care.

He felt he'd known as he'd shaped it that its lifespan was short and he grieved for it in the knowledge that the next tide would erase it without a trace.

Chapter Thirty-Four

During the night, the metal trolley came for someone in the end bed. How should Faye not weep?

All that she'd ever feared – darkness, pain, abandonment – and kept at bay by her own volition, had gained a foothold in her life. Cancer was a sharp chisel separating the layers and against its persistent force she could feel herself flake.

She would make no attempt to get to know the faces that intruded on her fear. She would let herself be cleaned, fed, wiped, but she wanted no part in it.

The physiotherapist called on her that morning, and forced her to move and cough.

She felt a cold rage at this chaos.

When she'd gone, a muffled blanket of hopelessness felled her and she had neither the desire nor the energy to crawl out from underneath it.

She was crying for her mother, for the first time ever, when a smartly-dressed man in his sixties with thinning hair approached her bed.

She turned her head. He would realise his mistake soon enough and move away quickly, embarrassed at her tears.

'Don't turn me away,' he said hurriedly.

She recognised the voice and started to sob. It brought her no relief; instead it was a curse that increased her tension so the wire of frustration binding her screamed tighter than ever.

'Eva said it would be all right.'

'Eva.' She struggled for control, reaching up with her hand for the tissues on her locker. 'Eva should know better. She knows how I feel.'

He misread the gesture and bent to embrace her in an awkward hug that bypassed the drip. 'Don't say that.'

Buried in his itchy jacket she could smell him, a mix of tobacco and Old Spice that she had forgotten she knew. He loosened his grip and his blazer lapel brushed roughly and damply against her cheek. His smell brought him back to her more vividly than his appearance, and now he was back she remembered how it was to lose him.

She was suddenly angry. What had he taken away from her with his leaving? He had taken the balance from their lives, the honing down of her mother's excesses, the confidence in prayers at night. He had taken away their belief that the world was safe despite ghosts in the dark.

She was going to tell him. But he was older and anxious, and nothing like the person she'd never ceased looking for in the street, paradoxically where she would never find him.

'I couldn't stay away,' he said. There was puzzlement in his eyes. 'Faye, I've been asking myself – why you? Why not me? I've smoked all my life, aye, and enjoyed it too.'

Yes, why not you, she thought as she turned to the window and noticed it had started to rain. Fat raindrops spattered, well spaced, on the glass. That was the dampness on his jacket. He had come without a coat and bare-headed, and his hair was thinning. She glanced through the glass at the yellowing sky and thought of sending him off to be rained on, but turning back to tell him she caught him shivering briefly. 'Why didn't you tell Mum yourself that you wanted to come back? Why did you leave it to me to mend it? I was too young.'

He looked as though he was at a loss to answer. He smoothed his damp hair awkwardly with the flat of his hand, confused. 'She didn't want me back. She stayed at her mother's until I left. She wouldn't come back while I was there.'

She saw that it was true, or likely to be. How could she now trust her memory of it? She'd remembered his weakness. What about her own, her fear of annoying her mother? That leaving his home and family for their sakes might have required strength had not occurred to her. What did, suddenly, was the futility of reproaching him. It was too long ago and inalterable. They had to start from now. She looked at him, almost a stranger. 'Are you remarried?'

'I haven't given up hope,' he said. He gave a little laugh as though it was a set line. He raised his left shoulder and stuck his thumb, with difficulty, into the waistband of his trousers, easing the strain on his waist. He was still standing, his stomach no longer held in. He looked worried and defeated. 'I'm sorry for everything,' he said.

The apology touched her.

If she'd seen him in the street, the handsome man in his thirties that had asked her to mention he was sorry, she'd have said what she'd practised saying, that he shouldn't have left them to the closed curtains, the constant dimness, the greyness that his absence had left behind.

But it was too late for that.

She reached for his sleeve and put her hand on it. His blazer, still damp, was beginning, as he warmed up, to smell of sheep. 'It's all right,' she said, 'I suppose it doesn't matter now.'

'Faye?' he asked quickly.

'Yes?'

'Would you and the children come to Disneyland Paris with me when you come out? I'd pay.'

She stared at him for a moment. Her eyes filled with tears at the absurdity, and she began to laugh despite them. 'Great. Now I really know I'm ill.' Disneyland! It was one of the few places she could honestly say she'd never wanted to go to. Not for her the pink plastic and make-believe, N-O-thank you, no way, José, and that's what she was about to tell him, when she saw the expression on his face. It had so little expectation of anything good that this bilious rush of scorn evaporated.

Well, why not. 'You, me and the children?'

He gave a brief nod. The skin under his chin folded over on itself. 'When?'

'When you feel ready,' he suggested.

She gave a nod. 'Thanks, Dad.'

She knew this was her father's version of the five-year diary, the man-made means her family were determined to anchor her down with.

She looked at him, this stranger, her familiar father. 'How old are you?' She felt ashamed at having to ask.

'Sixty-five,' he said.

She shut her heavy eyes for a moment. It was hard to take; life seemed to be spiralling by.

'Faye?'

They flickered open. 'Sorry,' she apologised fretfully, 'I sleep a lot. I dream.'

He leant forward. 'I'll go now. Can I come again?'

She nodded. Her eyes closed and she opened them with effort. He was bending close to her and she thought he wanted to say something to her so she turned her ear towards him to catch what he was saying.

It was a kiss, she realised afterwards. And she had dodged away.

*　　*　　*

After lunch she had another visitor out of visiting hours. She'd been asleep, exhausted by her father's visit.

She heard humming and opened her eyes and saw Richard Cross sitting by her bed wearing a suit, his red hair slicked back and a look of concern on his face.

'Richard?'

'Hello, Faye.'

Frowning, she shut her eyes. When she opened them again he was still there. 'Were you singing?'

'Yes. How are you?'

'Okay.' She felt herself sinking slowly back into sleep. Same old Richard. She hadn't known what to do as he'd sung to her in his flat before she'd taken that frightening, solitary dive into his life.

'Susie told me you were here,' he said, 'and I took a late lunch.'

'That's good.' She resurfaced and paused. 'I'd have put some lipstick on if I'd have known.' The thought of Susie drifted momentarily into her mind and out again.

'Nah. You look beautiful. You always look beautiful. I've bought you some chocolates to fatten you up. Thorntons. And some smokes.'

Next time she woke up, he'd gone. She could see the Thorntons box on the edge of the locker but the cigarettes had been removed.

He was her one lapse. He'd woo'd her with wine and song. Song and wine, more in that order, really.

He was wholehearted enough to relish a deathbed scene, she thought, and the name of the tune he'd been humming suddenly came to her.

It was the theme of *Love Story*.

Chapter Thirty-Five

On Thursday Faye felt well enough to go and look for Phil.

It took her three slow and shuffling visits to his ward before his bed was back from the recovery room, and she made her way to it, carrying her tubes in the sort of carrier used by milkmen for their bottles.

She pulled up a chair awkwardly and sat next to his bed. 'How are you, Phil?' Trying to sound cool, and trying to whisper, she pulled the chair a little nearer. She was aware of the men on either side of him, awake and interested and bored with daytime TV.

Not that it mattered to Phil how interested they were or how aware of it she was. She thought he looked as though the life had been knocked out of him. He was lying on his back, very still, eyes closed, his mouth slightly open. A tube was running from his arm, and another downwards to a pouch of urine. There was a drip above him, and the same collection of tubes that she had coming out of his side. She turned her attention quickly back to his face. He hardly seemed to breathe and she wanted to put her hand above his mouth as if he was a baby. She could see the sheet over his chest moving very slowly.

A nurse came to look at him, checking the drip. She smiled at Faye.

'Phil?' Faye said softly when the nurse moved away. She waited, but he didn't respond. He was far down in the dark territory of sleep. 'I could do with a smoke, Phil,' she said softly, 'seeing you like this.' She looked at the tanned face, skin tight over the cheekbones like the pinched edge of pastry. 'I don't think much of this, do you, Phil? I don't think much of it at all. You come in feeling . . .' she sighed, '. . . feeling shit, if you want the truth, and it gets worse, doesn't it.'

Phil moved his head towards her. His dark hair was flat against his forehead. He opened his eyes and she leant forward. They didn't look like his, they looked dark, blank and tear-filled. His gaze wandered a little, and rested on her. A couple of seconds passed and then he asked, 'How long have you been here?'

'Not long. I don't think you've been back long.'

He nodded so economically it was hardly a movement at all. He seemed to have drifted away. Then he asked sharply, 'What's the time?' as though he had an appointment to keep.

She glanced at her watch. 'Nearly seven.' She paused. 'You were in there a long time, Phil. Got your money's worth,' she said, hoping to make him smile.

He gave another brief nod and his gaze drifted and rested somewhere past her. She waited, but after a while he closed his eyes.

See, she thought, resisting the need to touch him to bring him back, the ward is like that. I was like that. People come here and they get knocked out and fixed up and they come back again, slowly, but they always come back.

She wished he'd hurry. He was her ally now.

Not Nick, not the children, nor her father who wanted to take her to Disneyland, nor her sister with her five-year expectations. How could they be? They were still safe, part of the mainstream who would last forever while she and Phil were in the war zone. She wanted him back to tell her tales of glory. 'Tell you mine, Phil,' she said, 'I desperately wanted a cup of tea that first night.' She smiled. One of the nurses had teased her about it. A minor victory.

She heard people coming in and she looked up and saw it was visiting time. An hour of awkward company amidst sporadic chatter and a scraping of chairs. Reluctantly she stood up. 'See you later, Phil.'

Walking back into her ward she could see Nick was already there, looking at her get well cards. He was dressed casually in a black jacket, t-shirt and jeans.

She greeted him and sat on the edge of the bed with her bottle-carrier next to her, pulling her robe over her knees. She wished she'd brushed her hair which had frizzed wildly. Nick turned to her with a card still in his hand. 'Susie sent you one?' he asked, holding it up.

'It came this morning. She rang for me, did she?' She could see the picture on it – a West Highland White puppy staring hopefully out of a boot on a pink tablecloth.

'Great taste,' she said. She watched him tuck the card back into the elastic straps.

He plucked at his lower lip and averted his face. 'She was asking about you. Yes.' He reached into the inside pocket of his jacket. 'Two more cards for you.'

She looked at the top one which was from Isabel. Red crayoned lines on pink card said, 'Get well Mummy'. It sounded like an order. There was a picture of Faye underneath: triangular body, orange hair, huge feet. I like the earrings, she thought. And the brooch.

Nick glanced at the card and pointed at the square in the apex of the triangle. 'That's an Elastoplast, by the way. She asked me where the lump was.'

In my throat, Faye thought. She looked at Samuel's card. It was purple and had a tab to pull, and when she pulled it the message appeared: Get Well Soon. She traced her finger around the big red heart that he'd drawn with a bandage round the middle. The feeling of separation came flooding back.

She looked up and to her surprise Nick was wiping his eyes. When he saw her looking, he averted his head. 'I'm sorry,' he said, his voice muffled.

'I know. I know you are.' His sorrow moved her and her eyes filled with tears. 'I'm sorry, too,' she said, 'I love you, Nick.'

'Me, too.' He took one of her tissues from the box on her locker and blew his nose briskly. Pulling himself together after a moment, he asked, 'Do you want me to put those cards up with the others?'

'It's all right, I'll keep them on the locker. I miss the children. I miss you.' She tried to keep her voice calm.

'Oh, Faye.' He took her hand in his, stroking the web of skin between her thumb and forefinger. 'Faye, we ought to talk about practicalities.' His eyes filled again and she gripped his hand tightly.

'I know,' she said. 'I've been thinking – I could get a home help for a while.'

'And a nurse,' he said. 'A MacMillan nurse.'

'The house will be full,' she said lightly, rebelling at the thought of a nurse. But what if he was right? Nick wasn't good with blood, or pain. Mucus made him retch. He couldn't touch dead animals, couldn't clean up the orange mess of his children's sick without heaving even though he loved them. Dark-brown dog excrement on a shoe, processed-pea green running from a nose – he couldn't eat if he thought about it. What sort of help was he going to be if he made her feel disgusting? She imagined spitting pink phlegm on the coals in the fire and watching it sizzle. But they didn't have a fire.

'I'd do anything . . .' his voice trailed away into despair. 'Faye,' he reached into his pocket again.

He was, she thought morosely, like a magician, pulling out surprise after surprise with a flourish from his black jacket.

He handed a sheet of paper to her, folded into three, and as she looked down at it he caught hold of her chin and tilted her face up so that she was looking into his sleepy, dark eyes. 'Don't look at it now,' he said, 'but remember you've got it.' He kissed her lightly on the lips. 'I'd better be off. Edith's going to mass tonight and I said I'd be back early. She's going to come and see you tomorrow.'

Faye smiled and watched him leave. He waved at her from the door. As soon as he'd gone out of sight she opened the letter; a love letter, she thought at first, but it was typewritten.

And at the top of the page it said: Living Will.

She skim-read it first, her eyes dwelling on the occasional phrase: 'In the case of gradual deterioration of mind and body . . . I direct that my dying should not be prolonged . . . refuse artificial feeding except for hydration . . . not be treated by radiation or chemotherapy if they be abhorrent to me . . .' Coming to the end, she forced herself to read it through again slowly. Another sentence caught her eye: 'I request that a "Do not resuscitate" notice be attached to my notes at all times.'

She began to cry.

She wanted to be kept alive no matter what it took. She wanted to be resuscitated, rescued, cured.

She put her arm over her face. She couldn't take it, she thought, as the tears ran freely down her throat.

Nick was trying to face the future, she knew, but it was somewhere she couldn't bring herself to look.

Perhaps she was afraid there wasn't one there to see.

Chapter Thirty-Six

Samuel lay on his bed looking at the pictures of aircraft on his wall and felt as if he was floating free of everything he knew. Not air floating, which would have been fine by him, he dreamt a lot about that, but floating in dark water, pulled away by the current. He knew it was useless to fight it, you had to go with it, but this was a frightening thought because it was hard to know where you would end up. His mother (my real one, not my new one, he said to himself stubbornly) had read him, just the once, the story of *The Steadfast Tin Soldier*. It was the worst story he had ever heard in his life. The helplessness of the soldier being washed along the gutter had frightened him to tears, tears which his mother hadn't noticed for pages, and her not noticing them, well that was frightening too.

And then she had, all of a sudden, and she'd wiped his cheeks with her warm hands, wetting his face more, and hurried off to the bathroom for streamers of toilet tissue and come back and wiped his nose, pinching it gently in the paper. Then she'd come back and sat on the bed and flicked right through to the end of the book and looked at the last page carefully.

'They all lived happily ever after,' she'd said, lifting her head to look at him. 'Sod Hans Christian Andersen. Come back Postman Pat, all is forgiven.'

He could tell by her smile that she wanted him to laugh. But she knew he was still frightened. '*I* hated the story of *The Little Match Girl*,' she'd said softly. 'I know how you feel,' and she'd bunched up the soggy toilet tissue into a ball.

He remembered being rather interested in the story of *The Little Match Girl*. He could guess what happened – what happened would be what always happened to children who played with matches. That wouldn't have seemed so bad, he thought. It would have been her own fault. She never told him that story, though. Probably they really did go back to Postman Pat.

He glanced at his watch. His new mother (call me Allie) was late.

He looked up, seeing a movement in the doorway of his bedroom.

His father rested his hand on the doorknob and smiled at him on the bed. 'Cheer up,' he said.

'She's late, isn't she?'

'Well, she's coming on the bus. I'll take you back to her flat. Don't look so worried,' he added.

'I'm worried about Mum. She said we could go and see her.'

'She's sleeping a lot. She's got tubes everywhere. You can go when she's had them out, if you like.'

The doorbell rang like a scream, startling them both.

'Here she is,' Nick said.

Sam got off the bed.

'It'll be all right,' his father said, 'and if it isn't . . .'

'What?' Sam asked swiftly.

'Ring me. I'll be here, I'm not going anywhere.'

Sam followed his father along the hall. He could see Alicia's blurred plump shape through the glass.

His father opened it and she was smiling as though she'd been smiling already. 'Hi,' she said, looking from him to Sam. 'Are you set?'

She still reminded him of his friends' au pairs. That's what they were like when they came to pick them up after school. They always spoke loudly as if it was important for other people to hear them talk, whereas the mothers were tired and quiet. Or was that only his? Allie even dressed like an au pair, in a long black baggy jumper, with a long black skirt underneath it.

'I'll get my jacket,' he said.

His father was behind him holding it and he hadn't realised. 'Shall I give you a lift?' he asked her over his head.

'There's no need, Adam's brought me in the car. We'll bring Sam back around seven unless you want him to stay over?'

Samuel felt his heart skip a beat.

'Not this time,' his father said. 'Seven will be fine.' He looked down at him. 'See you later,' he said, looking into his eyes. 'And ring me if you want anything.'

He nodded. He would.

He got into the back seat of the car.

'This is my boyfriend, Adam,' his new mother said.

The driver turned round to look at him and laughed. 'Doesn't look much like you, Tanya,' he said, turning back. 'Apart from the hair. Where to?'

'Home, of course. Do you like watching the TV, Sammy?'

'Yes.'

'What's your favourite programme?'

'*Live and Kicking.*'

'We'll see if it's on, shall we? We've got Cable. Have you got Cable?'

'No.' He was about to add an explanation but thought better of it – he felt more cheered up, now. Cable had some great stuff on it, Cartoon Network and the Disney Channel for a start – kids in school talked about it all the time.

'And later on we'll go to Sega World. Have you ever been to Sega World?'

He shook his head again.

'It's mega,' Adam said. 'I guarantee you'll love it if you like that sort of thing.'

'I do,' Sam said. Maybe it wasn't going to be bad at all. Maybe it would be brilliant. Maybe they'd let him bring Joe Curtis with him, and Ted Peacock and Chris Pavitt and Trav, someone he could have fun with and show off to. He was grinning.

'Do you like Kentucky Fried Chicken, Sammy?'

'Sure do.'

He was floating free of everything he knew.

And it felt fun.

When he got back that evening around seven-fifteen, his father was looking out for him, glancing pointedly at his watch as Alicia brought him to the door. 'I thought you said seven? And that's late enough for a school night.'

Alicia smiled. 'We were having a great time. Loosen up, Nick.'

Samuel looked with surprise at her. It had been hard to believe she and his father were brother and sister until now.

For a moment he saw his father frown but it turned into a shrug. 'Are you coming in? Go and call Adam, tell him to park in the drive.'

'I'm working tonight,' she said. She smiled at Sam and he found himself smiling back, couldn't help it. 'See you soon, Sam.'

He nodded and wondered whether she expected him to kiss her

but she didn't give him the chance, she went hurrying back to the car and Adam.

He waved at her from his father's side. Isabel was waving too.

'Bath time,' Nick said as they went in.

'Dad! I haven't had supper yet.'

'I'll make supper while you have a bath.'

'Do I have to go to bed at the same time as Isabel?'

'Just for tonight.'

'Dad!'

'Samuel . . .'

There was a tone to his father's voice that he didn't hear very often and that he didn't want to hear very often.

Still, the injustice of it hurt him.

He had a bath and he and Isabel had oven chips and spaghetti hoops and just as his father had said, they were taken to bed.

It was hard to sleep at only half past seven when it wasn't properly dark. He thought of Sega World and got his Game Boy out and put the light on it and played it under the covers.

He must have fallen asleep, because the bright and cheerful music from his game woke him up. He switched it off and the next thing he heard was a woman's voice at the door.

He got out of bed and listened. His father was whispering and Samuel wondered if his mother had come home.

He didn't think so, because if his mother *was* home, she would have come in to see him by now.

He opened his bedroom door and heard a woman laugh.

'Susie, shh,' he heard his father say in a loud, fake whisper, and they both laughed again.

Samuel closed the door carefully. He didn't want to hear any more. He wished he hadn't even heard that.

PART SIX

What? Is there no escaping death?

Cardinal Beaumont

Chapter Thirty-Seven

Unravelling death, she smells around her the scent of Parma Violets.

She is on her mother's knee and she is playing with Dotty. Dotty is heavy for a doll because she's filled with sawdust. The back of her head is made of black cotton and she leaks. Dotty has a plastic face and wears a red dress with spots on and black cotton shoes. She wears white knickers, sewn between her legs.

Faye slides off her mother's knee and sits on the carpet, on orange and brown starbursts.

Her mother and father are talking in hushed tones about Marie. She has seen Marie through the chicken wire on her gate, a little girl with a large head and not much hair.

She is afraid of Marie.

Marie belongs to the people next door. 'She attracts illness,' her mother says. 'Scarlet fever has made her large head bald.'

Faye hears the word neglect.

Her father says 'neglect' as if it is the worst thing in the world, and he tells them he is going next door to see the Williamses.

Her mother is ironing.

Eva is in the garden making perfume out of rose petals and water and pushes her away. Faye goes upstairs and sees the bottle of Parma Violet scent that her mother puts behind her ears. The sweet smell is very strong and there is a gap in the top of the bottle that wasn't there before.

Faye walks to the bathroom. The bath stands in the middle of a cold floor of chequered tiles and it has feet like claws curled ready to slash. She turns the tap on. Pop, pop, a delicate sound comes from the mouth of the bottle as the water drips in.

The clear green scent is clouding white.

She glances at the bath's clawed feet on the chequered floor. The feet are dangerously still but the squares start to dance and change colour.

She forgets the scent. On the way down the stairs she stops to press dimples in the pattern of the brown painted wallpaper.

There is a fuss going on in the kitchen. Her father is back and her mother is crying, her hand over her mouth.

'There was an angel crouched at the window,' her father says. 'She's pitiful to look at. I've told Peggy you'll help to lay her out.'

Dotty feels very heavy and limp in Faye's arms. She smells of Parma Violets.

She takes her out into the garden and pushes the bristly leaves to make a hole in the dusty hedge that separates the houses. She looks through it at the gate with the chicken wire. The garden gate bangs and she lets the dusty hedge bounce back into place before going inside, leaving Dotty abandoned in the garden.

In the morning, Dotty has slugs on her and is put in the bin.

Chapter Thirty-Eight

Edith had come with a bag of plums and a hymn book in her hand. Faye tried to show an interest but her own favourites, apparently, were anthems, and Edith said she'd bring an Ancient and Modern next time. She seemed very cheerful when she left.

Faye wanted to talk to Phil. Even with the Living Will in the bin she felt haunted by what she'd read. But she wasn't going to need it. She felt stronger now.

Looking at the other women in the ward, she felt isolated. They knew each other's names but she couldn't bring herself to join in the banter. She didn't want to belong to the hospital club. She wanted to go home. She could smell the flowers Eva had sent and they reminded her of Nick.

Opening her drawer she reached for her make-up bag and took a look at herself in her small make-up mirror. She wondered about putting on some lipstick and whether she'd feel foolish if Phil remarked on it.

'Going to see the boyfriend?' the woman who had been sick so often, Janine, asked her.

The hospital club members knew everything, or thought they did. Faye smiled stiffly and put her mirror back in her bag. She got out of bed and started the long slow shuffle into Phil's ward. From the doorway she could see him sitting up.

She could also see that he had company – an oldish man, balding, wearing an orange-check shirt. Could be his father, she thought. She turned round to go.

One of the men in an adjoining bed called out, 'Hey, Phil, your girlfriend's leaving.'

She cringed inwardly and carried on shuffling out in the hope of pretending she hadn't heard.

'Faye?' Phil's voice, hoarse, was calling her back. 'Come over here. There's someone I want you to meet.'

She paused. It would be easy to pretend she hadn't heard him; he hadn't said it loudly, hadn't got the puff for it, that was the truth. But she *had* heard him. So she turned round and went back towards them self-consciously.

'This is Ed,' Phil said as she got near the bed. 'Ed, Faye, fellow sufferer and ex-smoker, you can see it in her eyes.'

'Says the man with the permatan,' she said, grinning at him and then at Ed.

'Stand you both together, you'd look like a pair of petrol pumps,' Ed said, getting up and giving her his chair. 'Here you go.'

She thanked him and sat, her bottle-carrier on the floor. She'd save that joke for Nick. 'Well, Phil, I have to say you look better.'

'Yes, you were here yesterday, weren't you? I remembered, vaguely, when I woke up. Thanks.' He looked at Ed as the older man put down a chair next to Faye and sat, relaxed and at ease. Phil jerked his thumb at him. 'Ed here's a priest.'

'Oh,' she said. 'Look, I'll leave you to talk.' She pushed on the armrests to get to her feet. 'I can come back later.'

'Stay,' Phil said. 'He's a good bloke, aren't you?'

'Got qualifications in it,' the priest said, and grinned. 'And it's I who can come back later,' he said, getting up. 'Less effort for me.'

Great, she thought. Excommunicating a priest. 'I didn't mean to be rude,' she said. 'I only came –' she glanced at Phil, 'to see how you are.'

'Well, we were discussing funerals,' Phil said.

Coming from nowhere as it did, it took her by surprise. She looked at him and gave a little laugh. 'You should team up with my mother-in-law.' He didn't laugh back and she felt a sudden shock, as though she'd been drenched with cold water. 'But Phil, why?'

He tilted his head and his smile was kind. 'Ingrid's not fussed and it will make it easier for her if I've got it planned. I know what I want, the hymns, the readings, and my ashes sent up some time in a rocket, fireworks across the sky.' He smiled. 'I've found a man who can do it. What do you think?'

Faye looked at him. She could feel her face and body stiffen, blocking off emotion. 'But you're not going to die.'

He didn't answer.

'It's not funny,' she said, feeling her chin quiver.

He shook his head. There was no tilt this time as he looked steadily back at her, the trace of a distant smile still curving his suntanned lips.

'It's not funny,' she said again, shivering. 'You shouldn't think like that, you shouldn't think . . . because if you do . . .'

'You'll die and if you don't, you'll live forever? It's like making a will or carrying a donor card. You're preparing for an eventuality,' he said gently, eyebrows raised while he waited for her to agree.

She wouldn't. She covered her mouth with her hand. 'I don't want to belong to this,' she said, and pushed on the armrests to heave her body out of the chair.

Ed reached out to help her but she jerked away from his hands and picked up her bottle-carrier, keeping her head averted. She heard Phil call her name as she shuffled out.

A sympathetic male voice called after her from a bed close by, 'Come here, love, *I'll* kiss it better.'

Angrily she turned around, responding to the voice but saying in a rage to Phil, 'What's the point? What's the point, Phil? You'll soon be gone.'

She went past the nurses' station. The one with the dark hair looked up approvingly at her progress. 'You'll soon be home,' she said, 'the rate you're going. Don't overdo it, though, will you?'

Faye stopped. 'I'd like a shower,' she said. 'Or at least, to wash my hair. I want to get clean again.'

The nurse stood up and offered her a chocolate from a box next to her. She popped one in her own mouth.

Faye shook her head.

The nurse ran her tongue over her teeth and moved the chocolate to the side of her mouth. 'Go ahead if you're feeling up to it,' she said. 'I'll just check that the bathroom's empty.' She got up and went to have a look. 'You're all right, there's no-one in there. Faye, is something wrong?'

'No.' She went to her locker to get a towel, and went back to the bathroom. It was pale yellow, with a large white bath. Why did hospital colours all have to be pale, she wondered as she undressed and leant forward to turn on the shower, mindful of the tubes. Anything to do with her chest and back muscles was painful, but if she bent her knees she felt it would be easier.

The shower was powerful, coming warm now, getting to just the right temperature. Too hot. She leant forward again and adjusted it

187

down, blinking as the spray sprinkled on her face. It felt blissful and soothing but the floor was getting damp. It was fine, now, just right, but she had leant over too far and too precariously.

She felt herself go off balance very gradually, a slow inevitable process like the toppling of a rotten tree. The edge of the bath caught her knees and she fell forward into the bath, her arms jarring and sliding against the enamel.

The containers were still outside it, on the floor. She felt the excruciating sharpness of the pain as the tubes pulled in her side. Water deluged round her as, face down, the pressure of the water coming out of the shower hammered against her head and back. She was too weak. The water was gushing around her face into her mouth and nostrils, creating a torrent.

I'm going to drown, she thought in astonishment. She didn't have the strength to push herself up and she couldn't reach for the red cord to call for help. The force of the water was like a constant, unending blow. With a surge of survival instinct, she pushed herself backwards. The pain from the tubes was stabbing her side. She raised her right hand and groped for the red emergency cord and caught it. Seconds later the light rushed in through the open door and a nurse came hurrying over, switching off the shower and helping her up. Someone brought towels and they dried her as the water trickled down her face like tears. Aware of the sympathetic interest around her, she was helped to her bed, humiliated, her head thumping. The general opinion of the nursing staff was that she should have waited for the nurse to help before she'd gone in.

Left to herself at last she cried quietly and tried not to think of Phil. She tried not to think of the emotions that had upset her. It wasn't, it seemed now, that he was dying, but that she was going to, too, as if he was pulling her with him.

A nurse who had been checking her chart came over to see her. 'Feeling better?' she asked with a smile.

Faye nodded, turning her cheek on the damp pillow.

'It's normal to feel depressed, the anaesthetic does that. And you had a shock this afternoon.'

The unexpected sympathy cheered her slightly and Faye watched her go across to Annie. Annie was sleeping, propped up high. Her hair was messed. It looked like a dandelion that someone had gone and blown.

* * *

188

That night Faye went to the day room to watch *The Bill*.

It was dark outside, and raining. The room was cold. She was there because she wanted to be alone. She'd closed the screens around her bed but the nurses didn't like their patients to keep the screens closed. They liked to see what was going on, especially now that it was generally felt she'd tried to do too much too soon.

Against the reflection of the glass she saw Phil come in and her heart jumped as she switched her gaze back to the TV.

He came to sit next to her without saying a word, and sat back to watch the screen.

They watched the programme in silence until the two pairs of feet walked away to the theme music. It seemed poignant, watching it now.

Phil got up, using the arms of the chair to push against, and turned it off while the credits were still rolling to the beat.

'I was watching that,' she said, pulling her kimono closed.

'You watch the credits?'

'If you don't want to watch it, why don't you go back to bed? How did you know I was here, anyway?'

'There aren't that many places to go,' he said. 'And I want to talk to you.'

'There's nothing to talk about.'

'No games,' he said.

Faye looked at him, full in the face, for the first time that night. She pushed her curling hair out of her eyes. 'I don't know what you mean.'

He tilted his head to one side to look at her better. She could see the strands of white in his dark hair.

'Don't you?' He swallowed. 'Life's too short,' he said wearily.

The way he said it made her want to get up and run. She could feel her heart pumping in preparation. 'I don't want to talk about it,' she said.

'Walk out, then,' he said.

She folded her arms, keeping them away from her body so she didn't nudge the drains, and looked at the blank TV screen. Anything was better than looking at Phil.

'I have to face it,' he said. 'It's coming whether I do or not. I've lived the denial, Faye.'

'You might, but I haven't.'

'Bully for you.'

'Why should I care what happens?' Her voice rose with futile indignation. 'I don't even know you.'

'Yes, you do. You can't unknow me now.'

She rubbed her eyes but the tears still fell. 'What made you say that?'

He didn't answer. He looked away from her for the first time since they'd started speaking. He looked towards the window at the night outside where the rain was splattering against the windows. 'Ed's a good man,' he said after a while. 'Don't dismiss him out of hand.'

'I won't, but he's encouraging you to die.'

'Not true. He's just accompanying me part of the way.' He tilted his head. 'Give him another chance. Not now, but sometime.'

'You should fight it,' she said. 'I've got to, why can't you?' She stared at a polystyrene cup lying on its side on the floor. She nudged it with her foot. 'I don't understand religion. No-one's perfect.'

'No, we're human. It doesn't take your faults away.'

She thought of Nick. She was hating Ed instead of him. 'I thought that was the point. Perfection.'

'Forgiveness is the point.'

'Oh,' she said. She nudged the cup with her foot again. It rolled out of reach. 'I didn't know you were religious.' It sounded like an accusation.

'Hedging my bets,' he said.

'Yeah?' She looked into his eyes, and away again at the rain-splashed window. There were things she wanted to know about him, things she would like to ask, but it didn't seem the time. It would never seem the time.

His elbow nudged her as he felt in his pocket. 'Fancy a cigarette?' he asked.

Startled, she looked at the packet in his hand. He flicked it open and she saw ten sweet cigarettes lying side by side like thin pencils. They smelt of vanilla.

She took one out and examined the tip. She put it in the 'v' of her fingers. It felt a bit small, but wonderfully familiar.

Phil took one himself and put the packet away. He tapped the cigarette against his hand. 'Light?'

She sucked, and exhaled slowly into the air. They were companionable again. The candy got thin and her lips felt sticky but it was good, very good. The best cigarette she'd had in ages.

She watched him tap the ash onto the floor absently. 'Do you know yet when you'll be leaving?' she asked him after a while.

'Next week, same as you.'

'Yeah?' She looked at the last quarter of an inch of sweet cigarette and put it all in her mouth.

'I'll give you my address,' he said.

She was glad. Simple as that, she thought. No games. 'I'll give you mine.'

He took the packet out of his pocket. 'You want another?'

'I'm cutting down.'

He tilted his head and smiled at her. 'You'll be all right. You listen to the doctors. They give you it straight and if they say you're all right, you keep living.'

They sat in silence. When she could speak again she stood up. 'Well, I'll see you tomorrow.'

He nodded.

She got up with the sideways movement she was trying to perfect while the plumbing was still in place. 'Goodnight, Phil,' she said.

There was a silence.

'Hope so,' he replied without turning.

Chapter Thirty-Nine

Alicia was lying naked on Adam's bed. She'd put a pair of red panties over the table lamp, for atmosphere. The atmosphere smelt of scorching nylon. 'They won't let me have him,' she said.

Adam cupped his hand round her soft stomach. His voice was warm with affection. 'You're lovely, you are.'

'They won't let me have him, and he's mine.' She got hold of Adam's locks and looked at them. They were like felt, not hair.

'But they adopted him,' he said, jerking his head so that she would leave his hair alone. 'They're his parents now.'

She liked playing with his hair. 'He's mine. Nick made me take him back.'

'You were going to, anyway.'

'He likes me.'

'Everyone likes you, especially me.' He moved his hand up to the warm pillow of her breast. 'You can always have another child,' he said.

She thought about it carefully, how it would have to be; she thought of the ingredients that went into making Sam. Meeting Baz in Chilli's Night Club, liking the black-and-white triangles on his cotton shirt, going in his car, making holes in the condoms, going in the field on an autumn night. There had been a coating of frost on the grass. 'I don't know where Baz is,' she said.

Adam laughed at that. 'You're a funny one, Tanya,' he said. He still called her Tanya, he liked it better than Alicia. 'Dead sexy, you are. Don't have it with Baz, have it with me.'

'Then it wouldn't be another Sammy,' she said, 'would it?' She looked at her watch. 'I've got to get ready for work.'

'Not yet,' he said. 'You've got plenty of time.'

'I can't think,' she said irritably. 'I hate it when I can't think.'

Adam turned onto his stomach moodily. 'If you're that keen to have him, bring him here. Let him stay the night. See how you like having a nine-year-old around all the time.'

She smiled and tossed her hair over her round and naked shoulder. 'I do love you,' she said.

Chapter Forty

Sam looked at the small black travel clock by the side of the bed. It said eleven-thirty, half an hour from midnight, and he was trying to be calm.

First of all Alicia had gone to work and left him with Adam.

He didn't mind being left with Adam but after a while he'd got tired of playing with Adam's Nintendo and Adam had wanted to watch TV – was desperate to watch it, he said.

So they'd watched TV for a bit and then Adam had told Sam to get his pyjamas on and go to sleep.

He hadn't wanted to, but Adam was in charge.

Now Adam had gone out.

It was a small flat, small even for a kid, he thought, and Adam had said he was going out for some fresh air.

Samuel was keeping his eyes on the clock. It was eleven-thirty, pretty late, and Adam had been gone for an hour.

He wished he'd rung his father at ten-thirty, but it hadn't seemed so serious then, Adam going for a breath of fresh air. How long did a breath take?

Now it was serious but too late to ring. He imagined his father waking up and being annoyed, and having to wake up Isabel who would be grumpy, and probably crying. He imagined the fuss.

When Allie had asked his father if he could stay the night his father had said it was up to him, that he needn't if he didn't want to but that he must tell Allie why.

How could he if he didn't know why? Just that he wanted to stay in his own bed in his own house waiting for his own mother to come back.

He couldn't imagine saying that to Allie.

But he wished he had. He didn't like being left alone, not knowing when someone was going to come back. He'd tried to fix up the Nintendo again but he couldn't find the cable to attach it.

He wasn't sure he liked the flat. Everything in it seemed old and uncared for. The brown corduroy sofa had holes in it as though a cat had been using it for a scratching post. The carpet had old, shiny black chewing gum stuck in it. He felt as if he didn't want to touch things and was ashamed for a moment, but then it wasn't Alicia's flat, it was Adam's.

But where had he gone?

Sam decided to get dressed again. He would feel safer, dressed. He would feel ready. (For what? he wondered. Escaping?)

He put on his clothes over his pyjamas. If Adam – or Alicia – came back, he could jump into bed and pretend he'd been sleeping all along.

Or he could walk home. He could knock at the door of his house and pretend that he was homesick and that they had just dropped him off. He was pretty sure he knew the way.

He went to the door and turned the latch, not to leave, just to look out at the street to see if anyone was coming. But the latch wouldn't turn.

He tried it a couple of times, sure he was doing something wrong, turning it the wrong way. But it wasn't that, he knew. He had known straightaway, and fooled himself.

The latch wouldn't turn because Adam had locked it to stop him from getting out.

He sat on the Zed Bed and tried not to cry. The world seemed very large and empty, and he felt very small.

Back at his home, Nick had left the door open for Susie.

Once a barrier was smashed, well, that was it. It was gone.

The barrier that had kept him from loving Susie was so demolished he couldn't remember it, just that there had been a time when only their fingers and lips had touched and he was glad that time had gone.

And this – sin – was merely a sin 'until'.

They both knew that.

Susie came in, kissed him with warm lips, kicked off her shoes. She tip-toed up, barefoot again, smiling down at him as he followed her. He thought she might have brought something with her – wine, perhaps – but she hadn't and he was pleased. He only wanted her.

The television was on and he went to turn it off but she said, 'Don't; leave it. It's nice, we're like an old married couple,' and so he left it

195

and let her lean on him and buried his face in her soft hair, practising being an old married couple, 'until'.

She didn't ask about Faye.

They neglected to think of her; out of sight, out of mind.

This makes the future bearable, he thought later, as they undressed.

Skin against skin they slipped into the cold sheets in the guest room. He felt right about that.

He wanted to have nothing to reproach himself for.

Chapter Forty-One

The following morning, they came to take the tubes out. There were two nurses, one of whom seemed familiar with her flushed cheeks and sandy hair, the other the one who ate chocolate. Neither mentioned the shower of the day before.

'Will it hurt?' Faye asked warily as they pulled the screens around the bed.

'Hardly at all,' the red-haired nurse replied robustly.

It did. The pain was deep and hot and spiked, and as they pulled she broke out in a sweat.

'There,' one of them said, putting the tubes into a bag, 'that was all right, wasn't it? I'll just dress it for you.'

Still panting, Faye lifted up her t-shirt and looked down at her side. The two holes looked as if a couple of bullets had gone through her. The skin was red and puckered, ugly.

'You'll soon be as good as new,' the nurse said. She was good on platitudes.

Faye felt around the side of her body gingerly. She could feel a surplus of skin by the ribs under her arm, just above the stitches; the flesh was hanging over the scar. She was revolted by her own damage; if she had seen it on anyone else she would have moved away. 'You've sewn me up wrongly,' she said. 'Aren't you supposed to abut or something, like with wallpaper?'

The nurse had the dressing in her hand. 'Hold your top up,' she said. 'It will settle down, I promise you.' She smoothed the dressing over the wounds with professional rather than empathetic skill.

Settle down? Hard to see how, Faye thought, lying back on the pillow, nauseated. The bullet holes were still stinging hotly – a sensation like being flicked by rubber bands.

'Mr Angkatell is coming round the wards later. You'll probably be able to leave in the next day or so,' the nurse said, finally looking at her. Her pale face, marred by the startling pink of her cheeks, reminded her, Faye realised, of Edith.

When they'd left her, after pulling the screens back again, Faye shut her eyes. Hot tears rolled from beneath her eyelids – hot with the frustrated anger that had sparked up again. She couldn't wait to go home, but the thought of leaving the security of the hospital brought with it a new kind of fear. She wondered how long the insecurity would last. It occurred to her, not for the first time, that it might be forever, and the greater fear that followed that thought was that forever might not be long at all.

She looked up, hearing the sound of the screens opposite being moved back. Annie had had her turn. She could hear her groaning little moany puffs of air, sounding hurt. Her face was pale yellow against the whiteness of the pillows.

'Come on, Annie,' she heard the dark-haired nurse say, 'it wasn't that bad.'

Faye pulled herself out of bed, and, standing, she savoured the feeling of having been released from the encumbrance of the tubes. She went over to Annie's bed and said her name softly. 'Annie?'

Annie turned her face towards her. Her eyelids lifted slowly as though the opening mechanism had become as laborious as a drawbridge. 'I can't be bothered,' she said.

Faye found herself looking into pale, watery eyes. Annie's gaze latched onto hers. She shook her head slowly and closed her eyes again.

With me? Faye thought hopefully and looked at the woman's hands resting on her chest. With no fat to pad them, the veins lay unruly under the bruised skin. Returning her gaze to Annie's face, Faye thought she looked close to death. She was past disturbing, but she moved away from the bed before calling the nurse back. 'Excuse me!' she called, hurrying after her. 'Can I ask you something?'

It was the dark-haired one who stopped. She finished chewing something and swallowed, running her tongue over her teeth before she replied. 'What is it?'

'How long will she live for?'

The nurse glanced at the clock and then at Faye. 'Is this about you?' she asked softly.

Faye shook her head.

'Good. Because, Faye, it's hard to tell. Annie's seventy-three.'

It seemed old, but not old enough, Faye thought, and she went back to sit by Annie, whose mouth seemed to have sunk into her face.

She found herself wondering, as she had when Samuel was young, just where the energy had gone to.

She stood looking at her for a little longer. She would have liked to have kissed her cheek, and thought of Phil saying ruefully, 'When you tell people you've got cancer, they cry and try to hug you to prove they know it's not contagious.'

But it was contagious: the vulnerability and the resentment at having to face up to the fact of one's own death, and perhaps the greater resentment of having to face up to another's. After denial, acceptance.

She went back to her own bed.

She didn't know what was going on inside her, nor did they. They'd taken the tumour away but one or two cells could be already multiplying slowly, dissolving the glue between the healthy cells and stealing for themselves a juicy blood supply. Stop *that*, she thought, and tried to earth herself by reaching for the bowl of cherries. The sliminess told her they were somewhat past it, skin withered, seeping, bruised, with a slight smell of fermentation hovering around the glass bowl.

She heaved herself out of bed again and took the cherries to the bin and wiped the bowl out with a green paper towel.

'Not seeing your friend today?' Janine asked as she went past the foot of her bed.

Faye smiled and to save answering she asked impulsively, 'Fancy a walk to the coffee shop?'

'A walk? That's more like a hike. I'll get some money, we could have a sandwich. It'll be like playing truant.'

Faye put her dressing-gown on and got her handbag. She waited while Janine checked her face and put on some lipstick 'just in case'.

'Anyone else want to come?' Janine asked loudly. 'We're going on an expedition.'

Faye looked over at Annie, who didn't stir.

Freda volunteered, and the three of them started off on the long journey, the longest they'd made since being wheeled into theatre.

'Stairs or lift?' Faye asked.

'Stairs. We need the practice.'

They shuffled, laughing and groaning, down the stairs, along the corridor, past the chapel and to the coffee bar, where Janine treated her to a ham sandwich and a coffee. They were still there when the visitors started coming in and they posed, coffee cups aloft.

Faye could see Nick, Samuel and Isabel coming out of the swing doors and wished she'd been squashed in there with them.

'Hello,' she said loudly as they walked past. It was Isabel who saw her first, and laughed delightedly. Sam looked shocked to see her there and Nick looked at her blankly, as though she was an acquaintance he was trying to place.

It was so good to see them. She didn't care that Isabel was trying to get onto her knee and the cups were rattling in the saucers as the table was bumped.

'Careful,' Sam said loudly, mindful of his mother.

'Room for two,' Faye said to him, and he grinned suddenly and slid behind the table, not climbing on her knee but resting his head against her arm. She put it round him and held him close and looked up at Nick.

He was pulling up a chair. 'What a surprise,' he said, not quite managing to keep the disapproval out of his voice. 'Should you be doing this?' he asked with concern.

Janine caught Faye's eye. 'He can't take his eyes off you,' she said, and pointed at her lipstick with a wink.

Faye gave a wink back. She suddenly saw her sister and Janine got up with an 'Ow!' at her pulled stitches. The sister was carrying a holdall. 'I'm going back up,' Janine said, 'while I've got somebody to hang on to.'

'Can I have a Pepsi?' Isabel asked Nick.

'And a Kit-Kat?' Sam added.

'I'll come with you,' Nick said.

'No, let them go,' Faye said. 'Sam will get you a coffee.'

Nick made a big deal of getting a note out of his wallet. 'Make two trips if you have to,' he said to Samuel, 'and be careful with the coffee.'

'I *will* be,' Sam said indignantly.

Nick watched him for a moment before turning to Faye. 'Soooo . . .' he said.

She waited for him to follow it up, but the 'sooo . . .' seemed to be it. 'Four days,' she said. 'Are you proud of me?'

'I certainly am.'

'A little more enthusiasm, please,' she said, looking at him closely. He looked as though he hadn't slept for days. The skin under his eyes was finely wrinkled, like the skin on milky coffee.

'I'm worried for you, that's all.'

Faye looked from him to her coffee. A few beige bubbles were floating on the top and she dispersed them with the tip of her spoon. 'I know you are. I'm worried for myself.'

Nick looked over at Sam and Isabel still queuing at the counter. 'I worry about the children, too.'

He was making her uneasy. 'What's the matter?' she asked, putting the spoon back in the saucer with the exaggerated accuracy of a drunk. 'Have they been asking you things?'

'No, but – what's the matter? My wife's terminally ill and I've spent the last few days looking after the children, putting a brave face on it –'

'Terminally ill?'

Nick blew out a steady stream of air. 'Oh, phew,' he said, and rubbed his fingers over his upper lip. 'I didn't mean to say that.'

'It sounds as if it's not the first time you've said it.'

Nick steepled his fingers and rested his forehead on the pinnacle, a gesture of penitence. 'Look, Faye, I don't want to go into this now.'

She stared at the top of his head. His hair was catching the light, strands of copper burning amongst the fuscous. 'Have you spoken to someone? Have you spoken to the doctors without telling me?'

'No, of course not,' he said, lowering his hands. 'Of course not. I'm tired and I shouldn't have said it like that.'

There was a bang that startled her, and Isabel put the Pepsi can down hard on the table. 'One,' she said, and went for another. Faye could see Samuel walking across with one hand on the rim of the cup and the other holding the saucer, his tongue sticking out of the side of his mouth in concentration.

He pushed it across the table to his father and sat next to Faye. 'I saw Alicia again,' he said.

'Did you? Did you have a good time?'

'We didn't go to Sega World. Adam let me play with his Game Boy. But afterwards . . .'

Faye picked up her cup and sipped. The coffee was cool now. 'And afterwards what?'

'Oh, nothing.'

'You look tired,' she said. 'Both you and Daddy.'

'Do I?' Isabel asked interestedly.

'No, you look fine, fresh as a daisy. Except you've got your dress on back to front. Buttons go down the back, Nick.'

Isabel looked down the front of her dress. 'I like the buttons,' she said. 'Fresh as a paisy.'

'What are you all going to do this afternoon?' She was met with three blank stares. 'No plans?'

'We might go to the park,' Nick said. 'How about you?'

'Me? Oh, I expect I'll go to bed and then I'll wait for supper. That's what I usually do at this time of day. Will you bring my clothes tomorrow? Something loose, like the elasticated trousers I had when I was pregnant and a baggy sweater. Oh, Nick, I'm so tired.'

He gave her a gentle smile.

She wished she'd worn her watch. She wanted to go back to bed, preferably to sleep. Sleep was simple. She smiled at Nick and watched the children drink their Pepsis.

She loved them, but it seemed a long time since they'd come in through the revolving doors and she wouldn't be sorry to see them leave.

Chapter Forty-Two

The following day in the ward there was an air of expectation. Added to the festive atmosphere was the fact that the sun was shining, and the sky was deep blue and clear. Only Annie was still sleeping under the pale blue cover, waking only for tea, and for meals which remained uneaten.

Angkatell and his white-coated group had been seen emerging from the men's ward. Faye, having discovered the hospital shop, had bought three foil-wrapped chocolate cigars for Phil as her parting gift.

She tried to read one of the novels she had brought in. It was an old Jackie Collins, and Faye kept recognising bits of the plot as she read it. It was the ideal book, now she came to think of it, because she actually knew the ending.

There were three beds to go before hers. She kept the book up nonchalantly and swivelled her eyes as she watched them visit Freda's bed first. That didn't take long, and next they were standing around Janine. Janine was the one who had been so sick. Some serious talking was going on and she strained to hear. She could hear Janine's voice, light and steady, a soprano against the grumble of basses.

She looked up and saw Nick coming in, a carrier bag in his hand which he held up for her to see. John Lewis. His white t-shirt blended him in with the doctors who were converging on her. For a moment she continued to read her book but that seemed pointlessly nonchalant so she put it down and watched Angkatell heading the little shoal. She took in his electric-blue shirt, matching handkerchief, black suit – was that wise, in this ward? And a white coat over it, buttons undone, flowing like a trenchcoat as he walked. He smiled at Nick, who nodded his head gravely and came to sit by her and took her hand.

'Gerald Brown is an oncologist.' He took her chart from the end of the bed, glanced at it and passed it round.

'The tumour was contained,' Brown said, 'and the patient has had a lobectomy. The lymph nodes are clear and no further treatment is necessary at this point, although radiotherapy can be offered as an insurance policy.' He looked at Faye. 'We'll arrange for you to have regular checks; in the meantime, take it easy, listen to your body and ring us if there's a problem.'

Faye realised she was biting her lower lip. She stopped, and felt it swelling. She ran her tongue over it. She felt herself get lighter, as though she was floating. She held on to the rough, sage-green blanket. 'I'm cured, aren't I?' It came out higher than her normal tone. Reassure me, she thought, in case I've got it wrong.

Brown sat on the edge of the bed, one leg crossed over the other. His highly polished shoe caught the light as it swung. 'We call it a cure when there is no chance of the cancer coming back,' he said. 'In your case, there is no detectable evidence of cancer. There may be a recurrence but the checks will ensure we find it if there is. I know it's easier said than done, but people are often able to put it out of their minds until their check-ups. You're in complete remission. It hasn't spread to your lymph glands. Hopefully, that's an end to it.'

For the first time, Faye turned to Nick, her eyes shining with relief. She had a future and it tasted so, so sweet.

But Nick wasn't looking at her. He was staring at Brown. He looked stupefied.

Faye squeezed his hand but it was dead in hers.

'How long?' he asked.

'We'll know whether you're cured in three years' time.'

Three years, Faye thought. That was the time it took for one cell to multiply itself until it was a tumour the size of a golf ball. She wished she could fast-forward. 'Now that I'm allowed to, I'm scared to leave,' she said to Angkatell. 'I don't know if I can trust it.' But she would learn to trust the body in which she was living and give up watching every ache, wondering if it was all going to start again. 'I feel safe here.'

'Three *years*?' Nick asked. 'But she's got lung cancer.' He stroked his index finger repeatedly up his smooth neck as if he was in a Gillette advert, and lifted his chin.

Faye looked from him to the group of students. They were riveted. Brown was frowning. She glanced at Angkatell. His face was expressionless. She looked at Nick again.

Nick's mouth was open, his lower lip hanging heavy. He looked gormless with shock. 'It's *fatal*!' he said loudly. 'I've read about it! It's incurable! It spreads!'

Around them the whole ward fell quiet.

Angkatell felt for his tie, dull against the brightness of the electric-blue shirt. His voice was cold. 'Not in your wife's case,' he said.

The background conversation started up again, muted. Faye was staring at him, trying to understand.

Nick turned to look at her. He was frowning, looking at her as though she was some strange, unknown object. But it was he who was the stranger with the love gone out of his eyes.

He buried his face in his hands. 'Shit, shit, shit,' he said.

She felt as though the knowledge had always been there, lodged inside her. 'Susie,' she said.

Angkatell put his hand on her shoulder. 'I'll come back when I've finished the rounds.'

'You want me to die,' she said to Nick as the group moved away. It was a revelation and it astounded her. 'You hate me.'

He looked at her, startled. He stroked his hand over his hair. 'No,' he said. 'No, I don't. You don't understand, I thought – I thought it was planned for me. Things have always been planned for me. I was sorry about it, genuinely sorry.'

'*Sorry*? Get out!' she said.

He got to his feet. He had the puzzled look of a drunk recently awoken in a strange bed. 'How will you get home?' he asked. He hesitated a moment longer, then walked away from the bed with the John Lewis bag in his hand.

She didn't call him back.

Faye had changed into the dress she'd arrived in when Angkatell came back. He wiped his hand over his face in the gesture she knew well.

She was folding her pyjamas and putting them into her bag. 'He's a Catholic,' she said. 'He hasn't got the same feelings about death as the rest of us.'

'I'm sorry.'

She pushed her hair away from her face. 'How's Phil?'

Angkatell put his hands in his pockets. 'I could go on about patient confidentiality but it's easier to tell you to go and talk to him. See him before you leave. And don't forget to pick up your notes from the desk and give them to your GP.'

She held out her hand. 'I never thanked you,' she said.

He took it and she saw him smile. She was glad she'd managed to get out of him that last one.

Janine was pulling on a pair of blue cotton, baggy elastic-waisted trousers. 'I'm sure I've put on weight.'

'We never imagined we'd be glad of that, did we?'

'Where's Nick?'

'I'm getting a taxi. We fell out.'

'You live dangerously, don't you. I've rung my sister, she's coming in about twenty minutes.'

They looked at each other. 'It's been nice meeting you,' Janine said.

'Best of luck.' She had a lump in her throat. The period of enforced intimacy was over, the bond was broken. It wasn't as if they would miss it, the groaning in the low-lit ward at night, the discomfort. Faye went back to her packing.

Angkatell was talking to one of the nurses and looking at Annie. As soon as he'd gone, Faye went to see her. Her false teeth had been taken out and her lips puffed slightly with each breath. She looked decades older than when she'd come in.

The nurse came up and lifted one of Annie's bird-like arms, checking the pulse against her pinned-on watch.

'She doesn't look too good,' said Faye.

'She's going to be moved to the geriatric ward. I think she's given up.'

Annie fluttered her eyes and looked at the nurse. 'I'm very lonely,' she said in a clear voice. 'Very lonely.'

'You're in hospital,' the nurse said loudly, but Annie had closed her eyes and gone back to her lonely place.

'I'll come and visit her,' Faye said. 'How long will she be in the geriatric ward for?'

The nurse shrugged.

Faye put on a touch of bronze lipstick and drew a Nars bronzing stick across her cheeks . . . looking healthy! She sprayed herself with Eau Svelte and took the chocolate cigars out of the locker drawer.

'Is he leaving today?' Freda asked as she passed.

'I don't know,' Faye said. 'I'm going to find out.'

Phil wasn't in the day room nor in his bed. He was sitting in the armchair next to it. His eyes were closed although he was sitting upright. His skin was stretched taut over his tanned face – a sunbed tan, going yellow, she could see now. He had his robe on and her heart sank. He's staying in, she thought.

She pulled up a chair quietly and sat next to him. There was no hurry.

The television was on and the voices sounded clear and positive as though there was no such thing as doubt or uncertainty. A tea trolley clattered in the corridor. Behind her, someone was snoring gently as if not to disturb.

'Faye?'

She felt as if she had been drifting off herself and snapped back to the present with such speed that she was disoriented. 'Hi, Phil.' She felt shy, as though she'd disadvantaged him by appearing in her normal clothes. She felt as if she'd left him already.

'I must have nodded off,' he said, tilting his head to take her in as he spoke. 'You're leaving us.'

'Yes.'

'You're looking great,' he said. 'Fit and well.'

'Really? Oh, it's the make-up.'

'I've written down my address for you,' he said, and got a folded piece of paper from out of his pocket.

Faye took it and kept it in her hand. 'How long are you going to stay in? Angkatell said I should ask you myself.'

His eyes, which had not been on her, met hers.

She wanted to look away from what was in them. He was still silent. 'No games,' she said.

He scratched the back of his head thoughtfully, and didn't take his eyes from hers. 'Until my wife feels she can have me home.'

His eyes as she looked into them – why hadn't she noticed this before? – his eyes were as yellow as his skin.

'Well, I've got your address,' she said, consoling herself. 'And I've got something for you.' She'd put the cigars behind her on the seat and felt for them now, her fingers closing over the shiny paper, and handed them to him.

He took them, examining them closely. 'Havana,' he said. 'The best.' He offered her one back. 'Care to join me?'

She smiled as she took it and unwrapped it. Copying him, she held it between her thumb and forefinger, putting her mouth around the smooth, cloying chocolate. They breathed out in unison, exhaling the chocolate breath into the stale hospital air.

She watched him as he closed his eyes and smiled, remembering, perhaps nothing more than past cigars.

She was aware of being perfectly happy. Time seemed to stop. She sucked and ate the chocolate, comfortable and calm, watching him.

He opened his yellow eyes presently and smiled at her. She got up to go.

No words, not even a handshake.

And no goodbye.

She walked away.

Chapter Forty-Three

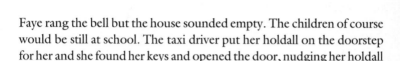

Faye rang the bell but the house sounded empty. The children of course would be still at school. The taxi driver put her holdall on the doorstep for her and she found her keys and opened the door, nudging her holdall in with her foot.

'Nick?' she called.

There was no reply. She went into their bedroom and opened his wardrobe door. There was more space in there than usual. She closed it again and lay on the bed and flicked on the lights. After the insipid green of the hospital ward the colours animated her with their vibrancy. Orange and yellow. She shut her eyes and wondered if the fish were all right.

She felt a sense of desolation and thought it must be something similar to the way Eve felt when she'd been booted out of Eden.

Still, she was alive despite him.

It was hard to think he'd so eagerly imagined life without her. And so easily imagined it with Susie.

She had been quick to dismiss the conversation recorded on the answerphone. She hadn't rung Susie to talk about her 'man trouble'. To think, Nick had said that knowing he was talking about himself.

She got up off the bed, leaving the lights on, and went upstairs.

The first thing she saw, dominating the far wall, was the portrait photograph for Edith's birthday. He'd put it where the light would fall on it. She went over to look at it. The gilt frame gleamed and inside the picture they gleamed too, looking out of it like brand new dolls in a box. There she was on the chair, laughing at something off camera while the future sniggered at her in some cosmic joke.

By her feet sat Isabel, dark hair curling, showing her teeth in a posey grin as phoney as her mother's.

Next to her, and a little way back, Samuel was smiling faintly, pityingly, at the foibles of man.

Only Nick was staring at the camera. Nick, the Good One. His hooded eyes were looking beyond the photographer, beyond the studio, beyond his wife studying it now on the wall; looking at the devastation that he knew was to come.

She could have walked once, but she was out of practice, she told herself, and anyway, parked right outside her house, light off, was a cab. Faye glanced through the passenger window at the driver, checking for signs of a flask, newspaper or polystyrene cup. The driver looked at her.

'Not free, are you?' she asked hopefully.

'Where do you want to go?'

'Mahler Industries, the High Street?'

'Yeah, go on.'

She scrambled into the back, hitting her head sharply on the door-frame.

'Watch that.'

Wryly she replied, 'Thanks.' The car smelt of cheap talc, the source of which was a scent-impregnated cardboard oak tree dangling from a plastic sucker with a hook. Faye felt for the seatbelt and took hold of the webbing tenderly. Tenderness was the key, she found. She didn't know how other people managed. But the belt locked in the casing before she could pull out enough to strap herself in. From experience she knew they could be coaxed sometimes but it needed patience and one could only be patient for so long, and after a few unsuccessful clicks which the cabbie ignored she let it be.

'Ever had sauerkraut?' the cabbie asked after a few minutes, inclining his head backwards for her to catch the words.

Faye looked up at the rear-view mirror. She could see the cabbie's eyes set neatly in the little strip of glass.

'Yes.'

'What did you have it with?'

It looked as if it was the cut-out piece of a blackmail photograph. 'Er, sausages and mash. Or frankfurters and mash.' Joke.

The traffic was light and the journey was taking no time at all. She should have collected her thoughts before acting, put them together neatly and decided on the purpose of her journey. She shook her head. Her stomach clenched when she thought of Susie. And they were now in the High Street.

'Right. You want a receipt?'

For a second she translated it as 'recipe'. 'No. Thanks.'

He was pulling up outside Mahler's. 'Two-sixty.'

Faye checked her bag and found three pound coins. She got out of the cab, ducking low, and handed them over. 'Keep the change. Your seatbelts don't work.'

He replied by rolling the window up and spinning a U-turn.

She turned to look at the building. Mahlers had replaced the revolving door with a double, one half of which, as she approached, was opened briskly by a man of retirement age, in uniform.

She thanked him and looked over at the reception desk. 'Hello, I've come to see Susie Jacks. She's expecting me. Don't ring, I'll go straight up.'

'Fine. You know where she is?'

'Second floor.'

'You can do my job any day.'

Faye smiled, noting that the receptionist's orange hair was defying gravity. She marvelled that some people's hair could be so obedient.

Faye stepped into the lift and wondered if she would ring Susie. She got out on the second floor. It smelt familiarly office-like – of polypropylene and synthetic carpets. It seemed the receptionist hadn't rung – Susie's office door was open and she was laughing with a girl Faye didn't recognise. The laughter was too robust to be fake.

Faye looked round and saw a couple of heads bowed over desks but no-one looked up. She got to Susie's door and tapped on it.

Susie's smile died. She ushered her colleague out past Faye, and beckoned Faye in, closing the door. 'Sit,' she said, heading for her seat behind the desk. She stopped and came back round Faye's side and pulled up a chair that had been placed against a wall.

The flurry of her actions was all that Faye could see at first, and they told her as clear as words that Nick had already rung Susie to tell her the news: Faye Knows.

The internal thump that came with this knowledge made her angry. She raised her head to look at Susie.

Susie was looking suitably grave. Her dark hair was fastened up. There was a loose eyelash on the apple of her cheek. Her face looked uncharacteristically blotchy. She met Faye's eyes and neither of them spoke.

Looking at her, Faye wondered what excuse she'd make for seeing Nick. Susie had been a close friend, once. She felt a squeeze of panic in her chest, not of loss but of being left; different thing. The squeezing was producing something bitter in her mouth. Her side was throbbing. 'How long has it been going on with you and Nick?'

'I don't know what to say,' Susie said softly, looking down at her knees. She was wearing a dark, chocolate-colour wool dress. She licked her finger briefly and picked up a piece of lint on it from just above the hem. She raised her head sorrowfully. 'We're in love.'

'Nick doesn't believe in divorce, I'm sure you know that.'

Susie shrugged. 'He didn't think he'd have to.' She put her hand on her heart. 'Faye, I'm glad you're better, and I want you to know I've been thinking of you – you got my card?'

'Yes, I got it. It's been going on for a long time, hasn't it?'

'Nick said you knew I'd rung him, you know, a few weeks ago. You dialled 1471, I suppose, traced the number back? We all do it, don't we.'

I don't, Faye thought. I didn't think I had to.

'Well, I'm glad you know. I wanted to tell you but I promised Nick I wouldn't. It seemed better for you to discover it by yourself. You see, I want him and you don't,' Susie was saying earnestly, looking up from her scrutiny of the dress stretched across her knees.

This statement took Faye's breath away. 'He's my husband,' she said. 'I've never not wanted him.'

Susie glanced at the door as though she'd heard some sound outside it. She looked quickly back at Faye. 'You told me it was all over, that you didn't love him. You said you only went back to him for Isabel's sake.'

'That was two years ago and I was fed up!'

'Do you think he didn't notice that it was all going wrong?'

Faye leant forward. 'It didn't "all go wrong",' she said. 'And we're fine now.' It seemed an absurd thing to say but Susie didn't pick up on it.

Susie pressed her lips together. It gave her a pious expression that didn't quite fit. She looked as though she was wearing someone else's face.

The phone rang suddenly, startling them both. Susie got up from her chair and grabbed the handset, listened and said, 'I'll get back to you.' She came back and sat down again.

'How long has it been going on? You didn't say.'

'"It"?' she asked fastidiously, and sighed. 'Since the summer. I rang up for you one evening and you weren't in, I think you were taking

212

Samuel to karate. I wanted to moan to you about work. Nick asked if he would do instead.'

'Oh, stop it,' Faye said warningly, getting off her chair. She could take the whole picture but she had no desire to look at the detail that made it up, not now, not yet, and certainly not recounted so specifically as part of Susie's love story.

'I do love him,' Susie added reasonably, 'if it's any consolation.'

Faye looked at her. 'That's a dreadful line. And it isn't. Why would that help me?' She hooked her fingers under the neck of her dress. Her skin felt hot against her knuckles. She moved her hand to her throat. 'It's not just about me, it's about the children, we are a family.'

'You didn't think of your family when it suited you, did you? Okay, it's not just about you but it's not just about me, either. It's about Nick, too. He wants to be with me.'

'Guilt free.'

Susie opened her desk drawer and took a peach-coloured tissue out of a small embroidered tissue-holder. She blew her nose. 'Sex and religion,' she said, tossing the crumpled tissue into the bin under her desk, 'they're so similar, aren't they? Giving yourself to another, it's so liberating not having to think for yourself.' She gave a short laugh and covered her eyes for a moment with her hand before looking at Faye. 'Well, I think he's beginning to. He can live with the guilt if he has to.'

Faye knew that something had shifted. She glanced at the window, perhaps for enlightenment. A row of spider plants sat there. Such plain plants, too, with their stripy functional leaves and their pallid flowers.

She returned her gaze to Susie. 'And he's slept with you?'

Susie didn't answer.

Faye nodded briefly and got to her feet.

'Faye, can we still be friends?'

'I don't think so, do you?' She walked out of Susie's office. She pressed the button for the lift and glanced down the office. Straightening up from a filing cabinet right down the other end of the room was Richard. He lifted his head and turned and looked straight at her. Funny how easy it was to recognise the shape of people.

She thought of him humming *Love Story* as she lay in her hospital bed.

She pretended not to see him and heard the ping, ping, ping of the lift door and hurried in, stabbing desperately at the button. Slowly the lift door closed and she felt grateful and safe, or under the illusion that she was. The lift sank and bumped into place. The door slid open. Ping, ping, ping. No-one was there. The receptionist with the gravity-defying hair waved as Faye stepped out, and the doorman opened the door.

She flagged down another taxi and got in without looking back. She thought she might have heard someone call her name: Richard, who had also found it quite easy to imagine her dead.

Chapter Forty-Four

Once Faye was home she rang Vicky to ask her to pick up the children from school.

When the doorbell rang a short while later she hurried downstairs in the crab-like movement that eased the picking sensation in her side. She opened the door and looked at four smiling faces. Vicky propelled her daughter Shani in through the door while Faye hugged Samuel and Isabel, overcome suddenly by heavy, sorrowful tears.

'Come on, come on,' Vicky said softly. 'Nice cup of tea. Or brandy?'

Faye gave an explosive, watery laugh. 'Oh, it's so good to be home,' she said, letting the children go and wiping her eyes with her hands. 'It seems ages.'

'It's been a week,' Samuel said, dropping his school bag on the floor. He gave her a worried glance.

'A long week,' Faye said.

Vicky retied her hair in a clip. 'I'll make a snack for these three. Four if you're hungry. Then you can tell me all the gory details.'

In the kitchen, as Vicky fried scampi, Faye told her that Nick had been seeing Susie.

The expression on Vicky's face saddened her. 'I didn't mean that kind of gory detail. Of all people,' she said at last. 'What will you do?'

'I don't know.'

'So the kids have kept you and lost him,' Vicky said, turning down the heat. Her face was flushed as she turned to Faye. 'Is it serious? I mean, he might have just wanted comforting, you know what I mean?'

'He wouldn't have done it lightly.' She sat down. 'I've been so complacent about him. I thought he would always be mine, no matter what I did, because I was his wife. Sometimes I used to think he'd married me because I loved Samuel. I mean, what did he see in me?'

'Oh, Faye, don't say that.'

'That's how I felt. That I never deserved him.'

'I don't understand how you stayed with him when he made you feel like that. Why didn't you leave?'

Faye gave a brief laugh. 'He didn't make me feel like that. I felt like that anyway.'

Vicky unhooked a slatted spoon from the stand and scooped the scampi out with unnecessary vigour, distributing it between the plates.

'But after Richard it changed. Then I stopped working and going out in the evenings and there was a lull for a while. Then I started doing the freelance lighting and life became interesting again.'

'And then he fell in love with Susie?'

Faye shrugged, hurt by the words.

The five of them sat around the table sharing a disjointed silence. A red glow lit the ceiling overhead to give an illusion of warmth.

'Where's Dad, did you say?' Samuel asked.

'I didn't say, because I don't know. I suppose he's still at work.' She stared at the chips, scampi and beans and found, as she stared at them, that she had no appetite. She speared a chip with her fork. 'What's the singular of scampi? I'll tell you. Scampo.'

'Thank you for sharing that with us,' Vicky said.

'Miss Maitland's engaged,' Isabel said. 'She's got a diamond ring.'

'Oh? What's her fiancé's name?'

'Paul. They're getting married.'

'Lovely.'

Samuel dipped a chip in ketchup. 'I stayed the night at Allie's,' he said miserably.

Isabel, wanting to continue her conversation, was kicking the table rhythmically, a new habit, Faye noticed, and one that was intensely irritating. 'Stop that,' she said, and repeated, 'You stayed the night at Allie's?'

He raised his eyes to hers, held her gaze, nodding. He looked as if he'd done something terribly wrong. Nick hadn't mentioned it, she thought. Why was that? 'Did you have a good time?' she asked, putting her fork down on the plate. It caught the red light and flashed in her eyes.

Samuel nodded.

Faye felt Isabel's foot nudge the table again and saw Vicky put a restraining hand on her daughter's knee.

Samuel dragged the chip lethargically through the red sauce, drawing a line on the plate with it and another, and another until it looked like a setting sun. 'Alicia had to go to work.' He raised his head to look from one to the other. 'Adam went out for some fresh air.'

'Alicia was working?'

He looked down and mumbled something under his breath.

'What did you say?'

He raised his head defiantly. 'I said I'd still rather have her as my mother than Susie. She's been here. I saw her.' He looked at her angrily. 'I know why Dad wants her, it's in case you die.'

'Susie's been here?' Of all the statements, why was that the one that shocked her most? 'When did she come?'

'It was late. I heard them talking. I heard Dad say "Susie".'

'And you stayed at Alicia's flat on your own?'

Samuel stared at the salt cellar and moved it nearer the pepper, like a chess move. He glanced at Shani who was the only one of them still eating.

'Did you tell Dad?'

'I thought it might make you angry with each other. Dad's grumpy anyway. Are you going to die? Dad thinks you are.'

'No, I'm not.'

Isabel looked at her doubtfully, her hand clutched round her juice. 'Daddy said you're going to be with Jesus.'

'I don't think Jesus would have me,' Faye said.

She heard Nick just then at the front door, his key rattling around the keyhole as though he was having trouble finding it. It was only five but she guessed he'd been drinking. He came slowly up the stairs and by the silence he knew something had happened and looked at them in turn.

'Vicky,' he said. His face looked closed.

Faye stood up. 'I know that Susie's been here,' she said softly. 'And that Alicia left Samuel on his own. You are a shit, Nick.'

Isabel and Samuel looked at her, shocked by the expletive. Vicky got to her feet. 'We'd better . . .'

Faye felt her fork tremble in her hand. It tapped against the table in a brief rhythm. She knew what her husband had been doing while she'd been ill. He had been packing her away, folding her up, dismantling her from his life, her good, pure, enlightened man.

She went to bed early, in the guest room. She saw that the sheets had been changed and she knew why. She put her head on the pillow and looked at the blue-and-yellow curtains through which the evening light still poured.

She heard him come in, later. The room was darker. He sat on the side of the bed and for a moment she was back in hospital and Angkatell was sitting by her, promising her safety.

Nick reached out his hand and placed it on the back of her neck. 'I didn't want to hurt you.'

She did not move away, but felt it heavy and warm and somehow dead. 'You wanted to be rid of me,' she said. 'I can't imagine how anyone, least of all you, could feel like that.'

'I didn't think you'd know,' he said. 'It just seemed . . . Susie ringing, and your being ill, I thought it was all meant to be. I was wrong.'

'Do you know how conceited that sounds?' She heard the sound of thunder growling in the distance. It stirred up some memory in her brain, but which storm she was remembering, she didn't know. Her thoughts were muddled but at other times the past came back clear and strong. Things she'd thought long-forgotten surprised her with their fierce clarity.

She had a theory about it; yeah, once she'd had a theory about everything. If you died suddenly, your life flashed before your eyes. And she believed this: that if you died slowly, it unravelled piece by piece, unreeling the past clearer than it had been lived, like moments filmed on video.

She'd gone back to her earliest memory but it all felt unfinished and unsatisfactory.

'I wish the old days were back,' Nick said. 'It was simple then.'

It wasn't his words but his tone that brought the tears into her eyes. She let them roll; there was no pity like self-pity, it could draw tears more efficiently than anyone else's suffering. 'Do you? Hell, Nick, I spend my time living them.' She wiped her nose with the edge of her thumb. 'What was so great about them anyway?'

When he didn't answer she turned and raised herself up on one arm to look at him better. In the fading light she could see tears silvering his eyes, pooling in the corners. He turned his head away from her.

'I knew who I was, then.'

She lay back down. She envied him. She'd never been sure who she was. For the most part her memories were all overlaid by guilt of one sort or another, spoiling the viewing, like looking at a mountain through smog. 'I bet you wish you'd never met me,' she said, turning to look at Nick. She could see his profile.

'Don't say that.'

'You should have found someone like Susie in the first place. Someone uncomplicated. You should have had everyday highs and lows, summer holidays and hangovers.'

'Someone ordinary, you mean.'

That made her smile. She was glad it was dark. Wowsers, ordinary, the worst insult of all. She wanted to continue the subject, the riveting subject of Susie's ordinariness, but her chest ached and her ribs hurt and somehow it didn't seem important enough to pursue.

'I never wanted anybody ordinary,' he said.

'Until now,' she said.

He stretched; she could hear his bones crack. He wanted to be gone, now, she thought, back upstairs for a Scotch.

'Anyway,' she said, 'I think you should make a go of it with Susie.'

'Leave here, you mean?'

'Yes.'

There was a long silence, during which she hovered on the brink of sleep.

'When you're better,' he said at last. 'I'll go then.'

It hurt so much to hear him say it.

'Your mother will like the photograph,' she said after a moment. 'Switch the phone off, could you? I want to sleep.'

She saw his dark shape bend and he kissed her on the eyes. He'd misjudged it in the dark. Or had he? He straightened and went quietly to the door. The only sound she heard was it closing behind him.

In the night she woke to hear Samuel crying.

He woke up when she went into the room and was surprised to find his cheeks damp. He didn't know what he'd dreamt, he couldn't remember.

She went back to bed but sleep eluded her, dancing around the edge of her mind, kept at bay by another emotion entirely: regret.

Chapter Forty-Five

Edith could see the change in Alicia; it was impossible to miss.

Just like her own father, she thought. Unto the third and fourth generation. The sideslip, not much wrong, not at first, not unless you were watching. It was a change that went deeper than the eccentric.

Derek had certainly been the Clever One, going to Boston on a Churchill Trust scholarship and never coming back. What had happened to her children? Nick had stopped going to church, now, so Samuel had said.

She'd asked Nick if he was disillusioned with God, thinking Faye's illness might have brought on an anger.

No. With myself.

That's what he'd said, Nick the Good One.

It wouldn't have been much to be ashamed of, to be angry with God. She had seen it before, in others. Others? She'd seen it in herself when her husband had died. She'd rather him be angry with God than with himself. 'You can take it,' she said, feeling for the crucifix around her neck. 'Nick can't.'

What would be left of Nick once the goodness was gone? There was a question.

But what would be left of Alicia if the madness left? She would be her own true person.

She had seen the long minutes her daughter spent looking at Samuel's photographs, looking for herself in him perhaps. Or looking for Samuel's father, whom she herself had never met, probably never would.

'Why did I leave Samuel?' Alicia said, coming in from the kitchen.

'You wouldn't say,' Edith replied, looking up from the red cardigan she was knitting for Isabel. 'You wanted to keep it to yourself. Alicia, one day Samuel might ask about his father. What was his surname?'

Alicia went to look at herself in the mirror over the fireplace, and gathered her red-gold hair in her hand, pulling it back from her face. 'I'm not quite sure. Edwards, I think. Baz Edwards.' She frowned at herself and cocked her head to one side. 'Stop looking at me like that, as if there's something wrong with me.' She turned from the mirror, her eyes hard. 'Why do you keep watching me?'

Edith concentrated on the stitches. She had to decrease for the sleeve. It was a nice colour red, scarlet, she would call it, although on the label it said flame, which she would have thought of as yellow.

'I'm talking to you, Mum!'

Edith looked up. 'It was a perfectly reasonable question,' she said. 'Nick's asked me more than once if I knew who it was. Samuel's going to want to know, I hope you realise that.'

Alicia turned back to the mirror and twisted her hair round her hand. 'When he asks, I'll tell him,' she said. 'Baz's mother used to come in to buy Brut aftershave to drink.'

Edith dropped a stitch. The thought of this – Baz – having a mother . . . 'Didn't it work out expensive?' she asked.

Alicia didn't reply. She held a hank of hair straight up over her head. 'Do you think Sam looks like me?'

Edith smiled. 'Yes, I think he does. He's a lovely boy.'

'He's mine,' Alicia said simply.

There was a knock on the door. Alicia went to open it and Faye came in, her face flushed.

Edith put down her knitting and got to her feet, startled. 'Faye,' she said warmly. 'Oh, my dear, what's wrong?' She folded her hands across her chest at the sight of her.

'I've really come to see you, Alicia,' Faye said. 'It's about Samuel. I don't want him staying with you any more. You can see him at our house whenever you want, of course. He likes you and I'm glad you're back.' Her voice tailed off as Alicia's humming got louder.

Shocked though she was, Edith turned to look at Alicia. She saw the small sly smile that crossed her face as Alicia continued to hum something tuneless and distracting to drown Faye out.

'I'm sorry, Edith,' Faye said, glancing at Alicia and raising her voice over the sound, 'but she and Adam left Samuel alone in their flat. He's too young.'

Alicia stopped humming. 'It was Adam's fault,' she said, tossing her red hair. 'He was supposed to look after him until I finished work. He promised. I got home just after one and Sammy was watching Cable. He was quite happy. He said he didn't mind.'

'Sit down, Faye,' Edith said, pleading. 'It really doesn't sound as though it's Alicia's fault. Blame Adam, if anyone, but it's nice for Alicia to see him on her own.' She could see that Faye shouldn't really have been out. Her face was white and she looked exhausted. She just hoped the hospital was correct in its diagnosis. It wouldn't be the first time it had made a – cock-up? Hash of it? – an error. 'Sit down,' she said again. 'Alicia, put the kettle on. Are you warm enough, Faye?'

Faye nodded.

When Alicia was in the kitchen filling the kettle, Edith said placatingly, 'She's much better, she really is, and I don't want –' to be responsible for her? To have her here? '– to make things difficult. Could you give her another chance?'

Faye's eyes seemed large and feverish in her pale face. 'Another chance?' she asked, and laughed. 'I don't want him staying, not while Alicia's working nights.'

'And Nick?' Edith asked.

'Nick – Nick's got no need to let him stay now.' She looked suddenly flushed. 'Thank you for keeping an eye on Nick and the children.'

'That's all right.' Edith pulled herself up in her chair. 'There's a memorial service, no tickets, that you might like to come to with me. It's in St Martin-in-the-Fields. You might enjoy it, you know.' She looked up as Alicia came back into the room looking edgy. There was a glitter in her eye.

She should have had a daughter like Faye, Edith thought; someone normal who could rely on her and ask her for the best butcher. She still went to Mr McMahone's. She was sure Faye knew how to pronounce it properly, but there again, she might not.

She glanced at her knitting.

'Can I take him out?' Alicia asked in an overloud voice.

Faye looked startled. 'Well . . .'

'He likes me.'

'Yes, I know he does. Of course, yes.'

Edith could hear the defeat in her voice. The girl was exhausted.

Alicia began humming again.

'I think I'll go now,' Faye said. She wrapped her arm around herself, holding her side.

Edith got to her feet. 'Won't you at least have a cup of tea? Alicia's put the kettle on.'

'I'm going for acupuncture,' Faye said. 'A friend arranged it for me. I've got an appointment at eleven. Bye, Alicia.'

Edith followed her to the door and watched her leave, her blue coat swinging in the breeze. Acupuncture? You'd have thought she'd had enough of needles, that one.

She went into the kitchen. The kettle was boiling with the lid off and the room was full of steam. Alicia smiled when she went in. It was a sweet and guileless smile, and Edith shivered.

Chapter Forty-Six

It was sunny, but the air was chill and the park was quiet except for a woman walking an old dog and scattering seed for the pigeons who jostled behind her, exploding into the air in an occasional flutter of wings. Her pet's posture summed up the word 'dogged'.

Nick reached for Susie's hand and pushed it down with his into the tiny space between them on the bench. It was lunchtime but neither of them was eating. Susie had said she wasn't hungry. It was a shame, he thought, because he was. The smell of fried onions was drifting over from the hot dog van and he would have liked to have had one. He could almost taste the pungency of the mustard offset by the sweetness of the ketchup. He groaned a little and Susie squeezed his hand.

'We should have gone back to my flat,' she said.

'What would you have made me?' Nick asked with interest.

'I didn't mean for lunch.'

He knew he'd offended her.

'You think of food instead of sex,' she said, taking her hand out of his with difficulty, as their fingers were enmeshed.

He was tempted to say how much easier his conscience would be if that were true, but wasn't sure of the veracity of it.

He suspected that she had brought him out here to this park in order to make him suffer. She was certainly suffering herself, shivering inside her thin beige raincoat despite wearing her jacket underneath.

'Untrue,' he said.

'If I'd have known . . .' She tossed her hair and averted her face.

'What?' he asked sharply. 'If you'd have known what?'

'How it was going to turn out. That we'd have to do all this waiting.'

He was amazed at her blatancy. 'But you always knew I wouldn't divorce her.'

She angled her head to look at him, mocking. 'Oh yes, because of your principles. I forgot. It was you who talked about marriage, remember?'

'Why did you start ringing me? And coming early to collect Faye? Just to see how far you could make me go?' he asked. The chill was getting to him. He could feel it creeping into his bones.

'You're so dense sometimes,' she said angrily. 'I fancied you, that's all. It was you who had to make everything so bloody difficult with your rules and promises. I knew things weren't going well between you and Faye and I couldn't see the problem. I still can't. What are you going to do, worry about her for the next three years?'

'I'm just staying until her first check-up. I don't think she even wants that, to be honest.' He looked at a squirrel who had come to check out the pigeon seed. The tail seemed to operate independently of the body.

'Leave her, then.'

'I can't.' I don't want to, he thought. He had to salvage something.

'She always comes first,' Susie complained.

'I don't think that's how she sees it.'

'That's how it is!' Susie snapped at him before turning away. 'You like being stuck in your comfortable marriage.'

'And what would *we* do?'

He heard her sigh. That, he supposed, was the reply. Take up where he and Faye had left off, of course.

'You said it was meant to be,' Susie said. Tears didn't sound far off.

'Don't remind me of my conceit,' he said softly, and got to his feet. 'Susie.'

'What?'

'Let's not worry about it now. Come on, I'll walk you back.'

'So where does that leave us?' she asked irritably, getting up. 'I want a future,' she said.

'I know,' he said sadly.

They walked along the path, not touching. He wanted a future, too.

And, of course, so did Faye.

Chapter Forty-Seven

Two weeks later, after an aromatherapy massage, Faye was feeling good and on impulse she decided to go and see Phil.

She'd rehearsed it many times, and put it off. Now she felt ready to impress.

In the taxi she put on some lipstick and ruffled her fingers through her hair. She looked at the folded square of paper with his address on that she'd kept in her wallet: Mendip Place.

The taxi cruised it slowly as she tried to see the house numbers. 'That's it, right there.' Phil's house was on a corner. The light was on in the porch although it was early afternoon. She paid the driver and walked slowly to the door and rang the bell.

A woman opened the door. She was tall, slim, and she looked younger than Faye. Her blonde hair was showing dark roots and she was holding a toddler on her hip, who was playing with the buttons on her denim shirt. Behind her the radio was on, playing Radio Five.

'Is Phil in?' Faye asked. It seemed a bit basic, so she carried on awkwardly, 'My name's Faye Reading and I was in hospital at the same time as him and as I happened to be passing I thought I might as well see how he was.' She winced. Rambling, she thought. 'If it's not convenient perhaps you could just mention . . .'

She saw the woman's expression and tailed off.

The woman's face had gone blank.

That and the silence told her.

The woman put her lips to the wispy hair on her child's head. 'Phil's dead.'

Faye already felt it in the pit of her stomach, a hard blow. Stunned, she looked at the child in the woman's arms. 'I'm so sorry. I shouldn't have just turned up.'

The woman looked at her through wisps of pale hair blowing across her face. 'No, he said you would. He was expecting you. Come in. He left you something.' She gave the ghost of a smile. 'He left everybody something, there are Post-It notes all over the place. Go through, that's it, first right.'

Faye walked on the springy pink carpet into a large sitting room and took a seat on a red leather sofa. Toys were scattered about on the floor. The woman put the child down and moved her hand to check the buttons that he had been playing with. 'I'm Ingrid,' she said, 'and this is Nathan.' The child looked up as she said his name. He had curly blonde hair and he walked over to a red and yellow Duplo tower and cheerfully knocked it over. Ingrid knelt on the floor next to him and began building it up again. She glanced up at Faye. 'You're all right now, aren't you? He said you were lucky.'

'Lucky?' Faye raised her eyebrows. She hadn't thought of herself as lucky. She'd thought of it as a nightmare. 'I suppose I am.'

She watched Ingrid build the tower and as her gaze wandered she noticed that there really were Post-It notes stuck on odd things around the room. Did Ingrid mind? she wondered, looking at her bent head. And what if people began swapping them round?

As though tuning in to her thoughts, Ingrid got to her feet and said, 'He's left you a record. I told him you wouldn't have a record-player, no-one does anymore, do they?' Her face crumpled suddenly and she began to cry bitterly and despairingly, not bothering in her grief to hide her face. Nathan lay on the floor and began to cry too.

Faye felt helpless. Tears rolled down her cheeks. She had no words of comfort, Phil's death was a bitter loss, beyond all consolation. How could she begin to console? How could she trivialise it with platitudes? He had gone and she could only cry with them, because he had gone and would not be coming back.

She watched Ingrid bend to take her son in her arms, comforting him even as her tears fell on his fine hair. 'He had the funeral he wanted,' she said, collecting herself, looking up at Faye through reddened eyes. '"Heartbreak Hotel", and "Come Down O Love Divine". He liked the line, "And o'er its own shortcomings weeps with loathing". We had lots of roses, I wanted flowers. People don't so much now, do they? Only I did. He liked flowers. I wanted flowers everywhere.' She dried her eyes with her hands. 'I'll get us some tea.'

While his mother was in the kitchen, Nathan toddled over to Faye with a toy Noddy car. She ran it up the front of his sweater and he giggled shyly.

Ingrid came back with strong, sweet tea. 'Everyone liked him,' she said, 'people have dropped by, people I've never met. It's wrong somehow. Bad people, you know, criminals, you can't get rid of too many of those and yet they seem to live forever, while someone like Phil . . .' she paused. 'He was a good man, you know.'

Faye nodded, holding the hot PG Tips mug, keeping the grief back as if the emotion would break her.

'He was good with people,' Ingrid said. 'The church was full. The priest read out a letter that Phil had written.' She wiped her cheeks. 'I'm sorry.'

'No,' Faye said, 'it's all right.' She had left the hospital without saying it. She had had two weeks in which to call him to say goodbye. Do the dead feel abandoned, too?

She could have come at any time. How well would they have got on, she wondered, playing once more against the props of their own lives? They had met, made contact, and parted again. They were friends for a time, and that time was over.

Nathan was banging his small fists on Ingrid's knee. 'Go and kiss Daddy, Nathan,' she said softly.

Nathan went to the sideboard and came back with a photograph held against his open lips. He gave it to Ingrid, who wiped the glass with her sleeve stretched over the heel of her hand and passed it to Faye.

Faye looked at a laughing Phil; younger, plumper, his head tilted slightly and his smile real as though he'd been caught at the punchline of a good joke. She wouldn't have recognised him as the man she knew, lean, his smile more knowing, his gaze more distant, with a tan that wasn't a tan colouring his eyes.

She wouldn't have expected the Phil she knew to be married to a woman with dark roots like her own or for him to have liked roses and Elvis.

But that was him, nevertheless, part of the whole person, the man who looked regretfully at the city at night and didn't want to play games.

When she finished her tea she stood up. 'Thank you,' she said.

Ingrid stood up too and took the mug. 'His ashes are going to be put into fireworks for the memorial service. March the third, St John's, Neasden. Could you leave me your address? And thank you for coming, he would have liked it that you did.'

Faye felt the heat rise in her cheeks and she found a business card in her handbag. Would he? Or would the intrusion have embarrassed him? The war was over for them both. All that was left was to mourn his passing.

Ingrid slipped out of the room and came back with the record, a forty-five in a paper sleeve, her name scribbled on the yellow note. Faye. She looked at the label. It was an old song, one she knew, 'American Pie'. Ingrid was right. He would have been glad to see her.

'Thank you for coming,' Ingrid said again at the door.

I didn't come for him, I came for me, Faye thought. I came for comfort, but there is none now to be had.

Ed was in his room at the hospital next to the chapel. It had two slate-blue moquette armchairs and a small bookcase with a tray and a kettle on top.

Reasons; that was what she was looking for.

Ed was wearing his dog collar, and he went to pour her a glass of wine.

The glass he handed to her was so delicate she thought it might snap in her fingers. 'I imagined you'd be unworldly,' she said. She put the glass on the table. 'Have you seen Annie lately?' she asked, centring the base onto a coaster.

'Annie died last week.'

'I can't stand it,' she said quietly. 'What hope is there for me?'

'A lot, I should think. What has your doctor said?'

'He says I'm doing fine. It's just, there's no-one to talk to about it.'

'What's there to talk about? You are cured, like Freda, like Janine. Why do you want to be like Annie and Phil, who were dying?'

Faye picked up the glass. It was cool in her hand, and the wine glowed dark and deep. 'I'm afraid to think I'm cured,' she said. 'I can't let myself believe it. If I do, and it comes back, I'll have to go through the same awful fear again. It's safer to live with it and not be disappointed. I don't suppose you approve,' she added.

'Why shouldn't I? That's how you feel, there's no right or wrong. You should tell your husband, though, and your children, how you feel.'

'It will upset them.'

'It will help them be supportive.'

'You don't know them. The house is filled with dread and foreboding.'

'And not talking about a fear makes it worse.'

'They're leaving me, all of them in their own ways, and I'm not dead yet.'

'Ally yourself with the living, Faye. Or in other words, let the dead bury the dead. Phil and Annie have moved on but you're still here where you belong.'

She took the bus home. The door opened before she'd got her key in the lock.

'Is Sam with you?' Nick asked her.

'What do you mean?' Why had she said that? Her mind knew all right and stopped her heart. 'No, of course he isn't. What's happened?'

'I was late picking them up, I forgot I'd promised to. They came home and Isabel said there was a phone call and Samuel told her he'd be five minutes.'

'How long had they waited for you?'

'I got to the school at quarter past and they'd left. Isabel said the phone rang and then Samuel told her he was going to the news-agent's.'

And he'd asked her if Sam was with her, knowing he was not. She pushed past him into the house. 'You've rung his friends?'

'First thing I did. The last they'd seen of him was at school.' He lowered his head.

'Waiting to be picked up.' She said it without bitterness but not without sorrow. 'What about Alicia? Have you rung your mother?'

'She hasn't seen Alicia for over a week. I drove to the flat with Isabel but there's no reply and we hurried back in case he'd returned.'

Faye thought about the humming in the kitchen that day. 'Ring the police,' she said softly. 'Alicia's taken him.'

230

Chapter Forty-Eight

'Where are we going?' Samuel asked, glancing at the mini-cab driver who had watched him get in. He had gone to the newsagent's and she had been waiting for him in the car. He'd imagined sitting there with her, having a chat about Nintendo, but the engine had started up and he turned round in alarm to see the street that led to his house getting smaller by the second.

'We're going for a trip,' Alicia said, looking at him from under the brim of her black velvet hat. 'Is that all right with you?'

She said it so lightly and sweetly that it didn't sound like her, but Samuel said, 'Isabel's at home on her own. I'll be in trouble for leaving her. Can we go tomorrow instead?'

'Aw,' Alicia said sympathetically, 'she's on her own, is she? No, we can't go tomorrow.' Her fingers pinched a pleat in her long, black skirt. 'See, Sammy, they don't want us to be together and we belong, don't we? We're going now.'

He looked at her and nodded slightly. He felt afraid.

'Of course we do,' she said. 'We belong. Blood is thicker than water, did you know that? It sinks.'

Blood is thicker than water. He knew the saying. His granny said it a lot but he couldn't understand what it meant or why sinking should come into it. It was one of those sayings that made him want to think: so what? 'Where are we going on the trip?' he asked, and saw the mini-cab driver turn his head to look at him, as though he thought he might be digging holes in the seats. Sometimes people's keys did that, but sometimes people did it on purpose, like graffiti. Some people just liked to spoil things.

Alicia leant between the gap in the seats and he noticed she wasn't wearing her seatbelt. 'Stop at Boots, Piccadilly, will you?' she asked the driver. 'You can go that way, can't you? Regent Street way?'

'It's your money,' the driver said, but he didn't sound pleased.

Sam was relieved to hear about Piccadilly as he knew roughly where it was – quite near Sega World. If he had to, he could get home from there.

'I need my stuff,' Alicia said to him.

Sam nodded, although he didn't know what she meant.

'When we get there, get me a bottle of Bennies, will you do that? Benylin, ask them for Benylin. They won't give it to me.'

The driver sighed audibly from the front.

Alicia looked up at him and then back at Sam. 'Say it's for your mother and that she's trying the make-up. Will you do that?'

Sam nodded and she patted his cheek. 'Of course you will. You'll do that for Mummy, won't you? Is that what you call Faye? Do you call her Mummy?'

'I call her Mum.'

'I'll be Mummy,' Alicia said, smiling. She reminded him of Isabel, it was like something she would say. Isabel was always pretending she was someone else. He didn't have to, he already was.

He looked out of the window as they passed Hamley's, and felt a leap of relief at seeing something familiar. Alicia was looking in her bag, trawling her fingers through heaps of coins, most of them fifties, from what he could see. Her bag must weigh a ton, he thought. She gave him six and the taxi pulled up.

'You'll have to hurry,' the driver said, 'I can't officially park here, you know.'

Sam opened the car door.

'Bottle of Benylin,' Alicia screamed at him as he walked towards Boots, and he nodded to show he knew. His mind was racing with options – to get the Benylin or say they wouldn't give it to him? To run and get the tube – three pounds was enough, he was sure. To ring home? But he shouldn't have left Isabel (and why not? Everyone leaves me). But those were just his excuses for not doing it.

He was worried about himself – and Isabel – but he was worried about Allie even more. She was in trouble already with his family for leaving him alone that night. He wished he hadn't mentioned it. His worries were best kept to himself because there had been a fuss. He went down the escalators to the pharmacy and asked for the Benylin at the counter. There was more than one sort so he picked the one for chesty coughs and the woman asked him who it was for and if they were taking any other medicines. He said he would ask his mother, and she popped it in a bag. He almost despaired. He waited for the change and ran back up the escalators and jumped into the taxi.

Alicia smiled.

They carried on travelling until they reached the station. Allie was getting edgy. She pushed him through the crowds and kept looking at clocks and she was impatient as they queued for tickets. 'Balham, adult and child, singles,' she said, and once she'd got them she held his jumper sleeve as they ran to the platform. He was hoping they would miss it, but the train was still there, large and alarming, its doors open to receive them.

They sat next to a man and as the train pulled out Allie started talking to him in a light, pretty voice, as though she knew him, or wanted to.

Samuel wondered where Adam was. He didn't even know if he'd got back that night after his breath of air. He supposed he had. He looked out of the window and watched the city change to the suburbs. The buildings looked dingy and grey. He wanted to get off at every stop, but was afraid for Allie as much as himself, talking to a stranger.

Every so often he was afraid for Isabel, too. He imagined her crying by the door (as he had wanted to when he'd been left). He felt sorry for her, and for himself.

The train stopped again. The stranger, whose name was Don, got up and stepped off the train. They got off too, but he hurried away ahead of them, taking the stairs two at a time. He seemed to be scared of them.

'Arsehole!' Alicia called after him angrily, and turned to Sam. 'Don't worry,' she said. 'We'll find somewhere to sleep.'

They walked from the station, down strange roads glittering with broken glass. He had never seen anything like it. He wasn't so much worried for her any more, but he was for himself. They stopped outside an hotel called Belview. Alicia pushed him forward and they rang the bell. A woman came to the door and Alicia said they were looking for a twin room.

The way the woman looked at him reminded him of the taxi-driver. 'I take payment in advance,' she said. 'You'll want to see the room.' Sam saw a payphone as they followed her upstairs.

The room reminded him of Adam's. It too had a brown carpet, and beds with pink covers like ploughed fields instead of duvets.

He sat on his bed.

The room had a kettle and Alicia boiled some water and made him a coffee, and herself a tea. She drank some Benylin straight out of the bottle and lay on the bed.

She still had her hat on – it almost covered her eyes. He watched her for a long time, sipping his coffee patiently, making sure she was asleep.

After a while he crept out of the room, letting the door close gently so that he could push it open again.

He went down the stairs and dialled his home number. The instructions on the phone said to press A when it was answered. He heard the phone being answered but he had no money to put in it. He could hear his mother's voice saying his name but although he replied over and over she couldn't hear him.

To be so near to her and for her not to know overcame him with grief. He tiptoed back upstairs and pushed open the door and watched Alicia lying curled up on the rumpled bed.

He just wanted to go home.

Chapter Forty-Nine

Faye slammed the phone down, torn apart with frustration. She was sure it had been Sam.

He might ring back. She felt demented from inaction.

When a policeman had come to take details, although he'd listened she knew he'd absorbed two details: that Sam was with his natural mother and that she was twenty-four years old. His attitude was that they were worrying for nothing.

Nick had gone to Sega World, looking. He'd wanted to get out of the house.

And she'd wanted him out. She paced the floor.

Isabel was watching a video, safe from reality. In her world, Henry the Green Engine was hot and bothered.

Where was Nick? How long would it take him to walk round the Trocadero? He might have gone to see Susie.

She could hear Susie's voice saying to her in the office, 'How did you find out? Rang 1471, I suppose. We all do it.'

Faye grabbed a pen and dialled. After writing down the number, she pressed three. The blood was thundering in her temples, making her feel her head would burst.

A woman answered. 'Belview Hotel.'

Faye cleared her throat. 'Is there a boy around there, aged nine? Red hair? And a woman? Please keep him, he's my son. He's been taken. Don't let him leave. What's your address?' She wrote it down painstakingly accurately. 'Oh, thank you.'

Samuel was lying on the bed when the tap came on the door.

He opened it to find the landlady regarding him with a worried expression. 'Your Mum's looking for you,' she said. 'Come downstairs with me.' She looked at the sleeping girl on the bed. 'Is she all right?'

'She's drunk some cough medicine.'

He looked in astonishment as the landlady led him out and locked the bedroom door on Allie. Standing on the landing, she shook her head as though she couldn't believe it either. 'I'll get a doctor. I knew you two were trouble,' she said, but she smiled at him. 'Your mother's on her way.'

The landlady, Dorothy, didn't let him see the police arrive. He was eating beans on toast in her kitchen when his mother and Isabel turned up.

He didn't know what to expect, but what he didn't expect was that she would look so happy to see him.

He'd never known he could make her that happy.

Talking to the police, she kept calling him 'my son', and although they'd seen his original mother they never once said that she was saying the wrong thing. And he knew now that Allie had no claim on him, sick or well. He felt sorry for her.

They rang home and he spoke to his father, who sounded happy too. It was a good effect to have on people, he thought.

PART SEVEN

How grand these rays! They seem to beckon earth to heaven.

Humboldt

Chapter Fifty

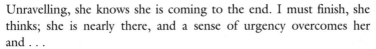

Unravelling, she knows she is coming to the end. I must finish, she thinks; she is nearly there, and a sense of urgency overcomes her and . . .

. . . she is very, very small. She is aware of something large looking at her and in its presence she feels like a full stop or the black dot of life in frogspawn; tiny, tiny, tiny.

She stops unravelling. She has untangled the whole thread of her life and it has led back to this, a smudge of insignificance.

As sorrow invades the smudge that is Faye she is aware of something she has only just seen. Inside the black shines a core of unsullied purity.

She has always been afraid.

But the shadow is not cancer, nor closed curtains, nor the losing of her son; it is fear.

For there to be shadows there has to be light, and she is like someone who has crouched in the shade with a weak bicycle lamp, missing the light that casts the shadow.

She has been hiding. But there is nothing to hide from. Nothing to be afraid of. Nothing to be *that* afraid of. Nothing to be ashamed of, with that pure core.

She moves cautiously into the light.

She feels delicate, newly unclothed, coming out of the hiding place, prepared for censure, misunderstandings, enemies, hurt.

In the light the landscape stretches out as far as she can see. There is nothing there except freedom.

She feels a rush of thanksgiving: *you've come back*!

She shuts her eyes as she hears the reply.

I never went.

Chapter Fifty-One

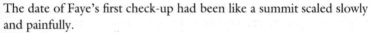

The date of Faye's first check-up had been like a summit scaled slowly and painfully.

Once it was over, she'd realised that other summits loomed. She was in the foothills yet, but the outlook was bright.

Nick had reached his own summit. He had done as he'd promised and stayed with her while she recuperated.

As she'd promised her father, she and the children were going with him to Disneyland Paris.

Eva, generous Eva, was thrilled. 'Something good for the diary,' she said. 'I'll want to see it when you get back.' Then she said it wasn't the only good thing for the diary. She and Frank had set a date. 'It just seemed right,' was her only explanation.

Faye accepted that. Some things did.

Nick drove them to the airport. Faye had suggested he move out the things he wanted from the house while they were away.

He had been silent during the journey.

They walked to the busy terminal and Isabel swung happily between her grandfather and Sam.

Nick waited as they checked in and went with them as far as the entrance to the departure lounge.

He stroked his dark, short hair as he looked at her.

'Take care of yourself, Nick,' she said, hoiking the strap of her shoulderbag higher.

'I've been a fool.' He said it in a voice so low that it seemed hardly meant for her, and yet it was. People were milling around them and he took her hand. 'I just want you to know I realise that.'

She didn't want to cry. She was trying to get out of the habit, she'd done too much of it lately, it seemed. She wanted to learn how to laugh. 'Nobody's perfect,' she said.

He gripped her hand tight. 'I thought I was. Self-deception is the worst kind of lie.'

She paused as an announcement rang out: last call for flight BA 553 to Paris. 'It's us.' She looked amidst the crowd of people for her father and turned her attention back to Nick, thinking over what he'd just said. 'Don't beat yourself over the head with it, Nick,' she said suddenly. 'Perfection isn't the point.'

'Then what is?'

'Forgiveness.'

'You've changed,' he said.

She glanced again at her father with Isabel in his arms.

'Constant adjustment is the key,' she said. 'There's never a time when you can say: that's it! that's me!, good, bad or crazy. I don't know if it makes sense. Look, we've got to go, Nick.'

He wouldn't let go of her hand. 'Could I stay?' he asked, almost without hope.

'Think about it. See if you really want to. Visit your priest,' she said softly. 'I'll ring you tomorrow.'

He released her then, and he watched as the four of them hurried away and were lost from his sight.

The Disneyland Hotel was right next to the park. It had a Peter Pan on the bedhead and ice machines in the corridors. The children were ecstatic. Everything in the hotel was shaded in pastels. The White Rabbit lurked around reception and tickled them.

It was a good place to be, and a good place to learn again how to laugh.

It was a warm day as they walked to the park. She could smell hot concrete and melting candy. She looked up at the pink castle dominating the blue sky. Pink and blue. Good colours, the colours of dreams. Everything seemed simple, and everyone happy. It should have been one big illusion. Why then were there so many happy faces? Even ancient grandmothers dressed in black lifted their lined faces to the sun.

They went on The Small World ride and she was fascinated with its bright and playful beauty. The jingle went round incessantly in her head.

The children were delighted with everything and Samuel bought a Minnie Mouse t-shirt for Alicia who, on a social worker's advice, was back with Edith once more. His generosity told the story. His uncertainty had left him. He was wholly theirs again now.

*   *   *

241

The following day Faye stood queuing in the shade outside the Phantom Manor, waiting silently, patiently, in the crowd with her father, ready, with him and her children, to be frightened by ghosts and hushed by gravestones and ageing pictures.

Laughter and fear and fun – the body took it all seriously despite what the mind knew to be true.

In the distance against the blue sky she could see Sleeping Beauty's castle glistening pink and sweet as icing sugar and the persistently appealing notes of 'It's a Small World' danced around like colours in her head.

She'd rung Nick that morning. He'd said three loving words; not the usual ones but ones that this time meant more. I'm still here.

They moved along in the queue and the grey manor loomed and her father patted her arm gently. 'We don't have to do this one,' he said lightly, 'look at the queue.'

In truth, it was no longer than any other. She looked up at him. He looked cool in his yellow polo shirt, cool, concerned, loving, smelling not of tobacco – he had given up smoking – but doubling up on Old Spice. The hairs at his temples were showing white and she felt another warm rush of gratitude at his risking knowing her before it was too late. She smiled at him and raised an eyebrow. 'Scared, Dad?'

'Of plastic spiders? I hope not.'

Smiling to herself, she looked at the faces in the lines of waiting people. So many faces, so many people, all ages, all different. She wondered if she was looking at someone who had shared the same disease, or who harboured it now and would lie at some future time waiting in a low-lit ward at night.

Shadows had their place.

Suddenly there was a stir in the crowd and she saw, making its way through towards them, Death, parting people as it walked. A black hood shaded the skull and people flinched from the black whirling cloak, billowing until, yards in front of her, it stopped, raised an arm and described an arc with a pointed bony finger at the faces in the crowd.

She waited.

Samuel stood by her side and Isabel took her hand tightly as the finger pointed at them briefly and moved on, and Death embraced a woman in the crowd. Posed for photographs.

And Faye put her hand on the bullet-hole scars on her side thinking, they can't make you as good as new. Organs can't grow back and scars can't be erased and the mind can't be wiped clean. But the patched-up people, all of us bound together by a hideous courage, carry on until next time and the next, while the last hurdle waits – and death is always the last place you look.